Part of the fun of traveling was watching scenery change as it whizzed by, like on a train. Simply continuing down a forested often grew tiring.

On a typical wagon ride, there wasn much else to do except stare out at the sig Roxine had brought some picture books with her, but reading them now might make her nauseous. She decided to save them for bedtime stories once they made camp.

Lytt and Luka enjoyed quizzing each other at first, but Luka had only recently moved to the village and couldn't get many answers right, so the game was over quickly. That was when Cayna took out a deck of cards.

It turned out there were all kinds of board games in this world, although it wasn't clear whether *Leadale* players or their Fosters were responsible for their spread.

LYTT

In the Land of Leadale

4

Ceez

[ILLUSTRATION BY]

Tenmaso

YEN ON

NEW YORK

L IN THE LAND OF EADALE 4 Ceez

Translation by Jessica Lange
Cover art by Tenmaso

This book is a work of fiction. Names, characters, places, and incidents are the product of the author's imagination or are used fictitiously. Any resemblance to actual events, locales, or persons, living or dead, is coincidental.

RIADEIRU NO DAICHI NITE Vol. 4
© Ceez 2020
First published in Japan in 2020 by KADOKAWA CORPORATION, Tokyo.
English translation rights arranged with KADOKAWA CORPORATION, Tokyo through TUTTLE-MORI AGENCY, INC., Tokyo.

English translation © 2021 by Yen Press, LLC

Yen On
150 West 30th Street, 19th Floor
New York, NY 10001

Visit us at yenpress.com
facebook.com/yenpress
twitter.com/yenpress
yenpress.tumblr.com
instagram.com/yenpress

First Yen On Edition: November 2021

Yen On is an imprint of Yen Press, LLC.
The Yen On name and logo are trademarks of Yen Press, LLC.

The publisher is not responsible for websites (or their content) that are not owned by the publisher.

Library of Congress Cataloging-in-Publication Data
Names: Ceez, author. | Tenmaso, illustrator. | Lange, Jessica (Translator), translator.
Title: In the land of Leadale / Ceez ; illustration by Tenmaso ; translation by Jessica Lange
Other titles: Riadeiru no daichi nite. English
Description: First Yen On edition. | New York, NY : Yen On, 2020.
Identifiers: LCCN 2020032160 | ISBN 9781975308681 (v. 1 ; trade paperback) |
    ISBN 9781975308704 (v. 2 ; trade paperback) | ISBN 9781975322168 (v. 3 ; trade paperback) |
    ISBN 9781975322182 (v. 4 ; trade paperback)
Subjects: CYAC: Fantasy. | Virtual reality—Fiction.
Classification: LCC PZ7.1.C4646 In 2020 | DDC [Fic]—dc23
LC record available at https://lccn.loc.gov/2020032160

ISBNs: 978-1-9753-2218-2 (paperback)
        978-1-9753-2219-9 (ebook)

10 9 8 7 6 5 4 3 2 1

LSC-C

Printed in the United States of America

In the Land of

Leadale

4

IN THE LAND OF LEADALE CONTENTS

THE STORY THUS FAR   001

PROLOGUE   007

CHAPTER 1
Daily Life in the Village, Restocking, a Journey,
and a Disquieting Shadow   013

CHAPTER 2
A Scheme, an Inquiry, Dealing with Sweet
Talkers, and Two Daughters   071

CHAPTER 3
A Demon, a Summons, a Tower, and a Project   111

ILLUSTRATION BY Tenmaso

CHAPTER 4

Preparations, a Thank-You Banquet,

a Festival, and an Idiot   171

CHAPTER 5

Retaliation, Fishing, the Road Home,

and Secret Talks   213

EPILOGUE   257

BONUS SHORT STORY

A Princess's Firsthand Experience   263

CHARACTER DATA   271

AFTERWORD   275

The Story Thus Far

A terrible accident had rendered Keina Kagami hospitalized and bedridden; one day while playing the VRMMORPG *Leadale* a power surge caused her life support to malfunction and she perished. The next thing she remembered was waking up in an unfamiliar inn and realizing she was in the body of her game avatar. Much to Keina's shock, the inn's proprietress, Marelle, informed her that Leadale was now made up of just three nations instead of the original seven from two hundred years prior. Keina thereby deduced that this modern era was far beyond when the game took place, and she had no idea whether other players she had known still existed. She then decided to live on not as Keina Kagami but as her avatar, Cayna.

Cayna, a Skill Master, visited her Guardian Tower, where her Guardian informed her that the rest of the towers were currently inoperable, prompting Cayna to journey across the continent in the hopes of learning about the other players who had abandoned their Guardian Towers.

As thanks for taking her under their wing, Cayna provided the people of the remote village with a bathhouse and mechanism to draw water from their well. Then she met Elineh, the head of a merchant caravan, and Arbiter, the leader of a group of mercenaries, and accompanied them to Felskeilo, a nation in the middle of the continent.

After registering as an adventurer, Cayna met Prime Minister Agaido and his granddaughter, Lonti, who asked for Cayna's help finding a runaway prince. She successfully captured the young prince, but not before dumbfounding everyone involved with her powers. Cayna also reunited with her children—or more precisely, the subcharacters she had submitted to the Foster System during the Game Era: her eldest son, Skargo; her daughter, Mai-Mai; and her youngest son, Kartatz, all of whom absolutely adore their mother.

Cayna then accepted a request from the Adventurers Guild and discovered that the Ninth Skill Master's Guardian Tower was in the Battle Arena. She activated the tower, and after many twists and turns, learned from the tower's Guardian that *Leadale* the game no no longer existed. The news sent her into a brief depression, but it also strengthened her bond with her children and made her realize this was hardly the time to be discouraged.

During an expedition escorting Elineh and his caravan to the northern nation of Helshper, Cayna stopped by the remote village and rescued a mermaid named Mimily, who had gotten lost in an underground water vein. Not long after this, Cayna and Arbiter's mercenaries defeated a number of bandits at the Helshper border who were part of a larger group blocking off the western trade routes.

Upon arriving in the Helshper royal capital, Cayna delivered a letter from her daughter to the continent's most preeminent merchant company, Sakaiya. There she met the founder, Caerick, and nearly fainted when he revealed that he is Mai-Mai's son—and therefore Cayna's grandson. A rift formed between grandmother and grandchild following a slight misunderstanding, and shortly thereafter Cayna encountered Caerick's older twin sister, the knight Caerina, which only added to Cayna's consternation.

However, Cayna soon got word of a Guardian Tower within Helshper and realized that in order to reach it, she would have to pass through the bandits' expansive territory to the west. Thus, with Caerick's help, she devised a plan to raid their turf.

Cayna came face-to-face with the bandit leader upon reaching the mansion-like Guardian Tower and learned he was also a player. She gave him a merciless beatdown in the hopes that he might finally realize this world isn't a game, but the moment before she could deal the final blow, Caerina and her fellow knights intervened, and Cayna let them take the leader into custody.

She then proceeded to reactivate the Thirteenth Skill Master's Guardian Tower and was shocked to learn it once belonged to her partner in crime and former fellow guild member Opus. The Guardian also gave her a book with a fairy inside. Certain this gift was definitive proof that Opus was still out there, Cayna took the fairy with her and decided to look for him.

On the way back to Felskeilo with Elineh's caravan, she ran into Kartatz attempting to build a bridge that would connect the eastern trade routes. With Cayna's assistance, the bridge was successfully completed in no time.

Once back in Felskeilo, Cayna took on an Adventurers Guild request to hunt down a horned bear, and Lonti and her friend Mye ended up accompanying her out of the blue. It soon came to light that Mye was in fact Myleene, crown princess of Felskeilo. The princess inadvertently let it slip that she had a crush on Skargo and then received Cayna's tentative blessing to court him.

Meanwhile, Lopus, Mai-Mai's husband and an alchemy professor at the Academy, became obsessed with Cayna's "ancient arts" and conducted several experiments to re-create them. However, his handmade potion ended in failure, and he tossed it into the Academy landfill. Unfortunately, the landfill was also a leftover Collection Point from a

Game Era turf war, and for reasons unknown, Lopus's potion caused a giant penguin chimera monster to appear. The monster subsequently threw the entire city into mass chaos.

Shining Saber, the captain of the knights sent to look for the princess, came across the adventurer Cohral in the Adventurers Guild. After discovering that they had been members of the same guild during the Game Era, the two players teamed up to fight the penguin monster just like they used to all those years ago.

The High Priest Skargo and a team of mages combined their strength to help in the fight as well, but it took everything they had just to keep the monster at bay. Kartatz was able to alert his mother to the danger in Felskeilo, and the penguin monster was subsequently destroyed thanks to Cayna's incredible magic. Cayna then obtained information on a new Guardian Tower following her chance encounter with Shining Saber and Cohral there.

She briefly returned to the remote village to further look into the possibility of relocating there. However, she ran into a group from the southern nation of Otaloquess and consequently earned the ire of a female member named Clofia. Their resulting duel saw Cayna soundly defeat Clofia, whose older brother, Cloffe, revealed the group were Otaloquess spies.

Additionally, it just so happened that Cayna's own niece had been Otaloquess's sovereign since the country's founding: Queen Sahalashade—Foster Child of a Game Era high elf, Sahana—who was like a little sister to Cayna. The fact that she kept inadvertently meeting national leaders at every turn left Cayna feeling unsettled.

Once she recovered from this shocking news, Cayna began searching for the Palace of the Dragon King. She followed Shining Saber and his knights halfway through their campaign, and her camaraderie with him sparked rumors that she was his fiancée.

The fishing village said to be near the Palace of the Dragon King was shrouded in an eerie mist. Here, Cayna encountered a female adventurer named Quolkeh and a dragoid named Exis, both of whom came to the village to investigate the local distribution of goods. The two of them happened to be players, and it was revealed that Exis was once Tartarus, a member of Cayna's guild.

The only person left in the fishing village was a little girl named Luka, and Cayna summoned her butler, Roxilius, to keep the girl company while she, Quolkeh, and Exis dealt with the bizarre situation at hand. After Exis defeated the Terror Skeleton and Ghost Ship, event enemies from the game, Cayna reactivated the Sixth Skill Master's Guardian Tower and then decided to adopt Luka and raise her in the remote village.

En route back to the village, Roxilius pointed out that they would need more help around the house, so Cayna summoned a maid named Roxine, who was a bitter rival to Roxilius. With Luka and this catty pair in tow, Cayna built a house in the remote village and started her new life.

Later, Cayna fulfilled her promise to take Lytt, the inn proprietress's daughter, on a sightseeing flight along with Luka and Latem, the son of Lux Contracting's owner. As the group marveled at the dazzling sights, they eventually came across Elineh's caravan under siege by a group of monsters. Cayna proceeded to crush the horde, save Arbiter and the caravan, and then return home to the village.

After discovering that quest enemies were ambushing the village outskirts, Cayna set off with Arbiter and his mercenaries to eliminate them. Meanwhile, Lytt, Latem, and Luka snuck out of the village to go make flower crowns only to be attacked by monsters. Just when all hope seemed lost, a White Dragon appeared from within a pendant Cayna had given to Luka and protected the children. The ensuing cacophony caught Cayna's attention, and she rushed back to the village. When she found Luka there safe, she then proceeded to break down in tears of relief.

Later, while in Helshper to buy goats and chickens, Cayna ran into Cohral and his party, who had accepted a request from Sakaiya at the Adventurers Guild. Cayna took the opportunity to introduce them to her great-grandson, Idzik.

After receiving word from Caerick that there was going to be a conference at the national border, Cayna returned home to find her son, the High Priest Skargo, already there.

Prologue

The man paused, and he examined every nook and cranny of what he'd been polishing. Even though he'd repeated this routine countless times before, he was wholly dedicated to inspecting every last corner to check if he'd missed a spot. The brown, orange, and black marbling created a lovely contrast; he never tired of looking at the object from every angle. Knowing that its perfectly smooth texture was thanks to years of polishing made the exhaustion in his arms all the more satisfying.

After placing the object back on its special pedestal that he set atop the desk in his room, he thought about how unique this object was.

It was one meter long with three strange fingerlike projections—a branch he'd obtained in childhood after the gardener had pruned it from a tree. It felt so far removed from the rest of the world as he, a young boy, knew it. In his limited knowledge, the boy had been overcome with repulsion and envy; he'd begged and nagged the elderly gardener for the branch until it was, at last, his own.

After reading some books and gaining further knowledge, he carefully removed the unnecessary parts of the branch, filed it down, and polished it repeatedly. It took him five years to bring the branch to its current form. He devoted himself to polishing it each day until its surface became as brilliant and glossy as ivory. By covering this branch in a special aromatic balm before polishing it again, he gradually created a marble pattern. What had started out as a mere tree branch was now the product of his years of dedication.

In order to save face, he chose not to reveal that this was only a tree branch but instead sometimes displayed it as some sort of rare *objet d'art* when he entertained guests. Its peculiarity only further piqued outsiders' interests. However, a part of him felt guilty knowing that this "rare object" was originally just a tree branch.

Perhaps in an effort to further the delusion, he'd collected every rare item he could get his hands on. He followed leads to antique shops catering to nobility, visited the Merchants Guild when he learned they had excavated relics from ruins, and resorted to underhanded means if commoners refused to part with the keepsakes of their deceased loved ones. So great was his tenacity that it seemed he'd lost his humanity somewhere along the way. As a result, rumors and deep-seated resentment of his relic obsession spread among high society.

His collection was extensive: It contained books and and weapons and armor along with various odds and ends. He built a secondary residence on the grounds of his mansion in the capital, where he displayed the items and opened an art museum of sorts.

He was warier than most when it came to potential theft, and he employed magic, as well as private guards, for protection.

A Grimoire Made from Many Felled by a Mage of Old

This book's every page was made of human skin, starting with the cover itself. After being consecrated and then tightly bound with a leather strap, it was placed inside a silver case filled with holy water. Some claimed an eyeball would occasionally rise to the surface and place a deadly curse on whoever met its gaze, though this was yet unconfirmed.

He had a number of items that he was quite proud of, but this one was top among the tomes. He couldn't confirm the rumors, but he was sure the book would unleash a stream of insults if he asked it to show him its contents.

A HELMET BELONGING TO THE KNIGHT CAPTAIN OF A RUINED NATION

Handling this item carelessly was said to inflict a grudge that would never abate until the victim tracked down and exterminated the descendants of a nation victorious in war. However, since it was uncertain whether the seven nations of the past had definite monarchies, the existence of the "ruined nation" in question was dubious.

This helmet sat atop a suit of armor that decorated his room. Visitors often warned him not to put such a thing in a place where anyone could so easily touch it.

A DRAGON SKULL STAINED WITH A LINE OF DUSKY BLOOD

Dragons were the stuff of legend these days, although apparently there had been confirmed sightings throughout the seven nations in years past. Any written accounts of dragons had long since disappeared, thus contributing to the general consensus that dragons no longer existed.

This particular dragon skull was on the floor in a corner of his room. Its mouth looked large enough to swallow a child whole, but according to archaeologists, it likely belonged to an adolescent specimen.

The items in the man's collection were clear proof of his extraordinary dedication, no matter what others might think of him otherwise.

His next target was a worn-out covered wagon.

The wagon itself wasn't a relic or anything of the sort. It had no checkered past that piqued his interest. What grabbed his attention was a single line from a book in his personal library:

"A wheeled mansion or castle traveled nations without the aid of a horse."

And that was precisely why he did not take lightly a rumor he'd heard from a merchant in his employ—that a commoner mother and child had been seen riding a horseless wagon.

His response was swift: He researched where the wagon was headed and what companies it purchased goods from, then devised a plan to procure the vehicle for himself.

His greatest downfall, however, was his failure to pay attention to the source of the rumor. If he had only investigated further, he would have learned this "commoner mother" was an adventurer with connections to the High Priest and on friendly terms with the founder of Sakaiya. His obsession with this wagon's rarity had blinded him; he was like a fool reaching for a dragon's treasure.

He had no way of knowing the disastrous conclusion that awaited him the moment he got his hands on that treasure.

CHAPTER 1
Daily Life in the Village, Restocking, a Journey, and a Disquieting Shadow

"*Phew*, that was indeed terrifying."

"I'm not convinced. Didn't I say it's just a spell that temporarily changes your appearance?"

Skargo, who had returned to his usual handsome self after a night as a hideous *Zhu Bajie* pig, was enjoying breakfast at Cayna's house upon her invitation.

Cayna, of course, had been the one to insist that he eat at her place. She'd realized she couldn't allow Skargo to fall in love with Marelle's amazing food, and so she'd rushed to invite him over for breakfast.

Cayna's only objective was to prevent the quality of the food from giving Skargo reason to relocate to the village, church and all. Because if he did that, Cayna's burgeoning anxiety would never cease so long as she lived here. After all, there was no question Skargo and his entourage would flock to her like moths to a flame.

The only other person eating with Cayna and Skargo was Luka. Roxine and Roxilius normally joined in under the family rule that everyone should eat together, but because they had a guest over, the two werecats were more than happy to serve the food instead. The menu was the same as usual—bread, salad, soup, fruit—which begged the question of whether having someone serve the food was even necessary.

Roxine glared at Skargo before retreating into the kitchen; Roxilius stood at attention nearby, occasionally refilling drinks or correcting Luka's table manners.

Luka was still too shy to engage Skargo in conversation, but she had started calling him "Big Brother"—a bit of welcome progress as far as Cayna was concerned.

Flattered by this moniker, Skargo cast Oscar—Roses Scatter with Beauty out of habit, effectively snuffing out any warm fuzzies Cayna felt. She stopped him with a glare every time he started up again. Old habits die hard.

Skargo succumbed to his mother's stares with a dry laugh. Unless he treaded lightly, Cayna would smite him with her Cursed Outfit Technique just as she had the night before. And his upcoming conference would likely end in failure if he showed up as a *Zhu Bajie* pig, leaving his role as emissary—not to mention his reputation as High Priest—in shambles.

"Mother Dear, I very much hope you won't turn me into *that* again…"

"Then quit using your Effect Skills for every little thing and just have a normal conversation. It makes no difference to me how you use them for work, but are you totally incapable of talking to your own mother without busting out these effects all willy-nilly?"

"No, of course not."

"Although I guess I don't have much room to talk, having left you to your own devices for two hundred years. Your future wife's got her work cut out for her."

Cayna put her hand to her cheek. The next instant, Skargo opened his arms wide, and a flower backdrop appeared behind him—which he quickly dispelled after a single steely glare from Cayna.

"…Pardon me," he apologized with a light cough.

Cayna felt a huge headache coming on. Twenty percent of her worries had to do with Felskeilo's future should a force like Skargo marry into the royal family; the other 80 percent was over how much Myleene would suffer if she ended up having to handle him. Wedding bells weren't exactly ringing just yet, but from what Cayna could tell, Myleene was hit with a severe case of first love. Considering Cayna had essentially encouraged this situation, she had no right to complain. But if the princess insisted on marrying for love, Skargo's proclivities were going to be a huge hurdle.

"Mother Dear."

"Uh-huh?"

Having finished his meal, Skargo dabbed at his mouth, his face quite serious. That gesture alone would render any unassuming woman lovestruck and squealing, but as Skargo's creator in every sense of the word, his pretty-boy looks had zero effect on Cayna.

"You mentioned something about a future wife just now. Might you have someone in mind?" he asked.

"…Now I'm not so sure."

"Whatever in the worrrld are you unsure about?! Whoever you introduce me to, Mother Dear, I, Skargo, vow to love and protect them with all my heart and soul!"

Skargo stood up and clutched his chest against a backdrop of white roses, his determined gaze focused somewhere off in the distance…

…only for Roxine to smack him in the face with a tray, sending him flying into the wall with a *wham*.

"Master Skargo," said Roxine, "you are frightening the young Lady Luka. I ask that you refrain from your comedy routine."

"…?!"

"Cie, aren't *you* the one who just startled Luka?" Cayna pointed out.

Roxine was spinning a face-dented tray on her finger. Luka was staring speechless between where her stepbrother had just been standing and where he currently remained stuck in the wall. Roxilius remained standing at attention, nodding wordlessly.

Scared by how accustomed she'd grown to ruckus first thing in the morning, Cayna put a hand to her cheek and sighed.

"Well then, I bid you farewell, Mother Dear."

"Yep. You'll probably be fine, but be careful on the road back."

"Yes, yes, certainly. Although I must say it is a pity that I cannot show you the fine man I have become."

"In what universe would an envoy bring his mother with him to a conference…?"

The knights accompanying Skargo thumped their breastplates in assertion that they would ensure his safe passage. They didn't seem to be part of Shining Saber's forces; Cayna was relieved that none of them referred to her as "the captain's fiancée."

After refreshing himself with magic following breakfast, Skargo had announced he would be departing for the national border within the day. Four carriages were waiting for him, the lead carriage so gaudy that it was impossible to miss. The entire delegation consisted of Skargo, ten knights, four civil officials, and several attendants. Such missions were typically flanked by a superfluous number of personnel, but since they were traveling with the High Priest, they kept the pomp to a bare minimum. In other words, little flavor and more substance.

Personally, Cayna thought Skargo was much too eager to share the delegation's sensitive information, but she could sense his trust in her and decided to hold back rebuke. Instead, she watched the rare spectacle of Skargo panicking terribly as Roxilius dug into him about leaking secrets.

"By the way," Skargo began, "Mai-Mai would be thrilled to meet Luka. If she had not been directly summoned by His Majesty, that sister of mine would have surely taken the initiative and paid a visit."

"Huh. Thanks, Skargo. You're right, I should definitely introduce her to Mai-Mai, too."

"Think nothing of it. Well then, Mother Dear. Let us meet again when the opportunity arises. Do take care, Luka."

With these parting words, Skargo waved lightly before stepping into the carriage. Cayna fondly watched the delegation depart. After they disappeared from sight, she crossed her arms and murmured, "Maybe Mai-Mai feels kinda left out?"

Mai-Mai's job required her constant presence at the Academy, so opportunities for her to meet Luka in the remote village were few and far between. If Mai-Mai couldn't come to them, they would have to come to her. Cayna had settled into her new home just days ago, but she didn't think an occasional bit of travel would be a problem. She considered bringing Luka with her the next time she went shopping.

Cayna had started calling Luka "Lu" after the incident with the White Dragon, but only because Roxine suggested, "Why don't you call her something a bit more familial? You are her family now, after all."

It took Cayna a while to actually put this into practice, though. She spent half the day deliberating over whether to give Luka a nickname until Roxilius finally had enough. The only reason she made any progress at all was because he dragged her over to Luka.

"Um," Cayna began.

"…Uh-huh?"

"So, L-Luka…"

"…Uh-huh."

"Can I call you Lu?"

"...Uh-huh!"

Cayna's face lit up like a Christmas tree, and she pulled Luka into a tight embrace. Behind them, dead-eyed Roxine and Roxilius collapsed to the ground in exhaustion; they'd been worried to death that this exchange would end up taking hours.

Cayna had gotten used to daily life in the countryside; she gradually renovated her environs just like she used to do with her base in *Leadale*'s Offline Mode. Of course, she always checked with the village elder or the other villagers before starting anything.

First, she improved the fence that kept the village safe from invaders. This fence was enchanted with a special charm that kept some of the monsters out.

Cayna began clearing the brush from the outside of the fence but was soon assaulted by the vegetation's wails, so she had Roxilius take over.

He mowed down trees and plants with such ease that the villagers thought he looked like a demon on a cleaning frenzy.

Next, an Earth Spirit leveled the uneven ground. The five-meter-tall chess pawn uprooted trees and smoothed over the soil with the fluidity of a real pawn moving across a chessboard. Cayna turned the pile of felled trees into lumber with her Craft Skills and evenly distributed them to each household.

She decided to hold off on any expansion, however. According to the village elder, the extra land would only go to waste since the village's population was in decline. Moreover, the area was managed by nobles, and apparently they didn't allow the village to expand their arable land.

"Wow," said Cayna. "So this land belongs to nobles..."

"Yes. They aren't too fussy about rules however, so we do ask for their input," the elder replied.

"Hmm. What's the name of these nobles?"

"They're the family of Baron Harvey."

"…Huh?"

The name immediately sounded familiar, and then Cayna's jaw dropped in sudden recognition.

Unless she misheard, the Baron had the same last name of Mai-Mai's husband, Lopus Harvey. Paying the Harveys a visit would be easy enough given her daughter's connections, but a mere adventurer like Cayna couldn't just go barging into aristocratic affairs. She slightly regretted even asking who oversaw the land, and Cayna thought it would be best to let the elder negotiate with the Baron's family.

Meanwhile, she felt the fence's enchantment wouldn't hold out against ogres like the ones from a few days prior, so she set up an extra layer of protection. Cayna placed stone stakes several meters apart outside the fence, set gargoyles atop each one, and modified their appearance.

Standard gargoyles resembled goblins with bat wings, but in *Leadale*, you could adjust them to look however you wanted. Cayna decided to turn these particular gargoyles into snow bunnies. With a few finishing touches—bodies made of snow mounds, bamboo leaves for ears, and small, red berries for eyes—the gargoyles were complete.

Since they were equipped with magic rhymestones, they'd automatically accumulate the MP needed to awaken whenever they were inactive. This way, Cayna could cut down on the time needed to refill them with the MP that kept them operational.

Humans and animals wouldn't find the gargoyles threatening; if anything, they looked more like a bunch of slapdash ornaments. But when activated, these bunnies were strong enough to make quick work of any local ogres.

A strained smile appeared on her assistant Roxilius's face. This amount of protection could keep even a fortress safe. "Lady Cayna, might this be a bit excessive?" he asked.

"Not at all. Life comes at you fast in this world. You can never be too careful." Cayna put her hands on her hips in a show of pride; Li'l Fairy assumed the same self-satisfied pose atop her master's head. She seemed in full agreement with Cayna's assertion. Pity that no one else could see her, though.

"Besides, Rox, this gives you one less job to do," Cayna added.

"What use am I if I'm without any work…?"

One of Roxilius's jobs had been to patrol the village's outskirts and eliminate any dangerous monsters. He and Roxine had divided any duties Cayna wasn't involved in amongst themselves: The latter handled the household affairs, while the former took care of the property.

"The kids are still cleaning the bathhouse as punishment. You're helping with that, too, right?" Cayna said.

"Well…yes."

Just then, Roxine showed up. She and Roxilius exchanged momentary glares before she turned to Cayna. "Lady Cayna, I have a favor to ask."

"Sure, what's up?"

"…Should you really be so quick to dole out favors to your attendants?" Roxine's tone quickly turned to exasperation.

Cayna smiled uncomfortably. "I mean, I've just been leaving you two to handle all the usual chores. I'm happy to help with anything if it makes life better for either of you."

Roxilius and Roxine looked at one another and shrugged. There were mutual mumblings of "She's a hopeless case" and "Even ideal masters have their limits."

"Well, I can't say how much better my life would be for it, but I'd like you to temporarily halt any restocking," said Roxine. "I need to calculate how long our current food stores will last."

"Oh, okay. Yeah, go ahead. I guess we better stop using Cooking Skills, too, right?"

"Yes, I would appreciate it." Roxine bowed her head and returned to the house.

"What were we talking about again?" Cayna asked Roxilius.

"We were discussing my work, although I have no objection to following your every order."

"A job for you, huh…?"

Cayna sank deep into thought. Eventually, she decided to suggest that Roxilius build an all-purpose storage room. The villagers were initially supposed to build it, but it was better to give the job to someone with nothing else going on. She could use rhymestones to control the humidity and temperature if need be, so there was no need to build individual cellars.

"Hey, the goats will need a stable for nighttime and when it's raining, right? And the barrels of beer will be fine in my Item Box, but we should also have somewhere to store the whiskey since it tastes better with age."

These proposals all came from Kee, but Cayna figured she should give Roxilius work to do as a "master worth serving."

The chickens would roam the village. Marelle had told Cayna that she was free to look in the bushes and take whatever she found whenever she needed eggs. The villagers weren't too concerned about the freshness of their eggs, so some would occasionally get an upset stomach. Kee suggested they come up with a method for sorting the eggs quickly.

"Understood. I'll get started straight away," Roxilius replied with a smile, satisfied to be entrusted with this new duty. He bowed respectfully and set to work on building a shed that very day.

Since most of his skills were combat-oriented, he excelled in manual labor.

Without a Craft Skill like Building: House, Roxilius couldn't construct buildings in the blink of an eye like Cayna could. She had tried giving him a scroll so that he'd learn, but it didn't help. Instead, he started from scratch using large carpentry machines and processed wood to construct the storage space from the ground up.

Cayna didn't expect Roxilius to do all the work on his own, so she created golems to move heavy loads and construct in high places. If they'd started building in the center of town, it would have drawn attention whether they wanted it or not. Since villagers with free time on their hands dropped by to help on occasion, it was completed much sooner than anticipated.

The final product was a two-story shed. The second floor was quite cramped, and half of the first floor was taken up by a stable that would fit perhaps two goats. Wooden rails extending from the second floor to the other half of the first floor allowed you to roll barrels sideways and then down between the two stories.

"What do you think, Lady Cayna?"

"It kinda looks like this one game where a gorilla throws stuff at you..."

"Huh?"

Roxilius appeared satisfied with the results, but Cayna's uncomfortable smile said she felt otherwise. Also, this setup was oddly familiar. Nevertheless, she treated the villagers who helped them to whiskey as thanks for finishing the job. The drunken men dragged in Roxilius, and it wasn't long before they had a raucous drinking party on their hands. Siblings, wives, and children came to collect the men who had sunk into a drunken stupor in the middle of the afternoon. It disturbed Cayna a bit that Roxilius returned to his butler duties the very next day without the slightest hangover at all.

Meanwhile, Roxine was polishing her housework skills.

Per Cayna's orders, she had stopped using Cooking Skills since they wasted too many ingredients. She then asked the village wives for help and learned basic cooking techniques. Cayna and Roxilius were shocked by this turn of events given how well they knew Roxine's personality.

"Don't be foolish," Roxine told them. "We can't afford to maintain a lavish lifestyle if we plan to settle in this village. In order to raise Lady Luka properly, we must learn to adjust our standards accordingly."

"You have a totally decent opinion?!"

"Why are you so shocked, Lady Cayna? You said so yourself, did you not?"

It was true Cayna had told Roxine to let Luka be herself, but she never expected Roxine to put so much thought into it. That motivated her even further to raise Luka.

She also had something else on her mind.

"So what do you think?" Cayna elbowed Roxilius.

"Unlikely as it may be, I simply can't shake this feeling," the werecat acquiesced, his gaze downcast.

Roxine was the real concern. She didn't look any different, but something about her felt off.

Cayna took the werecats' summoning bells out of her Item Box and rang Roxine's lightly.

"Maybe the real one will come out if I ring it again?" she said.

"That one might be a fake, too...," Roxilius replied.

"Well that's no help."

"What are you talking about?!" Roxine interrupted. Cayna and Roxilius examined her with an audible *Hmmm.*

"It's just, you haven't been nearly as sadistic lately, so we thought you might be a fake," Cayna said.

"Huh?"

A vein in Roxine's temple throbbed. Cayna had a bad feeling about that; Roxilius was looking up in thought and didn't notice she'd taken a step back.

"Oh, so you were thinking you'd just switch out the bitchy cat and—?!"

Roxine's petulant grumblings were interrupted by the clanging of metal. Roxine, who had drawn her weapon to unleash her power, had been cut off by Roxilius.

Roxilius's weapon was a common, one-handed sword. Roxine's was a hatchet. Not only that, it was a rare Tragic Night: Jason Blade. Cayna remembered giving it to Roxine when she asked her for it since Cayna didn't use it anyway. She never imagined that the were-cat would end up using it to kill a coworker.

"It seems the time has come for us to settle things once and for all!" Roxilius declared.

"Hey now! I can't have you guys waving weapons around!" Cayna shouted.

Scraping and screeching rang out as sword and hatchet crossed. Although their skill sets differed, their strengths were about equal, so there was an ongoing struggle for dominance. Cayna had tried telling them to get along, but just like in the game, they broke out into fights at the most trivial comments. Now even she wondered whether she'd teased Roxine too much this time. It was quiet as long as the two didn't move from their crossed weapons.

Just as Cayna thought to herself she should probably stop the fight before things got too serious, she heard a withered voice call out, "What's going on…?" behind her.

"Oh, Mimily. Something the matter?" Cayna asked as she turned around to find Mimily staring at them in shock.

"'Something the matter?' Shouldn't *I* be asking that?" the mermaid retorted.

A sword-wielding butler and hatchet-wielding maid engaged in ferocious combat was undoubtedly a shock to anyone unfamiliar with their usual pattern of behavior.

"Oh, this? Just a little difference of opinion."

"One that's turned to bloodshed?!"

Cayna shrugged as if this was just part of an average day. Mimily's head throbbed. Anyone else would call this carnage. Given how calmly Cayna was watching this fight unfold, Mimily couldn't help but think she was something of an oddball. She'd always had an inkling, but now Mimily was really starting to believe that Cayna was highly unusual.

"Guess I oughta let them blow off steam once in a while."

"*That's* the problem here?"

Mimily pointed at the savage scene with a trembling finger, but Cayna just smiled awkwardly and clapped her hands. It wasn't just her imagination that Cayna's idea of arbitration was more like feeding koi fish.

"Okay, you two, that's enough for today. You're upsetting the audience."

"Ack?!"

"Ngh?!"

Unbeknownst to Mimily, a coercive power hit Roxilius and Roxine with pinpoint accuracy. They immediately put away their weapons and straightened their posture while Cayna shot them a spine-chilling smile. And all this transpired the moment before Mimily turned back around.

""W-we're very sorry.""

"Right, great. You can't fight just because Lu isn't around."

The brutal atmosphere dissipated, and Mimily stared at the

shamed pair in confusion. She couldn't really understand what had just happened since she hadn't spent much time with the two, but she wasn't about to step into another household's affairs. After all, the maid and butler appeared to have turned frightening awfully fast.

"So what brings you to our home all the way from the bathhouse?" Cayna asked.

"Oh, um, I came for some bread," Mimily replied.

"Bread?" Cayna tilted her head in confusion. She obviously knew what bread was, but she had no idea why Mimily was suddenly saying she came to pick some up.

Mimily normally ate meals provided by the inn. However, she had been through a tough learning curve during her time there. Initially, no one in the village knew anything about mermaids. Cayna had left Mimily in the care of the village elder and Marelle, both of whom struggled with what to do with the mermaid. They figured she'd be fine serving food at the inn since she looked human from the waist up, but it turned out they hadn't given this quite enough thought. Who would've guessed the inn's patrons would turn pale and collapse at the sight of vegetable soup?

According to Mimily, her hometown's staples were seaweed and algae. Mermaids didn't eat fish, but shellfish were perfectly edible. After taking this into account, Marelle focused on making soups full of leafy vegetables to get villagers used to the concept bit by bit before eventually earning Mimily's trust. Once things had calmed down a bit, Cayna visited the inn and heard only a few idle complaints.

Considering all that Mimily had gone through, Cayna became a little upset with herself when the mermaid mentioned bread. She felt bad that she'd been so busy lately, running around looking for projects to do for the village, that she hadn't taken the time to check in on Mimily.

Roxine, however, responded to Mimily's mention of bread with, "Ah, that."

She withdrew into the house temporarily and brought back a basket with a cloth over top before saying to Mimily, "Shall we get going?"

Feeling curious, Cayna decided to accompany them while Roxilius chose to stay home.

Their destination was an empty house near the public bath. There, they found several other women waiting with plates and cloth-covered baskets just like the one Roxine was carrying.

"Oh, Cayna came with you, too?"

"What a sight for sore eyes. Will you be helping us today?"

"Umm, what's everyone here for?" Cayna asked. She had trouble answering the women since she had no clue what was going on.

As she stood there confused, several women took the covers off their baskets to show her the contents: several round, palm-sized white objects.

"Did you not know we're going to bake these, Cayna?" one woman asked.

Cayna thought back but had no recollection of this.

It seemed that Roxine was using this empty house for her own personal event. Several stone ovens like one might see in a pizza shop were lined up in the room. It was at this point Cayna finally figured out what they were being used for. She remembered always seeing cooking scenes like this on TV when she was bedridden.

"You've been making bread?"

"To be more precise, I've been teaching them how to create leaven, which we then use to bake bread. I had Lux make the ovens," Roxine answered matter-of-factly.

The villagers mostly baked a salty, hard, dark rye bread that could be softened by dipping it in stews and soups. The bread Cayna's household made with the help of Cooking Skills was a perfectly soft roll. When Roxine had brought some of this to the village, the women—Marelle included—were amazed. They said it was a delicacy, the kind of food only nobles ate.

In response, Roxine made yeast using the berries she'd harvested from the village's outskirts—a bit of knowledge she seemed to have picked up *outside* of the game's hardware. Cayna asked Roxine where she had learned such a thing, but Roxine claimed she didn't even know herself. It was as if Roxine had been equipped with some sort of external knowledge database.

"Well, it's not like I'll get a straight answer from you anyway, if even you yourself don't know where that info came from," Cayna concluded, giving up on the idea of pressing her for further information. "Besides, I'd just end up with a migraine."

"A wise decision indeed," Roxine replied, and an indescribable expression came over Cayna's face. After all, Roxine's vague response was the very reason why she decided not to think about this too much. However, she did wonder if her maid was intentionally dissing her. And considering this was Roxine, that was all too likely.

Nevertheless, Cayna was happy to see Roxine voluntarily contributing to the village's food culture. This change in Roxine, who never showed interest in anyone outside her immediate circle, astonished Cayna.

Since the ovens used firewood, the method was to light several at once. The current season presented no issues, but everyone would have to conserve wood once winter rolled in. Rather than warm each home individually, it was more efficient to burn a fire in one place.

"Now that you're here, Lady Cayna, we won't need to use firewood," said Roxine.

"I was wondering why you didn't say anything when I followed you here," replied Cayna. "You had every intention of putting me in charge of the fire, didn't you?"

"I cannot deny that."

"Some maid you are…"

Roxine's straightforward answer made it seem like a completely premeditated crime.

Mimily paid for meals via her laundry services, so she came to this gathering to take advantage of the shared bread.

Cayna reluctantly summoned a Fire Spirit to light the ovens and adjust the heat as Roxine instructed. However, watching the Fire Spirit in the hole beneath each oven raise one hand in the air and create a particular hero's signature pose with the flames was incredibly strange. The women were just baking bread, so using the Fire Spirit for this purpose felt totally wrong. Cayna didn't use magic rhyme-stones because you couldn't adjust the temperature well with them and they could run out of gas quickly if they were too small.

"I bet Opus would burst out laughing if he saw me doing this."

"You may well be right."

Even Kee sounded exasperated.

Cayna attempted to get by without leaving the village for half a month but started running low on supplies. Roxine's estimations were right on the nose.

The biggest contributing factor was the large volume of food they were consuming. This included the seasonings as well as the wheat used primarily for bread, which was a dietary staple. Since Cayna's household didn't have their own field in the village, they couldn't grow their own wheat. They could get food from Marelle in a worst-case scenario, but that would put Roxine in a bad mood. Vegetables weren't an issue since Roxilius had charmed the local wives; they gave him some of their own in exchange for small tasks. The meat caught by the hunter Lottor was divided evenly among the villagers, and Roxine brought back whatever animals she took down while gathering wild strawberries and plants.

There was also the matter of clothing and accessories.

Once the house was built, Cayna had made a large number of cloth-based items. Cayna herself hadn't been sure how much they'd need on a daily basis, so the quantity she had purchased had been completely inadequate. As she obeyed Roxine's demands of "I'd like a curtain here" and "A rug would be good here," Cayna ran out in no time. Luka also used fabric for her sewing practice, so the household truly did use up a great deal. Although processing items had its many uses, doing so also required materials. No matter how mighty one's skills might be, you couldn't create something from nothing.

"Hmm. I knew it—we'll have to go to Felskeilo or Helshper and buy some more."

It looked like she also had the option of reaching out to Lux Contracting and ordering from Sakaiya directly. However, it would take her goods over ten days to arrive.

"Come to think of it, I'll also need fodder for the goats," said Cayna.

"Do not worry on that matter," Roxilius assured her. "As long as they do not disrupt the village's crops, it seems they are free to eat the weeds and grasses. We can always feed them hay as a stopgap measure."

"I'll…walk the goats," Luka added.

Cayna planned on keeping goats for their milk. Roxilius had apparently found out from the villagers the best way to care for them, and as soon as Luka heard this she volunteered to help as well.

"Shouldn't that be my job?"

"Your miscellaneous chores are our duty, Lady Cayna," Roxilius replied.

"Besides, shouldn't you be looking for Opus?" Roxine asked.

"…That's true. I wonder if that jerk's still around."

Opus's existence seemed questionable, but Li'l Fairy was the key to finding him—at least, that's what Cayna thought. She needed a way to communicate with the fairy, something she hadn't quite figured out yet.

Li'l Fairy popped out from Cayna's hair and beamed. The fact that only players could see her was a source of frustration.

"You're one big swirl of mystery, too," Cayna told the fairy as she watched her flit about happily.

Li'l Fairy was slightly under twenty centimeters tall and could fit in the palm of Cayna's hand. She had long, light green hair and blue eyes, and the four wings sprouting from her back were a translucent light green. Her face looked like that of a ten- to twelve-year-old human girl. The fairy lived in Cayna's hair, and when she did come out on occasion, she was usually all smiles.

Cayna and the other players could touch her, but she seemed to pass through everything else. The fairy was sensitive to noise and hid at any intense or loud sound. She didn't need to eat and smiled every morning as she watched everyone eat breakfast. Even windy days had no effect on her, and she could always sit on Cayna's shoulder with ease. Cayna had no idea if Opus ever named the fairy, so she simply dubbed her Li'l Fairy. Since the fairy glowed with a faint phosphorescence every time Cayna used her skills or magic, she wondered if she was connected to the game's system.

"Yeah, there's gotta be some connection."

It seemed that the change in the system Cohral had talked about had happened right after Cayna met the fairy, and she'd also acted strangely back when Cayna used Special Skill: Oracle. It might even be possible that Cayna wouldn't have been able to use the skill without her. Based on his actions during the game, Cayna had a sneaking suspicion Opus was an administrative player. Not that she had any proof.

"Did Opus purposefully leaving you behind have something to do with the system?"

She had a feeling the truth went far deeper. After all, Li'l Fairy's response to this question was to immediately turn to Cayna and puff up her cheeks before turning away haughtily to sit on Cayna's shoulder.

Cayna felt like she offended the fairy in some way. At this point, though, she could do nothing more than talk to her, pat her head, and apologize in earnest. By the time the fairy had cheered up and was flying around in happy circles, Cayna went back to her room and collapsed into bed from mental exhaustion.

A knock soon came at the door, and Cayna sat up listlessly. "Come in," she said.

Luka popped her head into the room, then went inside and walked over to Cayna.

"Mommy Cayna..."

"What is it, Lu?"

Luka hugged Cayna's leg. Cayna picked the girl up and took in the child's warmth.

"Were you talking...to someone?" Luka asked.

She must've overheard Cayna apologizing to Li'l Fairy. After a moment's thought, Cayna set Luka down next to her.

"Uhh, well. I might've mentioned this before, Lu, but I can see fairies."

"Uh-huh."

"And I made one of those fairies mad at me. I was apologizing just now."

"Mm...?"

Luka didn't seem to follow. After all, she couldn't see the fairy herself. It was hard to believe in something you couldn't see. Fairies in storybooks were visible only to children, but in this case it was practically the opposite.

"Are fairies...scary when they're mad?"

Cayna pondered Luka's question for a moment. The easier answer would be, "*They're a bunch of meanies!*" but if she made Li'l Fairy mad again, it'd only wind up being more work for her.

"Uhh, well...they'll pull your hair while you're sleeping, take your fork when you're eating, and sit in the middle of the page when you're reading a book," Cayna replied, choosing her words carefully as she gauged the fairy's reaction.

Li'l Fairy plopped herself right on Luka's head and stared at Cayna, which made Cayna more than a little nervous. She was still in the realm of gentle ribbing, but if provoked, the fairy might shoot a magic spell in a random direction, something Cayna was eager to avoid.

Luka looked sad, so Cayna patted her head and said, "It's all right. Watch this!" She then cast Illusion Magic. Small bits of phosphorescence gathered from around the room to converge right in front of Luka. They gradually took a humanoid form and solidified to become a second Li'l Fairy. It was a carbon copy of the real one, so the size was exactly the same. It was impossible to touch since it was an illusion, but Luka could without question see this "Li'l Fairy."

Luka stared wide-eyed for a few moments before reaching out her hand, which passed right through the illusion.

"Oh, sorry, Lu. It's just a picture, so you can't actually touch her."

"This is...a fairy?"

The illusion spread her wings and arms as if she were flying. The real one gleefully struck the same pose.

Luka gazed curiously at the two smiling fairies.

"This fairy looks the same as the one that flies around me. The real one is right next her making the same pose," Cayna explained.

Luka looked between the illusion and the empty space that the real fairy occupied and giggled softly.

"Show me...the real one someday..."

"Sure. I promise I'll introduce you."

Cayna spent the rest of the day chatting with Luka until they eventually fell asleep together. The next day, Luka asked if there was any way to keep the fairy illusion around.

"Hmm. I guess it's not impossible. But what for?"

"I want Latem...to sculpt her."

Cayna couldn't help but sympathize with poor Latem for the huge request he was about to get. She'd cheer him on but wouldn't help him out of this one.

Cayna used the Copy skill to print the illusion on a piece of paper and handed it to Luka.

"It's fine that you want him to create a model of her, but be sure to help him out, okay, Lu?"

"Uh-huh!" Luka replied giddily. She was no doubt eager to hurry up and invite Lytt to come along, but the three kids wouldn't be able to meet all morning.

After Cayna finished eating, she gave orders to Roxilius and Roxine.

"I'm leaving the house to you two for now. No fighting."

"In a worst-case scenario, I can gather provisions from around the outside of the village," replied Roxilius.

"You'd only gather meat," Roxine scoffed.

Elineh's caravan visited the village just once a month or so, which Cayna hadn't factored into her recent move. That further contributed to her household's heavily depleted stockpile.

Roxilius and Roxine had apparently anticipated this situation, as they were actually having a civil discussion for once.

"That was sooner than expected," Roxine stated.

"I didn't think we'd have these shortages," Roxilius replied. "Since our water and fire are supplied by magic, we should be consuming less fuel than other households."

"I imagine it has to do with our food consumption."

"Indeed. Lady Cayna is used to three meals a day, after all."

"I think it would be best to split breakfast and lunch into a total of 1.25 meals."

"Yes. Two and a quarter meals seems reasonable."

"I think that's a fine idea. So two for us ladies and a quarter for the mangy cat."

"Aren't you the one who should be on a diet? Scaling the fence must be quite difficult for you now."

"Hsss!"

"Shaaa!"

Cayna had just warned them not to fight, but fighting came as naturally to the two as breathing. She couldn't take her eyes off them for a second.

Just as Cayna felt a migraine coming on, Luka stepped between the pair before they could come to blows. Moved by what a good little girl Luka was, Cayna patted her head and showered her with praise.

"Are…we going out…?" Luka asked.

"Yup, that's right. You still have to meet Mai-Mai."

"Who's…Mai?"

"She's my daughter—and your new big sister!"

As Cayna tossed a whiskey barrel onto the shed's second-floor rail, a thought struck her. If all that needed doing was loading barrels up and down, there was no need for a ladder; she could just use the Leap skill. Luka had been very curious about the whole process, so Cayna leaped to the second story with Luka in her arms. The little girl seemed to enjoy watching the barrels roll down the rails with a *thunk, thunk.*

The magic rhymestones installed in the shed kept the humidity and temperature consistent. Kee had crunched the numbers since he knew how these things worked, but because he was merely a disembodied voice, Cayna had to do all the installations herself.

"All right, that should do it for today."

Cayna held Luka and leaped down to the first floor. Li'l Fairy wiped the sweat from Cayna's brow as if to say *Good work.* The fairy had more time on her hands than anyone else in the village, with Cayna at a close second.

Once Cayna put Luka down on the ground, Luka told her, "I'll go...help Cie," and went over to the house. She couldn't quite pronounce Roxilius and Roxine's full names, so they'd said she could call them by simple nicknames: Roxine became "Cie" and Roxilius became "Li." Luka voluntarily helped Roxine with housework; cleaning the bathhouse with Roxilius became her punishment.

As Cayna wondered what to do next, she heard the sounds of a ruckus entering the village. There was a host of neighing horses and rough footsteps, as well as the thuds of wagon wheels along the ground and the clamor of people coming together all at once. Even if they'd been apart for some time, she knew all this meant that a good friend had just arrived.

Elineh's caravan had appeared for its usual visit. Their timing was perfect, since she had been at a loss for what to do about her stockpile issues, so Cayna headed on over.

As always, the caravan crew unloaded luggage and set up simple stores in the plaza by the entrance of the village. The sharp-eared villagers had already begun gathering and waiting in anticipation for the shops to open.

Cayna greeted the crew with a polite bow and looked around. She soon spotted her target, Elineh. He was chatting with Arbiter and the other caravan members in a corner lined up with wagons.

"Hello, Elineh."

"Oh, Lady Cayna. It has been quite some time."

"Hey there, miss."

Elineh and Arbiter greeted Cayna warmly when she waved and headed over to them.

"Ah yes, I have the goats and chickens you requested from Sakaiya, Lady Cayna," said Elineh. "An attendant has gone to deliver them."

"That's great. Thank you very much."

"Think nothing of it. This is business, after all. I have already collected the transport fee. The goods you ordered are higher than the market price and have earned me quite a profit."

Judging from Elineh's ear-to-ear grin, Caerick must have paid him a little extra. Cayna was well aware that goats and chickens themselves didn't have too high of a transport fee, so her expression turned sour.

"He'll be in trouble if word gets out that he tends to trivialize cost and has no desire to make a profit," she said.

"C'mon, the guy's showing a little devotion to his grandma! Just take it," Arbiter replied.

"……"

The moment Arbiter called Cayna "grandma," the temperature around them instantly dropped. Elineh and the co-captain quickly backed away from him, and the next moment, he found himself under the spotlight.

"I beg your pardon, Arbiter. What did you just call me?"

"Hold on, just wait a sec! Calm down! Okay, I take it back! It was a figure of speech! A figure of speech! I'm sorry, I was wrong, I'll never say it again, forgive me!"

Before he knew it, Arbiter was surrounded by a wall of water that was smooth as polished glass. Even though it was a warm day with the sun shining bright, that spot alone was cold as a jail cell in midwinter. Arbiter let out a flurry of panicked, wailing apologies.

Cayna had intended to merely rake him over the coals a bit, so she soon released Arbiter from his watery prison. He clutched at his chest.

"This is why I always tell you to think before you speak," his co-captain admonished.

Arbiter got a taste of Cayna's frightening powers after she cornered him with such swiftness that he couldn't even hope to flee her clutches. Feeling the sun's warmth on his skin once again gave him a momentary reprieve before he was attacked from another angle.

"Honestly, sir, you truly are hopeless. Commenting on a woman's age forfeits any right to complain, even if you are stabbed repeatedly from behind," the co-captain said as he brandished his short sword. When Arbiter instinctively paled and froze up, the co-captain cheerfully told him, "It was a joke." However, his sword stayed right where it was.

Cayna left the co-captain to take his stress out on Arbiter and began discussing matters with Elineh.

"You wish to come with us to Felskeilo?" Elineh asked her. "That's all right with me, although I thought you had your own methods of instantaneous travel."

"I'm bringing some people with me, so I was thinking we could take a leisurely trip in the wagon."

"In that case, you're welcome to join us. How can I ask for anything more than having a powerful mage to accompany us on our journey?"

Elineh readily accepted, but something else seemed to be worrying him. He furrowed his brow.

"Having said that, I'm afraid the wagons don't have much room for sleeping. You will likely have to sleep outside in the hammocks again. Is that all right?"

Elineh's expression turned apologetic, but Cayna replied, "That's totally fine," and waved her hand with a smile. "I have my own wagon this time. I got it from your store."

"Ah, the one you purchased the other day. I hear you've made some marvelous renovations. It's become quite the talk of the town."

Rumors traveled eerily fast. Those were merchant networks for you.

"People are talking about it even though I only rode it once, from Felskeilo to here?"

"A sensible person does not judge an item based on its rarity alone. What matters most is how well it serves one's purposes." Elineh suddenly drew close. His expression was serious; his tone changed. "Please take care, Lady Cayna. Many are after this wagon of yours. I hear several nobles have already set their sights on it. If you do travel outside this village, perhaps you might be better off going to a neighboring nation?"

Cayna looked at him blankly for a moment, then murmured, "Ah, right, right," and struck her fist against her palm. A cunning smile rose to her face. For those who knew her well, such as Exis, the malice in that smile and the chaos it so often brought were cause for much concern.

"The great and mighty nobles, huh?" said Cayna. "That sure does sound like an interesting quest…"

"'Quest'?"

"Ah, nothing, just talking to myself. Anyway, I really do appreciate the warning, Elineh. If I hadn't known, I'm sure something ridiculous would have happened."

"Yes, please be careful. After all, I would be very troubled if something were to happen to a dear customer."

"Right, duly noted. I'll keep an eye out. I wouldn't want to worry you."

Elineh put a hand to his chest in relief and left Cayna. However, he didn't seem to realize that his idea of "being careful" was drastically different from hers.

After listening to them from nearby, Arbiter shot Cayna a reproachful look as she giggled.

"Hey, miss."

"What is it, Arbiter?"

"If somethin' goes wrong in the capital, just lemme know. I'll get in touch with my old workplace."

Cayna's eyes widened. She laughed softly and replied, "Thank you very much," with a dip of her head. "Wow, Arbiter, you're super nice. Makes me wonder if there'll be a natural disaster tomorrow."

"Hey now! Is that what you say when people are tryin' to be nice?"

"I kid, I kid. I'll just go ask Mye for help if I get stuck in a jam."

"Don't you dare go botherin' the princess, dammit!!"

The other mercenaries started causing a stir when they noticed Arbiter chasing Cayna around and waving his spear at her. But since their co-captain—who was normally the first to mediate whenever a fight broke out—decided not to get involved in this two-person game of tag, they simply watched the events unfold. Needless to say, as soon as Arbiter directed his spear tip at them and yelled, "Quit lookin' at us like that!" the men scattered like baby spiders.

Cayna managed to escape the ghastly game of tag that had unfolded and headed for the inn.

She greeted the villagers who had just finished eating and were on their way to the fields, and then entered the building.

"Good morning!"

"Ah, if it isn't Cayna," said Marelle. "Mornin'."

"Good morning, Miss Cayna," said Lytt.

Cayna exchanged greetings with the mother-daughter pair and

approached the counter. "Mind if I have a quick word?" she asked Marelle, who tilted her head in puzzlement. Cayna asked if she could borrow her daughter.

"Borrow Lytt?" said Marelle. "I hope you're not recruiting her for your beer-brewing business."

"No, no. I'm taking Lu to meet my older daughter, and I thought Lytt might like to join us. It doesn't seem like she has many opportunities to visit the capital, so I figured this would be a good learning experience for her. Would that be okay with you?"

"Hmm. Well…"

"What if I have Cie help you out with the inn? Or maybe I can give you a barrel of beer for free?"

Lytt froze in confusion. Marelle glanced between her daughter and Cayna, but finally caved to their earnest stares.

"You sure know how to make a deal, Cayna," she said with a sigh. "All right, I accept. You can take Lytt with you."

"I'll have Rox bring you a barrel a bit later. Okay, Lytt, time to start packing for our trip. We'll be traveling with Elineh's caravan."

"Huh? Huh? Whaaaa?!"

Lytt didn't comprehend what was happening. Dumbfounded, she blinked her eyes in a fluster, and Marelle patted her back to calm her down. Marelle had heard Elineh's caravan was spending the day in the village before departing tomorrow.

"You're going with Mr. Elineh?" Marelle asked. "Well, I would've said yes a lot sooner if you'd mentioned that."

"Hmm, really?"

"Really. Why wouldn't I be more worried at the thought of you three girls going off on your own?"

When Marelle put it like that, Cayna could see where she was coming from. Marelle had never seen for herself what Cayna was capable of, so naturally she was nervous about Lytt accompanying her.

Cayna flexed her arm and made her case to Marelle in order to put her at ease.

"You have my word that I'll eliminate any harm that might get in Lytt's way. You have nothing to worry about. Besides, we'll be using my wagon this time. And Rox will also be with us, so we'll be perfectly protected."

Roxilius was only half of Cayna's level, but his combat abilities alone made him a worthy defender.

At her mother's urging, Lytt went off to prepare for the journey. Once she was out of earshot, Marelle bowed her head. "Thanks for this, Cayna. She's in your hands now."

"Don't be silly, Marelle. I owe a lot to Lytt. Plus, she's my friend. Of course I'll keep her safe."

"It's like the village is back to its old lively self ever since you showed up."

"I feel a little bad for turning the place upside down. I'm afraid the elder might keel over."

Cayna shrugged, and Marelle burst into laughter. Her husband, Gatt, poked his head in from another room to see what all the commotion was about and joined in the laughter when he heard the reason. Lytt came back with a small rucksack that contained a change of clothes and tilted her head in confusion when she saw the adults in stitches.

Elineh and his crew would be departing the following day, so Cayna told Lytt to meet her by the caravan early that morning. After checking that Lytt was adequately prepared, Cayna left the inn. She had invited Latem as well, but he didn't get permission to go since Lux was still mad at his son for the previous runaway incident. He seemed upset, but he was most likely already familiar with big cities since he was born in Helshper.

"In-invite me next time, 'kay?" he asked with a tight smile. He probably would have acted more like his usual self if his mother, Sunya, wasn't right behind him, monitoring him to see if he might say something careless.

Cayna had initially chosen Roxilius to accompany them, given his good social skills, but Roxine insisted she take his place.

"If you three ladies will be traveling together, then I shall join you. An oaf like him doesn't understand the inner workings of a woman's heart. It would be extremely unwise to bring him along."

"But there's gonna be lots of people. You're okay with that, Cie?"

"If you are referring to the worthless insect rabble, I shall not grow hostile. If push comes to shove, I can simply spray insecticide."

An easy-enough solution, although Roxine was essentially making terroristic threats. But since Cayna wanted to take Roxine out of the house every now and then, her proposal couldn't have come at a better time.

Roxilius offered no objections, although his scary murmurings of "I wonder how many she'll turn to trash beyond all recovery..." left quite an impact on Cayna.

"Please look after the house, Rox. And before we get back..."

"Yes, I understand. I am to accept the alcohol and magic tools that are to be delivered from Helshper. Worry not—it will be done."

"Thanks, I appreciate it."

Roxilius bowed respectfully, and Cayna answered with a light wave of the hand.

Hopefully their trip would prove uneventful, but if Luka ended up in any sort of danger, there would be no quelling Cayna's resulting rage.

"Opus was always good at dealing with this sort of thing."

Not that she could ask him for advice now. Cayna wound up wracking her brain over how to avoid the nobles' unreasonable demands.

Roxine, meanwhile, was taking care of their luggage with Luka, who stared wide-eyed as Cayna clutched at her head and mumbled to herself.

The next morning, each member of Elineh's caravan went slack-jawed when Cayna rolled in with her wagon. Of course, Lytt, who had arrived early to wait for them, was no exception.

"H-hey, miss... Whatcha got there?" Arbiter asked, pointing at the horse head neighing behind Cayna. Though it produced the typical sounds an actual horse would make, the horse-shaped head was not part of a real animal—it was made of wood and had a grain finish. Even Arbiter had seen horse golems in his line of work before, but never one with a blinking, braying head.

It stuck out from driver's seat. The fact her wagon ran on no horses at all was fundamentally strange. That technically made it just a plain cart.

Luka rubbed her eyes sleepily as she popped her head out from the loading bed. Realizing she had the attention of the entire caravan, she jolted and ducked back inside.

"This is my wagon. Something wrong with it?"

"""" ......""""

Where to begin? There wasn't anything *specifically* wrong; its very existence was the issue. Elineh's mouth twitched even though he'd already heard the rumors describing this wagon.

"Pardon me, Lady Cayna," he said. "This is the wagon we discussed previously, correct?"

"Yes. The very same."

Fascinated members of the caravan surrounded the covered-wagon golem and observed it closely. For the most part, the covered wagon was ordinary and no different than the way it had been when Cayna first obtained it. What *was* different, however, was the wooden horse head sticking out of the driver's seat, which was the focal point of this golem. Every vital point was embedded with a magic rhymestone, but it was the head that unified the wagon and allowed it to move. It also guaranteed a pleasant ride.

A barrier spell behind the curtain kept the interior at a comfortable temperature. The cushioned interior was big enough for three grown adults to sprawl out and relax, and the wagon itself barely swayed when in motion, thanks to a spell that eased the jolting of the wheels and axles. If any nobles knew of these features, they would surely try to snap up the wagon at once. But there was a catch: This wagon needed a little something extra in order to function properly.

"To be honest, this thing eats up magic like crazy. It practically needs an external MP tank," Cayna explained.

The average person would end up fainting if they used spell after spell and depleted their MP all in one day. Unless you were someone like Cayna, who boasted an inexhaustible supply, it was impossible to keep the wagon running from the village to the capital.

Many people in the group worried about Cayna and warned her to keep an eye out for any nobles who would want her wagon for themselves. But there was no time to waste by standing around and taking in Cayna's vehicle; Elineh's subordinates promptly got the caravan set up, and they were soon on their way. As the villagers saw them off, Lytt spotted her mother among the crowd and waved excitedly. Luka also leaned forward out of the wagon to wave at Marelle. When Cayna joined in and waved, too, Marelle returned the gesture with a strained smile.

"Now, if you don't mind me."

"Come on in."

Once the caravan began to depart, Elineh visited Cayna's covered wagon. He was all smiles and made it very clear they weren't going

anywhere until he could have a look. Cayna had no reason to refuse him, of course, so she gladly welcomed him aboard.

"Goodness... You really don't feel the swaying at all, do you?" he said incredulously.

Sitting on one of the many cushions that covered nearly the entire floor, Elineh marveled at how little vibration they felt beneath them.

The cushions were the results of Luka's sewing practice. Roxine's training seemed to place more emphasis on creating things than patching up clothing. The shapes depicted in the center of the cushions weren't entirely clear, but this made them even more enjoyable to look at.

Luka and Lytt opened up the back curtain and sat next to each other, their eyes agleam with curiosity as they watched the scenery pass them by. Roxine stood at attention making sure they didn't fall.

Everyone's luggage was suspended on hooks placed along the wall of the covered wagon. This was mostly a decoration meant to dispel any suspicion. Cayna had her own Item Box, of course, and Roxine did as well, so they kept the luggage in the wagon to a minimum.

Cayna took out a small table, upon which Roxine soon placed cups of black tea. Elineh's eyes went wide with surprise as he was offered a drink that seemed to come out of nowhere.

"I've always wondered, Lady Cayna—where do you and your friends store all these things?"

"Oh, it's an ancient art of sorts. I don't think there's a way to learn it anymore."

"I see. That makes it all the more interesting..."

Cayna couldn't tell anyone about her Item Box. She'd learned that calling it an ancient art kept people from prying any further.

"I wonder if there will be any vacant inns in Felskeilo this time of year," Elineh said, changing the subject when he suddenly realized there were more urgent matters at hand.

"'This time of year'? Is something going on in Felskeilo?" Cayna asked.

"Yes—ah, but of course you wouldn't be familiar with it. It's called the River Festival."

Since Cayna had told him when they first met that she was from the middle of nowhere, Elineh wasn't the least bit surprised she didn't know about this festival and proceeded to explain in detail.

Unlike most other cities, the royal capital of Felskeilo was bisected by a great river: the Ejidd River. Consequently, the city depended on this river for survival. Felskeilo citizens lived shoulder to shoulder with the water; its benefits and adversities shaped them as people. Thus, they held this festival annually in the royal capital to offer the river their gratitude.

"The most exciting event is the boat race at the end of the festival. Anyone, old or young, can participate. The race is just two simple laps around the sandbar, but each year it remains a highlight that has you on the edge of your seat."

"Really? I'd like to see that."

"I myself participated with friends many times as a child."

"Huh? You did, Elineh?"

Cayna worried that his small kobold frame would have put him at too much of a disadvantage. Yet the smile on Elineh's face as he fell into his vivid childhood memories told her that he enjoyed being momentarily transported back to another place and time.

"I was always eliminated in the preliminary round, however…"

"Oh dear…"

Elineh smiled awkwardly and scratched his head, but he didn't look the least bit upset. In fact, he seemed perfectly content. Cayna could tell this vignette from Elineh's life brought back happy memories.

"But despite all my failures, that race helped me learn the joys of teamwork."

As Elineh described his youth in earnest, Cayna couldn't help but smile, too. He was different from his usual self, and she found it rather interesting.

Noticing Cayna's grin, Elineh looked down sheepishly.

"Goodness…look at me, rambling on and on about my younger days. Do keep this between us, Lady Cayna."

"I will. That side of you is safe and sound with me, Elineh."

Cayna looked over at Roxine, who had been listening in, and the werecat nodded lightly. Roxine would never tell a soul. Cayna couldn't think of anyone the maid could tell even if she wanted to.

"Hmm. So it'll be hard to find a room, huh…?" Cayna wondered aloud.

Since she now had a human child with her, she doubted she could stay at her usual inn. The guests she'd met there didn't seem to take too kindly to humans.

Maybe she could use the inn she had arbitrarily chosen when she brought Luka along last time. It was a pretty classy establishment near the river. She remembered paying one gold coin for a night. However, even though money wasn't an issue, Cayna wasn't into such fancy places, so she decided to forego that option.

"What do you say I show you somewhere you can stay?" Elineh offered.

"Huh?"

Elineh's offer took a moment to register with Cayna; her mouth hung wide open. She had assumed his company didn't dabble in real estate.

Elineh was proposing she rent a vacant house that his company used. Incidentally, he told her, it was quite normal for merchants to be involved in a variety of merchandise. Elineh's company handled quite a bit of real estate that ranged from small cottages to entire housing complexes.

"I'll lend you a one-family house."

"Are you sure that's all right?"

"Of course. And should you take a liking to it and want to use it as a home base in Felskeilo, I can certainly make the proper arrangements for purchase."

"Well, I'd at least like to try before I buy. But I'll gladly take you up on your rental offer."

After that, he instructed her on proper precautions before settling into the home. They would draw up a formal contract after arriving at Elineh's company.

There were only two rules: *Don't break the equipment. Clean the house after use.*

"That's it?" Cayna asked.

"Yes, although we do strictly enforce them. You must reimburse us for anything you break."

"Understood. We'll clean the house top to bottom and return it to you in prime condition," Cayna replied with utmost confidence.

Elineh smiled pleasantly. "When you say that, Lady Cayna, it makes me fear I will end up with a brand-new house altogether."

"What're you talking about? I mean, sure, I could do that, but I won't. That would be a lot of work."

She could use several skills in her arsenal to make a weathered home good as new. However, since doing so would require her to use both MP and HP, she'd be completely wiped out by the time she was done. Cayna personally thought the idea was full of disadvantages and therefore was not something she wished to do at all.

She tried to ask for as much detail about the River Festival as she could, but since Elineh would be making the rounds as a sponsor, he didn't know much beyond the main events.

"I believe Sir Arbiter would be more helpful in that regard."

"Huh, I see…"

She enjoyed spending the rest of the day discussing Felskeilo from a merchant's perspective with Elineh until they reached the first campsite.

Luka and Lytt naturally couldn't keep up with such conversation, and Cayna found the two peacefully fast asleep together in no time.

Just as Roxine was putting a blanket over them, the caravan stopped for a short rest. Elineh took this opportunity to apologize for "overstaying his welcome," and he alighted from the wagon golem.

Then, as they camped along the main road that night…

Several bonfires were lit since their group was quite large, and everyone had dinner. Roxine was a big hit with the merchants in Cayna's circle after exhibiting her culinary talents.

Just as Cayna was thinking that it'd be nice if Roxine was able to get along this well with others, Arbiter approached her group with a bottle of alcohol in one hand. An unpleasant look appeared on Roxine's face, and she brusquely got to her feet.

"Well then, Lady Cayna. I shall look after Lady Luka and Lady Lytt. Please do your best to care for the inebriated."

"Thanks, Cie. Good night, girls."

"Good night, Miss Cayna!"

"Good…night…"

Arbiter was still sober, and he didn't give the slightest reaction when Roxine dealt him the low blow. His gaze shifted between the children returning to the wagon and the bottle; he seemed to be deliberating over whether to have a drink. He noticed Cayna's giggling and called out to her.

"H-hey, miss!"

"I don't mind if you drink. We all need ways to relax. What's holding you back?"

"Uh, I'm pretty sure that maid of yours hates me…"

"Cie's like that with everyone. She's really softened up a lot recently."

"You call that 'soft'? How?"

Arbiter scowled, and as he watched Roxine's receding form slip into the night, he started gulping down the beverage.

"*Phwaagh!* That one hit is what I live for. I've been reborn."

"…'One hit'?"

She figured one bottle and one drink were essentially the same thing for anyone who loved alcohol.

Cayna brought out roasted beans and grilled, salted fish from her Item Box to pair with it. She had bought them during her last shopping trip in Felskeilo and stocked up when she got hooked on several flavors. Ever since summoning Roxilius and Roxine, Cayna had been eating her favorite foods without even having to ask for them, so she completely forgot to take these out.

"Man, these are some good snacks. You make these, miss?" Arbiter asked.

"No, I bought them a little earlier."

Arbiter's face turned strange at her honest answer, and he sniffed the beans and fish.

"Don't seem like they've gone bad."

"They're perfectly edible. I guarantee it," she assured him.

Storing them in her Item Box prevented any degradation, so there was nothing to worry about. However, Cayna doubted she could tell Arbiter as much.

"I heard from Master Elineh that this'll be your first River Festival. That right, miss?"

"Uh, well, yeah. I mean, I'd only just left the countryside when you and I first met."

"That feels like forever ago. You've got one hell of a presence."

"What's that supposed to mean?" Cayna demanded. Arbiter took a swig of his drink and gave her a tight smile.

When she thought long and hard about everything she'd been through so far in Leadale, she realized she actually relished all these ups and downs. She felt much better and more alive than she ever did when she was stuck in a hospital bed.

As she ate her snack, she listened to Arbiter give a general overview of how to best enjoy the River Festival. The booths in the residential district were more leisurely and family-oriented than those on the main drag. There was plenty of fun to be had, but there were also plenty of pickpockets, so it was best to keep your wallet close. The boat race around the sandbar at the end of the festival was also worth checking out. Cayna wished Arbiter didn't encourage gambling, though. He told her about the different types of entertainment that could be found at the festival in great detail. Half of these involved food and drink, so it was rather obvious where Arbiter's interests laid.

"It'll be my first time going to anything like a festival. I can't wait."

As soon as she said this, Cayna realized her slipup but couldn't cover for herself. It was probably better not to say things that hinted at her time in "this world."

"Don't elves have festivals?" Arbiter asked.

"Y-yes, we do, but I'm a high elf, so...we can't really join in and goof off with the rest of the elves."

She relayed to him a sight she'd witnessed in one of the game's quests. It was a specifically for high-elf players, and the mission was to successfully pull off an elf festival. The quest itself wasn't very hard. The basic premise was that you had to eliminate obstacles that got in your way. But even if the festival went off without a hitch, the player could only sit on the throne and watch the festivities unfold. It left a sense of dissatisfaction that made one feel there could have been more to it, but it was a quest that seemed like it would have come from a player.

"That so, eh? I guess even you've got your own hidden troubles to deal with, miss."

It seemed that she had fooled him. Cayna felt a wave of relief.

Arbiter cut a pitiful figure as he nodded along to Cayna's explanation and tilted his bottle dramatically in order to lick the last drop of beer that trickled out. Unable to watch him any longer, Cayna handed him some beer from a small barrel she had set aside.

"Oh, is this…? Are you sure?"

"Seeing you struggle like that is just… Well…"

"Shucks. Sorry for kinda forcin' you into it."

Arbiter clutched the small barrel gleefully, and soon a couple of mercenaries appeared, lured in by the beer. They'd detected it in no time flat.

"Aghhh! You're so mean, boss, keepin' the good stuff all to yourself."

"Shut it! This was a gift."

News traveled in an instant, and soon enough even more mercenaries packed around Cayna's bonfire. Members on night patrol duty who were unable to leave their posts could only look on in jealousy. They hoped Arbiter would save them some since he'd been given his share for free.

"Got any more, miss?" he asked Cayna.

"Nope."

"""" """"
 ......

Part of the fun of traveling was watching the scenery change as it whizzed by, like on a train. Simply continuing down a forested road often grew tiring.

On a typical wagon ride, there wasn't much else to do except stare out at the sights. Roxine had brought some picture books with her, but reading them now might make her nauseous. She decided to save them for bedtime stories once they made camp.

Lytt and Luka enjoyed quizzing each other at first, but Luka had only recently moved to the village and couldn't get many answers right, so the game was over quickly. That was when Cayna took out a deck of cards.

It turned out there were all kinds of games in this world, although it wasn't clear whether *Leadale* players or their Fosters were responsible for their spread.

They had playing cards, *karuta*, *Hyakunin Isshu* (Cayna was impressed this world still had each poem intact), Go, shogi, chess, Reversi, the Game of Life, mahjong—it really was a wide array. Cayna had spotted them for sale in a corner of Sakaiya, to her astonishment.

Even simple card decks or *karuta* were fairly expensive since they were printed on thick, high-quality paper. No doubt the people in the remote village couldn't easily afford them. Elineh's caravan sold similar products, but the villagers apparently didn't go for them because on top of being pricey, they didn't know how to use these items.

Cayna first spread out her cards to show the designs. The kings and queens were cutesy little cartoon characters, but otherwise it was a pretty standard deck. The only other difference was the Joker card, which was now depicted as a cartoon ghost. Cayna had heard from Idzik that the designs on these cards were geared toward children, and that the adult version had separate designs.

Still, Cayna had to wonder why the store manager himself had been attending to her in the board game section. She understood he had been showing hospitality, but the store employees had been shocked. She distinctly remembered how he had insisted he had better things to do. When Idzik eventually offered Cayna the card deck for free, she quickly turned him down and paid the full price, even though he insisted they could spare the expense.

"Okay, let's first try a game called Concentration," Cayna said.

Lytt was confused. "Concen…"

"…tration…?" Luka finished her question.

Cayna turned all the cards over and demonstrated how the game worked. Roxine helped out with the explanation, and soon they were ready to begin playing in earnest.

Cayna had always thought she had a poor memory, but her skills and high specs apparently made up for it. She'd matched up four pairs of cards and then purposely played a few unmatching ones so that the kids had a chance to get ahead. After Roxine got three pairs, she too picked several unmatching cards in order to test the girls' memory. It seemed Roxine's recall abilities were just as good as Cayna's.

Aside from Luka and Lytt, Li'l Fairy also appeared to be having some trouble. Cayna had thought she was just spinning in circles over everyone to watch the game, but she would fly around certain cards with a smug look on her face, which guaranteed they wouldn't be a match when flipped over.

"Number oooone!" Lytt cheered.

"N-number two…," Luka stammered.

For their very first match, Lytt came in first and Luka in second. Cayna was third, and Roxine was fourth. From then on, Lytt and Luka continued to alternate between first and second place. The one time Lytt told Cayna and Roxine to get serious, the two took almost every card. Although they'd done as Lytt asked, it was a little immature of them to actually follow through.

The next card game they played was a version of Old Maid simply called Ghost, so named for the designs on the joker cards. It was a very odd feeling for those who knew it as Old Maid.

For this game, the outcome was obvious from the very beginning.

"Aww, come on! Why are Luka and Miss Roxine so good at this?" Lytt whined.

In three rounds, only Lytt had suffered crushing defeat. Luka and Roxine switched off between first and second, and Cayna was soundly in third place.

"I can tell...by your face," said Luka.

"You are very easy to read, Lady Lytt," Roxine agreed.

Lytt didn't stand a chance against Roxine, who had a mean poker face, and Luka, who was still fairly inexpressive.

"Lytt, you grin way too much when your opponent is about to take the old maid—I mean, the Ghost," said Cayna. "It's a dead giveaway."

"Nghhhhhh!"

Lytt moaned in frustration. Laughter erupted in the following match when Lytt pulled at her own face. The final outcome could only be described as unfortunate.

Leaving the depressed Lytt to Luka and Roxine, Cayna stepped down from the wagon. Kenison had asked her to come out and see Arbiter.

"What is it, Arbiter?" she asked.

The caravan had grown wary of something and was moving at a reduced speed. Cayna approached the mercenary group; Arbiter looked very concerned.

"Seems like we're being followed by something that's staying back at a set distance. Any idea what it could be?" he asked her.

"I can't say I do, no."

Cayna and her group had paid to come along and were thus treated as guests. Naturally, it also meant they were to be guarded. Even so, if asked, Cayna had every intention of helping guard and mount a counterattack. She had conveyed this when she joined the caravan.

"Well, hopefully it's just bandits or somethin'," said Arbiter.

"Captain...we'd better investigate their movements a bit more," his co-captain chided.

Arbiter's expression soured. It seemed that he'd been hoping to somehow avoid rebuke.

Cayna offered nothing in his defense, instead summoning a Wind Spirit and sending it in the direction that worried Arbiter. As she shared the spirit's sight and searched the surroundings, she discovered a host of thieves stalking them.

"It must be because us merchants all travel at once whenever a festival draws near," Elineh explained as he came by on his wagon. "They're after our earnings."

He shot a melancholy glance from the driver's seat to where the bandits had apparently gathered.

"I do wonder where they pour in from each year...," the co-captain grumbled as he rubbed between his brows. Bandits were no different from cockroaches, and they were treated just the same: as a scourge.

"They'll most likely attack us under the cover of night," Cayna said.

"We won't wait till night. Let's clean 'em up quick. You'll help out, right, miss?" Arbiter asked.

"Sure thing." Cayna was willing to lend a hand, but then when Arbiter suggested they just jump right in and drive the bandits out, she and the co-captain voiced their objections.

"We can't do that," Cayna insisted.

"Miss Cayna is right. To either capture or take out half their numbers, we will need to weaken the bandits' forces. Rushing in without a plan will only give our opponents the advantage. If they escape, it will be our own failure."

"Well, why don't we temporarily halt their forces? Master Elineh, what if you pretend one of your axles is broken and need to stop?" Arbiter suggested.

"Pretending we'll be immobile for some time? I do not mind. Since Lady Cayna is here, we can entrust her with our safety," Elineh replied.

Arbiter then made a rather crafty proposal that made one wonder why he wanted to blindly rush in to begin with. Elineh himself was quick to give permission and went along with the idea like an old partner in crime.

"Anyway, I'll leave you to keep us safe."

"Anyway, I shall leave our safety to you."

"Why are you two in sync?!"

Arbiter and Elineh grinned and patted Cayna's shoulders, while Cayna stood there in shock.

The co-captain issued orders one after the other, and the mercenaries moved into formation to stop the bandits from escaping. Cayna attempted to join the frontlines as well, but as soon as Arbiter said, "You've got kids. The last thing they wanna see is you caught up in a bloodbath," she quickly fell back.

Instead, she showered everyone with buffs: Attack Power Up, Defense Power Up, and Acceleration Up. She also cast a healthy amount of Invisibility on the mercenaries who were assigned to carry out the ambush. When Arbiter saw his subordinates flowing with power from every pore in their body, he heaved a resigned sigh.

"I dunno why these bandits even bother when we have her around," he said.

"This will undoubtedly turn out just like the incident at the national border," the co-captain agreed.

They then fleshed out the details of the plan to thwart the bandits.

After bouncing ideas off one other for a little while, the mercenaries notified the caravan, making sure to add that everyone needed to feign ignorance.

The caravan resumed its usual pace and continued on its way. Then, just as it reached the next campsite…

"Heeey! Hold on!" the mercenary acting as the decoy hollered so that everyone nearby could hear. The wagons stopped one by one. When the caravan came to a complete halt, the merchants poked their heads out of the wagons and asked what was going on. They were all cringe-worthy actors, but luckily they didn't need to be star performers. All they needed to do was trick their target.

"Something's wrong with this wagon axle. Someone, come help me out!"

This too was loud enough for everyone in the area to hear. Since the caravan was in the middle of the forest with nothing else around, the sound traveled a great distance.

The person they chose to be the decoy was apparently quiet by nature and not comfortable yelling. When Arbiter flatly told him, "It's all on you," he had accepted the role while smiling through his tears.

Not aware of the situation, Luka and Lytt leaned out the wagon to see what was going on. After Roxine's gentle urging, they reluctantly returned inside.

Several people gathered around the mercenary who had raised the call. Half of them were illusions Cayna had created with magic; they were meant as stand-ins for the mercenaries who had been cast with Invisibility and were now entering the forest to carry out an ambush. The bandits, seeing so many of the mercenaries crowded around one section of the caravan, chose that moment to leap out from the forest in droves. They'd intended to take the caravan by surprise, only to be overwhelmed from their rear by the mercenaries who had been lying in wait.

"Gah?!"

"Gwagh?!"

"Wh-what the—?!"

Most of the defeated bandits had either died blissfully unaware of their failure or otherwise didn't realize what was happening until right before they met their demise.

"I—I give up! I surrender!"

"P-please! Spare me!"

The survivors all quickly realized their situation, threw down their weapons, and surrendered.

"I can't tell anymore if we're playing dirty or not…," said Cayna.

"No use pointin' it out, miss," Arbiter replied. "This is just how it works."

"It's rough when they swarm in like this," Kenison added.

"You folks quit your rambling and tie them up already!" Arbiter yelled to his men.

""""Yessir.""""

The dead bandits were buried in holes right there while the survivors were captured so they could be taken to the capital. Their hands were tied behind them, and they were connected to ropes that trailed behind the wagons. To prevent any escape or resistance, a giant, double-headed snake that unsettled everyone was wrapped around the bandit group at their torsos.

Since Cayna was hesitant to let the children see the snake, she moved her golem wagon to the very front of the caravan.

"…Hey, miss, what's that?" Arbiter asked.

"A goghoda. They say if one bites you, you're dead before you can take even a few more steps."

The snake occasionally gave the bandits a good lick with its long tongue and stared directly into their eyes, making the men's faces go from a pale to deathly ashen color. A goghoda was a level-450 snake monster from the Underworld area; it often appeared as ornamentation around the arms and necks of the area's devil midbosses. Since the snake enjoyed being an accessory, Cayna summoned it and asked, "Could you please be their accessory in place of this rope?" and it happily agreed. Cayna really wanted to ask the snake if it was happy that way.

Arbiter felt sickened after watching the whole thing play out from start to finish. Who would tie someone up with a snake instead of a rope?

However, since they were on a main road, the caravan couldn't very well shock the passersby. Therefore, when given the order, the snake used a camouflage technique to disguise its body as a fat rope.

"Well, we're almost to Felskeilo. We can take it easy from here," Arbiter said.

The co-captain heaved a long, deep sigh as Arbiter quickly shifted into relaxed mode. By his look of resignation, this seemed to be an ongoing occurrence. Sensing his anxiety, several mercenaries patted the co-captain's shoulder and offered to help him out.

"...Arbiter," said Cayna.

"Hey, what's up? Why the look of pity?"

"I really do feel bad for the co-captain, so let's try and keep our focus."

"It's fiiine. As long as I'm a solid wall, me and my men can relax. There's nothin' to worry about!"

"I don't think being a solid wall should equal abandoning your job," Cayna pressed him solemnly. The mercenaries within earshot smirked.

Arbiter then beckoned Cayna to come closer. She was hesitant but obediently lent an ear.

66

"There's something strange going on in Felskeilo. Be careful," he whispered.

Cayna couldn't hide her unease. He was being too vague; she had no idea she was supposed to be careful of. Arbiter was basically telling her to be ready for anything and everything.

However, the biggest question of all was how he had managed to get this information while accompanying the caravan.

The Felskeilo royal capital was as lively as ever. Several other groups were lined up and waiting to go through the east gate, but the caravan was immediately allowed passage once the influential merchant Elineh displayed his permit.

Cayna had dispelled the snake beforehand, and the bandits were handed over to the guards at the gate. A monetary reward would be sent to the inn where Arbiter's group was staying. Cayna's horseless golem wagon astonished the guards, but they let her pass without further questioning. It grabbed the attention of others in line as well, and they all watched it go by with shock on their faces.

"Darn it. I should've put it in my Item Box before we got to Felskeilo," Cayna muttered.

She was hit with a wave of regret as soon as she saw just how people were staring wide-eyed at her mode of transportation.

"I think passing through this crowded street will be a bit hard on Lady Luka and Lady Lytt," Roxine said, and with good reason. The main streets were much more packed than when Cayna first came to the royal capital. Passing through the crowds now would now take twice as long as last time.

Shop employees loudly touted their wares and attempted to entice people in. Others danced in the sun while onlookers cheered them on and clapped to the beat. Some people carried large loads on their heads and shoulders or worked together in threes to move cargo. There were shoppers, sightseers, adventurers, and patrolling knights. The streets were overflowing with people from all walks of life.

Carriages traveled down a separate road, but the road's boundary line was vague, and for some reason people would dash out toward them from the pedestrian side. The caravan slowed to avoid hitting anyone, and as they moved along, the mercenaries arranged themselves to form a sort of wall.

Lytt and Luka had never seen such a conglomeration of people before, and their eyes sparkled in awe and wonder.

This was Luka's second time to Felskeilo, but she'd barely taken in the sights on her first trip since she hadn't been sure what was going on or how she was feeling. Cayna and Roxine observed with smiles on their faces as the two girls giddily asked, "What's that? How about that?" in a way one might expect girls their age to act.

The caravan made its way through town and arrived at Elineh's business. One wagon after another came to a halt behind the store where Cayna had earlier obtained her wagon, and employees bustled along in swarms as they transported their loads. They, too, were astonished to see the horseless golem carriage, but when the caravan merchants whispered, "Not a word to anyone," they nodded and returned to work.

"We can look after your wagon for you, Lady Cayna. What would you prefer?" Elineh offered Cayna after she climbed down from the wagon and stretched.

"It's okay, you don't have to go that far," she said. "Wouldn't it terrible of me to put that much on you after you've already told me everything else you're supposed to take care of?"

Once she made sure Lytt and Luka were out of the golem wagon, Cayna put it back in her Item Box. After seeing it disappear before his very own eyes, even Elineh, who had heard of such ancient arts, couldn't hide his surprise. He didn't question her further, but the look on his face made it clear that he was dying to know more. Cayna's ability to stow away entire wagons was part of her charm.

Cayna quickly signed the lease for the house they would be renting, and just as Elineh offered to have an employee give them a tour, Arbiter appeared with a subdued look on his face. It was hard to believe he was the same person who just a short while earlier enthusiastically exclaimed, *"I'm goin' straight to the bar!"*

"What is the matter, Sir Arbiter?" Elineh asked.

"I got a tip a bit earlier—looks like something weird is going on. I'm hearin' there's some worry about holding the festival."

"What?!" Cayna cried.

She had thought the festival was already happening, but it turned out it was still in its preparation stages. The sponsors were aiming for a bright, fine day to hold the actual event.

"So the energy level hasn't even hit its peak... What kind of situation could endanger the festival?" she asked.

"I already sent Kenison to the Adventurers Guild to find out. They'll let us know once they've got further details, so you should let the kids take a break in the meantime," Arbiter replied.

Luka and Lytt, whom Roxine had pulled away from Cayna and the group's conversation, were now staring at her. The sparkle in their eyes hadn't faded, and their expressions showed eager anticipation. Cayna couldn't possibly forbid them from going out when they looked at her like that. She thanked Elineh and Arbiter, and the girls were led to a house not far from the Elineh's business.

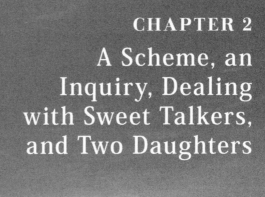

CHAPTER 2

A Scheme, an Inquiry, Dealing with Sweet Talkers, and Two Daughters

"This is a house?" Cayna asked.

"Well, it is rather big, but it used to be a small store," one of Elineh's employees replied as they gave Cayna's group a tour of the enormous two-story house. It was maybe about half the size of Marelle's inn, and even that qualified it as larger than a house. The employee handed them the key and said, "Please use it as you wish," before leaving.

The first floor had a wide storefront area, two smaller rooms, and a kitchen. One of these rooms had been converted into a dining room and was outfitted with a table that seated six. The second floor had three rooms that were about thirteen square meters total. Cayna, Luka, and Lytt would sleep in one of the rooms on the second floor, while Roxine would use a small room on the first floor. As they walked through the house and Cayna investigated the kitchen, she murmured that they would some need firewood.

In the meantime, Cayna took beds out of her Item Box and plunked them in the intended bedrooms. Roxine had utensils and food in her own Item Box, so they were fine in that regard. However, they still seemed to be lacking a few things.

"Hmm, guess I better go shopping," said Cayna.

"No, I shall take care of any errands," replied Roxine. "Lady Cayna, you should show the girls around town first."

Although the girls had been cautioned not to go exploring on their own, they were completely focused on going outside. At that moment, they saw a group playing music as it passed by a nearby road, and their eyes followed after it. Li'l Fairy was captivated as well; she floated through the wall over to the musical group before flying back in a hurry. She would probably be the first to get lost.

Leaving the shortage of supplies to Roxine to handle, Cayna decided to take the two girls out into the lively city. Using her memories of chasing Primo as a guide, she brought them to the riverbank.

However, since the citizens were constantly adding more piers to the riverbank, these swelled out several dozen meters farther toward the river than they had originally. Even so, the incident with the penguin monster had destroyed a wide swath of it, so the people must have rebuilt the extensions afterward. If seen from above, the piers created a serrated pattern.

Normally, there would be countless small boats bobbing along the river in addition to the large galleys that required many rowers. However, in that moment, they couldn't spot a single boat. Several small ones were tied up along most of the piers, and the surface of the oddly quiet river simply reflected the sun's rays.

"Huh?"

"Wow, this is amaaaaazing!"

"So…big."

Cayna tilted her head at the strangeness of the scene, while Lytt's heart soared as she gazed at the river. Luka had visited once before, but it'd been such a whirlwind that she didn't remember much—although most of that whirlwind may have been her interactions with the High Priest.

The flow of the river as it moved around the sandbar was gentle, and on calm days one would likely mistake it for a large lake. The church on the eastern end of the sandbar stood out conspicuously even at their current distance. It had the remarkable elegance of a white-walled palace.

"I wonder if this 'something' that's going on has anything to do with the boats being docked?" Cayna pondered aloud.

"Miss Cayna, Miss Cayna! What's that? That over there!"

Lytt's enthusiastic shouting interrupted Cayna's train of thought, and she looked up to see what the girl was pointing at. Calmly soaring over their heads was a giant laigayanma with people upon its back. Since the boats were out of commission, a number of dragonfly transport services were in operation up above.

"Those are dragonfly rides. You can ride a laigayanma to go sightseeing and cross to the other side of the river."

"Wowww!" Lytt squealed.

Lytt couldn't take her eyes off the dragonflies flying above her. She had apparently taken a keen interest in them. Since there was always the chance she might fall off the pier while she was busy staring up, Cayna pulled Lytt toward her.

"Mommy Cayna…"

"What's up, Lu?"

Luka tugged on Cayna's cloak and Cayna crouched down to meet her gaze. "Why…are there no boats?" Luka asked.

"Huh? Hmm, that's a good question. There must be some reason for it."

"Yeah…"

As you might expect from someone born in a fishing village, she immediately noticed there were no boats on the river. Luka's a genius!

"Cayna, please stop pretending to be surprised by a child's suspicions."

Cayna had a feeling Kee was giving her an exasperated stare, and her thoughts turned serious.

This certainly seemed to qualify as the "something strange" Arbiter had mentioned.

"Maybe something scary came out of the river?"

"Something…scary…"

"Ah! Sorry, sorry! There's nothing scary in there, nothing at all!"

Luka's expression darkened just then, and Cayna quickly pulled her into a hug. Realizing with a panic that her comment had probably reminded Luka of the disaster that occurred in her home village, Cayna's own regret made her want to kick herself for failing as a mother.

However, Luka suddenly removed herself from Cayna's embrace and smiled softly.

"I know…you're strong, Mommy Cayna."

"Lu…," Cayna said, trembling with overwhelming emotion.

Lytt hugged Luka as well and giggled. "Yup! Miss Cayna is suuuper strong. After all, she's a bad witch."

"Ack?! Lytt, I told you that was a secret!"

Lytt and Luka stared blankly as Cayna began panicking.

"But I already told her before…," said Lytt.

"Mommy Cayna…is not…a bad witch," added Luka.

"Ahhh! You two are such angels!"

Once again on cloud nine, Cayna held them both close. This only brought more attention to her, and the passersby on the pier watched the scene fondly—although Cayna never noticed.

After they finished viewing the river, they left the pier. The three avoided the crowded main streets and instead passed through the residential district, where many people had set up stalls selling drinks and meat skewers. Lytt and Luka grew thirsty from all their frolicking, and Cayna bought them drinks made from squeezed fruits. Each one was an incredibly cheap two bronze coins. They seemed to be diluted with water, but the fruit flavor still shone through. The girls returned the wooden cups once they were done, and the three enjoyed browsing the shops along the residential district while listening to the hustle and bustle of the main road. Cayna bought the girls wooden hair accessories made by the local women, and both Lytt and Luka were in a fantastic mood.

"I do not detect any danger in the area."

"Probably 'cause there are so many people here."

Cayna was holding the girls' hands and listening to Kee's report when a group of children crossed in front of them. She saw a familiar face among the group and yelled without thinking, "Primo! Did you run away again?"

"Huh? Agh?! It's the monster lady!"

Primo jumped in shock at the sight of Cayna's face, pointed at her while yelling this rude moniker, and ran away as fast as his legs would carry him. He dove into a narrow alley between two houses and disappeared out of sight. His reaction seemed to remind the other children of who Cayna was, too, and they scattered in every direction.

"He sure got out of here fast..."

"Do you know him, Miss Cayna?" Lytt asked.

Hardly a few seconds had passed between her calling out to him and the group making a break for it. Lytt and Luka—both unaware of Primo and Cayna's connection—were dumbfounded by the group's swift escape.

"Mon...ster?"

Luka seemed to take issue with this nickname. Cayna smiled and patted the girls' heads and decided to bring them up to speed. Of course, she skirted around the part where Primo was actually the prince.

"I took on a request from the Adventurers Guild to catch a rich kid who'd run away from home because he hated studying. That boy you saw just now was him."

Cayna chose to blame Primo's flight on his hatred of studying. Lytt and Luka frowned.

"But studying is fun," said Lytt.

"Uh-huh…I love…reading books," added Luka.

The diligent students' reactions warmed Cayna's heart, and she hugged them both.

Cayna couldn't go after Primo since she had to keep her eyes on the girls. She told herself she'd report him to one of Shining Saber's patrolling knights as soon as she spotted one.

After they went around the stalls buying meat skewers and such and returned to the rental house, they found a large pile of firewood in the kitchen. Roxine had apparently finished quite a lot in a short amount of time; the chairs in the second-floor bedroom had even been replaced with floor cushions.

Luka and Lytt sat on these cushions and enjoyed taking a load off their feet. As Cayna watched over them, Roxine called out to her.

"You have a guest, Lady Cayna."

"A guest?"

A table and chairs were set in the vast and empty-looking storefront room. Sitting there was Kenison.

"Sorry for the wait. Everything all right, Kenison?"

"Uh, yeah, I'm just here on an errand for the boss."

Something seemed to be bothering him, and he was being evasive. He stared absentmindedly into the teacup in front of him. When Cayna stole a glance at the cup, she found it was filled to the brim not with tea but with salt. The surprise of it temporarily left her stunned.

There was no need to ask who had brought it out; she already knew. This maid of hers had a knack for making Cayna look bad.

"…Um, I'm very sorry about my maid."

"Ah, it's okay. I just came to deliver a message."

After her sincere apology, Kenison stood and smacked his hand against his chest. He grinned sheepishly at his instinctive knight's salute, and Cayna burst out laughing.

"This is about what you asked at the Adventurers Guild, right?" she said.

"Yes. It looks like the boats aren't allowed to sail because a large shadow appeared under the river's surface several days ago."

"A large shadow... How big was it?"

"They say it reaches from this riverbank all the way to the sandbar."

"What?! That's gigantic!"

As far as Cayna could remember, even the *Leadale* game didn't have an aquatic monster of that size. The only exception might be a high-level Green Dragon summon, but those couldn't dive underwater since they were flying types.

A chill ran down Cayna's spine when she considered what else might be lurking in this world.

At the breakfast table the next morning, Lytt and Luka excitedly discussed where they might go and what they might see that day. Although Luka's speech was as stilted as ever, it didn't mean she didn't have her own opinions. It seemed that Luka's responses of "yes" or "no" to the things Lytt liked or wanted to see fueled their conversation.

"I wanna see those people that throw the balls. What about you, Luka?" Lytt asked.

"The...balls?"

"Yeah, when we were in the carriage trying to get through that crowd, I saw people some throwing balls."

"...I...didn't see them."

"I wanna get a closer look. Luka, will you come with me?"

"...Okay."

"Yay! Let's check it out together!"

Cayna couldn't immediately imagine what Lytt was referring to, but she guessed they were talking about street performers of some sort. Most of Cayna's knowledge came from TV and the Internet. If someone was throwing balls, she could only think of circus performers like clowns juggling balls on a unicycle. Cayna reminded herself not to get more keyed up than the kids she was escorting.

Roxine, who had been serving them, took notice of something and left the table for a moment. She came back shortly thereafter and asked a disturbing question: "We have a most boorish guest at the door. May I dump water on him so that he'll leave?"

"Don't be so violent first thing in the morning. Who's the guest?"

"Your typical stuck-up noble's flunky butler."

"A butler?"

Cayna told Luka and Lytt not to leave the house and made her way to the entrance. Roxine stood at attention at the front door and acted as a blockade to prevent this boorish fellow from stepping inside.

When they first arrived at the rental house, Cayna thought to fortify it with at least some magical defenses. Any lowlife who tried to sneak in from the second floor would be caught Venus flytrap–style by a magical creature disguised as a roof. There was a chance they might be flattened by the sheer force of it as well. Those foolish enough to try and sneak in the back entrance would be stopped by a magic trampoline and sent flying sky-high. The intruder wouldn't be flung far enough to land in the river, but a fall from that height wasn't exactly survivable. Roxine and Cayna had come to an executive decision: Any trash who brought harm to children had no human rights. Neither of the two had the least bit of mercy or compassion on that matter.

When Cayna cautiously stepped outside, she was met by a thin, aging butler with a bushy white beard who was dressed in a suit. He bowed as soon as he saw her.

"I do apologize for troubling you so early in the morning," the butler said.

"No, that's all right," Cayna replied. "May I ask who you are?"

"My apologies. My name is Marnus. I am a butler in the employ of a distinguished individual."

"I'm Cayna, an adventurer."

"Yes, I am aware." With his right hand on his heart and his left behind his back, the butler Marnus gave a slight bow.

"Well then, what business does a distinguished individual's butler have with me?"

Cayna had meant to give him a bright and completely normal smile, but Marnus took a step back for some reason. His age and many years of service had taught him that such a smile was like an invitation into a dragon's maw. His cheek unconsciously twitched, and his perfect facade as a composed, emotionless butler cracked. Collecting his pride to keep Cayna from noticing his agitation, he adjusted his posture and faced her once more. This all occurred within the span of a single second.

In actuality, the source of the pressure that nearly broke him had come from Roxine, who was standing behind Cayna. Unable to stomach any butler who treated her master as a mere commoner (at least, that was how it seemed to Roxine), she fixed him with a healthy dose of Intimidate. Even her weakest attack might cause a puny human like Marnus to keel over from shock, so she tested just how far she could push Intimidate onto him.

Roxine figured she'd gone too easy on him since he managed to recover. She clicked her tongue and ended the skill, then obediently took a step back, fearing Cayna would take notice if she tried to push it any further. However, she was fully prepared to attack the butler at a moment's notice if push came to shove.

Kee had already warned Cayna of Roxine's actions. She internally sighed.

I swear, Cie...

"You never know what this butler's master might be after. If you give Roxine the order, she will murder this master in their sleep."

In the middle of the festival?! That'd cause total chaos! Where do you and Cie get such disturbing ideas?!

She wasn't happy that both Kee, her longtime mental companion, and her maid were way too willing to initiate violence. If she allowed either one of them to run wild, there was no doubt she'd get stuck in a pattern of paying for it later. Cayna already had enough experience with that when *Leadale* was just a game, and she was plenty sick of it.

"Can I help you?" Cayna asked.

"Ah, yes. Actually, this individual I work for very much desires the wagon in your possession. Would you be so kind as to sell it? You will be well compensated, of course."

Ah, there it is, Cayna thought, remembering Elineh's warning with annoyance.

"So how much are you willing to offer?"

"Right—would five hundred gold coins suffice?"

Five hundred gold coins was equal to 50,000 silver coins—not even one percent of the money Cayna had left over from the game. Those five hundred gold coins could buy her 125,000 nights at Marelle's inn with her special discounted rate. She could certainly stay there that long given her high-elf longevity, but whether the inn would even allow it was another question altogether.

"That's chump change. Make me a better offer."

"Ngh?! What did you say?!"

As soon as Cayna shot him down point-blank, the elderly butler showed emotion for the first time. His clenched fists trembled in disbelief, and his sleepy eyes suddenly opened wide. Roxine didn't waste a moment in stepping forward and informing him the conversation was over before shooing him off.

"Your negotiations were unsuccessful," she told him. "I bid you adieu."

"We still have more to discuss!" the butler cried.

"Any further disruptions and I will not hesitate to use force. Is that all right with you?"

Roxine directed this question not at Cayna, but at the elderly butler who didn't know when to give up. Marnus's spine froze under Roxine's icy glare. He was wracked with chills an instant later, and it was as if he had witnessed his own mercilessly shredded future.

"Y-you will surely regret…turning down a deal such as this."

He stammered a vague threat and left. An incident like this normally meant hired thugs and an attempt to kidnap children were on the horizon.

"Hopefully he's just some cookie-cutter villain," said Cayna.

"Say the word and I shall ensure he takes his final breath tonight," Roxine replied.

"Who told you to kill anyone? He'll probably give up if we just leave him be."

"You're quite the optimist, Lady Cayna."

"Well, I can't imagine anyone who could get past our combined defenses."

"This is true, but still…"

A maid grumbling with nonstop irritation because she wouldn't get the chance to kill was something truly terrifying. Cayna figured Roxine would be less likely to go on a rampage if she had her prioritize the children's welfare.

"Tomorrow I'll swing by the Adventurers Guild and see if I can get any details about what's happening. We can touch base after that."

"I suppose there's no stopping you. I understand. The children will be safe with me."

"It'd also be nice to stop by the Academy despite all this craziness. We can take a dragonfly to the sandbar."

"Wouldn't it be faster to use a summoning?"

"That'll bring the knights over in full force!! The festival will be in danger for a whole other reason!"

Aquatic summonings weren't the most subtle creatures. Blue Dragons, for example, got bigger as their level increased. Then there was an eight-armed starfish massive enough to easily block Felskeilo's eastern gate; a hermit crab whose spinning-drill shell was slightly larger than Cayna's rental home; and an octopus that could wrap its tentacles around the royal castle and still have room for more. Cayna couldn't guarantee these summonings wouldn't cause any less of an uproar than that one penguin monster had, so she quickly vetoed Roxine's suggestion.

When Cayna and the two girls went into town that day, they were once again dumbfounded by the sheer number of people. The girls were tuckered out by the time they made their way through the crowds, watched knife-throwing performers, and went around the numerous stalls. They stopped by Elineh's company on the way home, where Cayna bought a large supply of cloth.

Meanwhile, in an unspeakably dim part of Felskeilo that was once a redevelopment zone.

The stretch of ruined houses had been turned into a castle and sightseeing attraction literally overnight, and during the day it was the second-most-crowded place after the market. At night, however, it was nearly desolate, with nothing more than a campfire and a guard outpost. In between this zone and the residential district was an even more desolate area where people eked out a living: the slums.

The destitute also frequented a spot just past the city's southern gate, where squatters who had been denied residence within the city gathered. Naturally, since they were outside the realm of soldier protection, the chances of being attacked by a monster here were significantly high.

These squatters wouldn't stand a chance in the city's slums—it was a rough crowd in there. But as tax-paying citizens, the slum's more unsavory inhabitants couldn't simply be kicked out.

To the soldiers tasked with patrolling the area, the group was considered a thorn in their side.

That night, these unsavory inhabitants put their secret plans into action.

They occupied a house said to have been built by a prominent merchant of days past. In its heyday, the building had been a three-story palace; now, it was half-destroyed and a mere shadow of its former beauty.

Several men were gathered in the basement around a tiny fire thick with animal fat, their faces warped with unsettling grins as they discussed their devious plot. They sat huddled around one man, who cut an especially severe figure amongst these notorious fugitives.

"We got the go-ahead from our contact," rasped the fierce-looking man with a deep scar across half his face—the leader of the Parched Scorpions, a shadowy organization in Felskeilo.

"Heh-heh-heh-hehhh. What kinda job ya got dis time, boss?"

"Hope there's a girl involved."

The first of his subordinates to speak was a slender man twirling a dagger around his hand. He seemed like the friendliest of the syndicate's members. All the more reason he was such a scoundrel for associating with this bunch.

The subordinate who spoke without an accent was a short kobold man. His fur was gray, and perhaps because he didn't groom properly, it was terribly ruffled every which way, like a bad case of bedhead.

"There's girls involved, but they're children," the leader replied.

"Oh-ho? Then this job is right up my alley," came a friendly-sounding, youthful voice that belonged to a surprisingly large man. His face was sharp, and he had a muscular figure. He looked like the type who carried steel girders on construction sites.

A man like him was a pedophile beyond all saving.

"It's a hostage situation, so be gentle," the leader warned.

"Does that mean our target is a merchant?"

"Seems she's an adventurer. There's also a maid."

"An adventurer...and a *maid*?"

The man who asked this with a dubious look possessed no unique characteristics. Even if you were to pass him on the street, it would be difficult to identify him as a villain. He was also the type not easily spotted in a crowd. It was no exaggeration to say he was the most average of the average. He put his completely generic features to use as a pickpocket.

"The client wants something from the adventurer lady, and our job is to abduct the kids and get her to accept their demands," the leader explained.

The less assertive subordinates nodded, grinning fiendishly. Even getting a small share of the profits would be fun.

"Lucky her, bein' surrounded by girls. Are the kids hers?"

"No idea," the leader replied. "Find out yourself if you're dyin' to know."

"Feh-heh-heh-heh. I don't mind one bit either way."

"We strangle the maid and capture the kids, right? Sounds like a pretty easy job to me."

"Lemme fool around with the maid before you kill her. That okay, boss?"

"Sure, as long as she's still alive by the time everyone else is done."

"Aw maaan!"

Their excitement grew as they talked about everything they'd do once the job was done, but this was because they did not have any detailed information on who they were dealing with. Underestimating women and children and seeing them as targets who were easy to control was proof of a typical scoundrel.

"Listen up, you bastards! Don't go embarrassin' me!"

The leader slammed his fist against the wall as he roused his men. The subordinates all nodded—some smugly, some emotionlessly, others with their mouths twisted in wicked grins.

"Just wait for the good news, boss."

"Kidnapping's my specialty."

"Heh-heh…love me some women…"

"Sheesh."

They exited the basement one by one, sneering at what a simple hit this would be…all without ever realizing that something hiding within the darkness had heard their every word.

The fact they hadn't noticed was reasonable enough. This "something" was a bug no larger than a fingernail. The black cricket's compound eyes faintly flickered red before the insect flew after the boss, who was the last to depart.

The next day.

The plan was for Cayna to visit the Adventurers Guild to gather information and then meet up with Roxine and the kids to head over to the Academy. Roxine would watch over Lytt and Luka until then.

"Be sure to scold them if they start whining, Cie," said Cayna.

"Yes, please leave it to me."

"I'm not gonna whine!" Lytt pouted.

"Me…neither…," Luka agreed.

The two girls gripped Cayna's cloak. She slowly eased their hands away, then handed the pair twenty bronze coins each.

"You've both been studying hard, so take this and buy yourselves a treat."

"Huh? But I can't take all this…"

Lytt counted the coins in her hand and tried to give some back to Cayna. Luka wasn't really sure what to do and seemed worried about both the money and Lytt's behavior.

"You don't have to use it all at once or anything. Keep it so you can buy food or souvenirs at the festival," Cayna told them.

She'd initially meant to give them each a silver coin, but Roxine and Kee had said that was far too much and would only make the girls targets for pickpockets, so she'd shaved it down little by little.

If she gave them their full allowance from the start, they'd end up spending it all on the first day.

With that in mind, Cayna felt the girls would benefit from planning out their expenses. She could always give them a bit more if they ran out, which was bound to happen if they ended up staying in Felskeilo longer than anticipated. It was critical that Cayna resolve this bizarre river conundrum in order for the festivities to wrap up in a timely fashion.

Before that, however, Cayna had to fulfill her mission of introducing Luka to Mai-Mai.

"Worst-case scenario, maybe I'll have to use the Silver Ring," she wondered aloud.

"Lady Cayna, your ring is likely to make a terrible situation even worse, so I please ask that you refrain," Roxine insisted.

"Right-o…"

Even Cayna herself couldn't say with any certainty what would happen if she used her most powerful magic. Roxine hinted at the resulting destruction and urged caution.

"Well, I better going. Thanks again!" said Cayna.

"Take care," replied Roxine.

"Have a safe trip, Miss Cayna."

"See you…later."

"Yup, see you guys later!"

Although she was only going out to gather information, Cayna felt filled with spirit when the children and Roxine saw her off. She started for the Adventurers Guild.

But first, she had to cut through the insanely packed streets.

Cayna looked around and saw people climbing up on the rooftops of nearby houses. She decided to follow their lead, using Leap and Wall Walker to jump high over the crowd. Those who noticed her pass overhead caused a stir, which only further added to the pedestrian bottleneck.

When she entered the Adventurers Guild, it was surprisingly busy. The last time she came, the guild's usual mess of adventurers—such as Cohral's group—had been the only ones hanging around.

This time, there was not only a wall of requests but a second signboard as well. The latter was set up like some sort of special shopping display, so this was likely something other than the usual requests. It seemed to be the main focus; people were constantly coming and going to check it. Many young solo adventurers would tear off several requests at once, take them to the counter, and quickly rush out. Neither their armor nor equipment was very adventurer-like, so they seemed to be people who specialized in completing requests that were within the city and wouldn't get them into any fights.

"What's all this?" Cayna said.

Upon closer inspection, she realized the requests on this second signboard had to do with the upcoming festival. Many said things such as *"Help find lost children,"* *"Help mind the store,"* and *"Help manage lines."* Something like *"Take care of whatever strange thing is in the river"* would have definitely caught her attention if it existed.

And there weren't just a few of these requests; dozens upon dozens were artlessly bundled together and bound with string.

"Ooh, they're like little presents!"

When she turned to the counter, her eyes met those of a familiar employee.

"Ah, Cayna."

"Almana! Long time, no see."

Almana, the beautiful redheaded employee who had first registered Cayna as an adventurer, turned to her and waved.

"Excuse me, Almana, but there's something I'd like to ask—" Cayna approached the counter when Almana leaned over and firmly took both of Cayna's hands into her own.

"Huh?"

"I have you now, Cayna!" said Almana. "Actually, I'd like you to do me a favor!"

"Uh, 'have me'? Huh? What? What's going on?!"

"Listen to me, Cayna! You're my only hope!!"

"H-hold on, don't pull on me! Whoa, hold on, wait, I have no idea what's going on! Why are you taking me away?!"

Adventurer and guild employee. Two beautiful women. But it was their loud tug-of-war match that grabbed everyone's attention. This eventually began obstructing business operations, and both were separated by other employees. After being sent to a small interview room, the women were finally able to calm down and talk.

"Sheesh, Almana. What was that all about?"

"I'm sorry...," Almana apologized as she set a drink in front of Cayna before sitting down herself.

"I just had something I wanted to ask you," Cayna clarified.

"Oh? What might that be?"

"I was wondering the Academy is still open. I'm thinking of going to see Mai-Mai."

"Yes, despite the current situation, the Academy is still holding classes," Almana replied. She'd seemed bewildered at first but then remembered that despite looking seventeen, Cayna was actually the mother of Mai-Mai, the Academy's headmistress.

"Anyway, what was it you wanted from me?" Cayna asked.

"Right. I was wondering if you might investigate a strange phenomenon."

"'Investigate'?"

"Yes."

Cayna furrowed her brow as Almana explained the details of the odd incident.

It happened just as the festival was approaching and began with a sighting of a fish shadow the size of a galley. The Kingdom of Felskeilo dispatched soldiers and boats to search for and identify it.

As curious onlookers watched from the piers with bated breath, an enormous shadow appeared out of nowhere. Its length reached all the way from the riverbank to the sandbar. These rubberneckers weren't the only ones panicking either. Those out on the boats felt the same way, and multiple vessels had capsized. No one was hurt, fortunately, but the enormous shadow suddenly vanished in the midst of the uproar. The Kingdom quickly prohibited all boats from sailing out, but there had been no more sightings of the giant shadow since then.

"So why are you asking me to look into this?"

Once Almana finished explaining, Cayna asked the biggest question on her mind. In her humble opinion, she wasn't that far off from a beginner adventurer. Although she was registered with Felskeilo's

91

Adventurers Guild, she didn't really have that many requests under her belt.

"I heard the stories, Cayna. You earned great recognition for subjugating that group of bandits along the western trade route, didn't you?"

"...Uh."

Indeed. Although she hadn't officially taken on a request per se, there was no question she had completed one by collaborating with Caerick's plan. He was supposed to explain the details of the matter to the Adventurers Guild and make sure her name wasn't revealed in connection with the request. However, Cayna hadn't actually forbidden the guild to speak of it outright, so it was only natural that the information spread through the organization and among the employees.

"Besides, Cayna, can't you walk on water?"

"Uhhh..."

She had walked on water with everyone in town watching in order to corner Primo. That must have been the main reason why Almana picked her for this undertaking.

"In other words, you reap what you sow."

Kee's comment left her at a loss for words. Disappointed, she hung her head in resignation. Her only saving grace was Li'l Fairy, who patted her head to console her.

"I understand," Cayna said. "It does seem like there's no one else more qualified."

"So you'll accept it?!"

Almana leaned forward, rapturous. "Too close, too close!" Cayna shouted, and pushed her back. "Let me go see Mai-Mai first. I have to introduce her to my daughter."

"Yes, yes, of course. If you have accepted, I will wait as long as... Huh?"

Almana, who had taken out forms she came well-prepared with, immediately stopped her in her tracks. She turned her neck with the *crick, crick, crick* of an ill-fitting door and ruminated over what Cayna just said.

"You're introducing your daughter to Lady Mai-Mai?"

"Indeed I am."

"Um...? Do you mean to say you have another daughter?"

"That's right."

The shocking truth froze Almana solid. Her mind raced in circles; she wondered how she could still be single and childless when this (high elf) lady who looked even younger than her already had four children. She soon became unresponsive.

"Uh, hello? Almana?"

Cayna's statement had rendered Almana nearly comatose. She collapsed onto the floor, eyes still open, before another employee came by and carried her to the breakroom.

"She seems to be experiencing some sort of shock. Was it something you said, perhaps?" the employee asked.

"I haven't the slightest idea."

Cayna lacked the self-awareness required to understand that she herself was to blame. She agreed to come again another day to take on a request and then decided to meet up with Roxine and the girls.

After seeing Cayna off, Roxine locked up the rental house and took Lytt and Luka out into the busy city.

They first went to see the ball-throwing street performers Lytt had spotted from the carriage.

Their initial problem was finding out where to cut through the mass of people crammed into the streets like sardines. The crowd moved even more slowly than the children did.

Roxine would have been able to cut in easily if she were on her own, but with two children who weren't used to city life, this was a much more difficult task. She let the girls decide what to do next.

"Girls, I believe the performers you're looking for are somewhere among this rabble. I mean, this crowd of people." Her true feelings had slipped out, but she went on explaining indifferently as if nothing had happened.

Luka and Lytt stared out at the sea of people and thought it over. They had no idea where everyone had come from, and the masses continued on with no end in sight. For the two girls who were just experiencing a packed street for the first time, being caught in the middle felt life-threatening.

"What should we do?" Lytt asked.

"Mm…," Luka mumbled.

The girls stared at the crowd for some time before telling Roxine they should give up.

"Lady Cayna can mow them all down to create a path when she gets here."

"N-no!"

"Mommy Cayna wouldn't…do that…"

When Roxine enthusiastically proclaimed her master could easily commit a crime, Luka and Lytt defended Cayna's innocence. The group lost any hope of crossing the main thoroughfare and headed to the residential district Cayna had brought them to the day before.

Like yesterday, the festivities weren't limited to the main thoroughfare; there were citizen-run booths all over the place, too many to see in just a single day.

"Hmm."

"…Lytt?" said Luka.

"Well, what do you think, little ladies? I'll give you a discount!"

One such booth run by a young man sold sold an array of stuffed animals: dogs, cats, birds, goats, rabbits, hornless bears, swans, and even unfamiliar monsters like chimeras and wyverns. None of them caught Lytt and Luka's eye, however, so they slowly made their way booth by booth in search of souvenirs they could buy with the allowance Cayna provided them. The girls anxiously pored over each booth's wares.

Meanwhile, Roxine had issues of her own to deal with.

She was a knockout beauty, personality be darned. Men captivated by her stunning looks approached her, one after another—all a bunch of sweet talkers.

"Hey there, wanna have a good time with me?" one nice-looking man purred. Roxine shot him a steely glare; he trembled, then stopped in his tracks, stiff as a board. A muscular guy had the audacity to shout, "Trust me to support you!" to which Roxine replied, "Your very presence disgusts me," and sent him flying with a single slap.

After being so easily pummeled by a dainty maid, he felt unworthy of his beloved muscles. Now just a shell of a brawny man, he turned pale and curled up despondently on the street corner.

"Honestly... The trash around here are absolutely clueless," she spat when another new sweet talker appeared.

"Maaan," he said. "You're a lot feistier than you look, miss."

"More trash? Get lost."

The young man laughed flippantly as he approached and did not recoil at all under Roxine's glare. Far from it, in fact; he took her arm and rubbed the back of her hand against his own cheek.

"Those are some fierce eyes you got there. I liiike 'em," he said. "You could take gooood care of me."

Roxine's eyes were now devoid of any emotion. The sweet talker surreptitiously drew his hand.

He was skilled at this range. His dagger was close enough take Roxine out with one blow, but she grabbed his hand before he could attack.

"Whaaat?"

"Heh-heh-heh," she chuckled. "You mean to strike me down? How laughable."

"Gwagh?!"

She crushed his hand, dagger and all, and the sweet talker was ready to scream. Not a moment too soon, Roxine grabbed his jaw and slammed his mouth shut to keep him quiet.

"Keh-keh-keh. I can't have you interrupting the girls, now."

She grinned demonically, and the sweet talker turned white as a sheet. He'd thought she was some dainty young woman, but here she was, nullifying his swift, foolproof attack. He could hear his jaw cracking and breaking in her grip; the agony kept him from fighting back.

Having grown bored of the man's tears and repeated mumbled apologies, Roxine let him go. At that very same moment, she quickly dislocated his shoulder and hip, and he crumpled to the ground.

"Huh? What's wrong with that man, Ms. Cie?" Lytt asked.

"Oh, he merely appears to be drunk. Pay him no mind, ladies."

"…Drunk…?" Luka asked dubiously.

The pathetic womanizer's muted cries of "Hyah-feh-heh, hyah-feh-heh" mixed into the throng and faded away.

Truth be told, Roxine had sensed a swirl of conspiracy around them as soon as Cayna had departed. If someone was going bring such nastiness their way, she had no choice but to deal with the situation accordingly. Anyone bold enough to catcall her and go out of their way to get close was most definitely an unsavory character.

One man who tried to grab Luka and Lytt had his arm shattered into splinters. Roxine turned it an impromptu show by yelling loud enough for everyone to hear, "Oh? What's that? You're going to show us an amazing trick? You'll fly weightless through the sky?" before flinging him toward the main road—all the while making sure no one noticed that *she* was the one putting on the show. The crowd clapped and cheered as the large man flew in a perfect arc; whether or not the man heard the crowd was anyone's guess, as he'd already passed out by that point. Roxine heard a scream from the main road and took that to mean he did not land safely.

Then there was a pickpocket who tried to sneakily reach out for the girls only to collapse to the ground when Roxine crushed his ribs with one swing of her arm. It had been so spur of the moment that she put way too much force into it; several of his organs had likely ruptured, but he wasn't dead, so that was good enough. Roxine told Lytt and Luka that he was just another drunk, and the three were on their way.

Close to ten "drunk" men ended up splayed out on the ground along the way. Roxine considered them mere trash, and soon enough she forgot about them altogether.

"Would you two mind telling me what you purchased today?" she asked the girls.

"I got a souvenir for Latem!" Lytt replied.

"This…is for…Li," said Luka.

Roxine peered into Lytt's bag to find a small plush wyvern; Luka had chosen a bear. Roxine felt a momentary flash of jealousy when Luka told her who the bear was for, but she then offered to take the girls' bags for them. She deposited them in her Item Box but pretended to put them in her knapsack.

Lytt and Luka chatted excitedly about where they should go next. Roxine was forced to be the bearer of bad news.

"We promised Lady Cayna we would meet up with her soon. Let's be off."

"What?! Already?" cried Lytt.

"…Okay," Luka said with an obedient nod.

Lytt, on the other hand, whined that they hadn't yet seen

everything. But spending more than twenty minutes hemming and hawing at each booth meant they could make only two stops before it was time to meet up with Cayna.

"Let's come here again tomorrow," Roxine said, and Luka chimed in with "We'll...look some more." Lytt had no choice but to quietly give up her shopping expedition.

Once they returned to their rental home, put away their things, and used the ladies' room, the three of them headed to the dragonfly boarding zone where they would be meeting Cayna. She was already waiting by the time they got there, and when they approached she knelt down and gave the girls a hug.

"I apologize for the wait," Roxine said with a dip of her head, to which Cayna replied, "You can't help these huge crowds," and smiled.

"Lytt...had trouble deciding...," Luka explained, and Lytt retorted, "Nuh-uh! Too many men kept trying to talk to Ms. Cie."

"Ah, um...," Roxine stammered.

"Well, Cie's very pretty, so you can't really blame them," Cayna said with a nod. Roxine shifted her gaze to the ground, red-faced.

Never expecting the werecat to be embarrassed, Cayna vowed to keep in mind that this would be an effective method of stopping her when necessary.

There was a line of about twenty people at the dragonfly boarding zone. From what they could see, this stop employed about ten laigayanma and their Insect Tamers who came and went in rotations. The laigayanma were about four meters from head to tail and could carry a maximum of three riders each. Since one Insect Tamer needed to hold the reins, that meant each dragonfly could only take two guests each. The Tamer sat on the neck, while the other riders sat right behind the wings. Guests had to sit facing backward so they wouldn't be hit by the laigayanma's wings. Apparently, there was also a special sightseeing route that stopped at each dragonfly station in the city.

"Guess we'll have to split into pairs," said Cayna.

"In that case, please ride with Lady Luka. I shall accompany Lady Lytt."

Since Roxine had soundly decided the pairs on her own, Cayna promised Lytt she would ride with her on the way back.

She removed her sword and cloak ahead of time since they were likely to get in the way. One round trip per person was ten bronze coins, and you were given half of a ticket tally when you arrived at the opposite shore. If you showed this, you'd be able to get a ride back. Roxine took care of the payment.

The young Insect Tamer was overcome with shock when Cayna asked him about the in-flight safety precautions.

"Aren't you the girl who walked on water?!" he said.

"Agh, people know me here…"

The riverbank's residents had yet to forget Cayna, "the girl who walked on water."

"I remember back then," the Insect Tamer continued, smiling. "I looked down below and saw someone walking on the river's surface. Nearly lost control of my yanma from the shock! It's a fond memory of mine." A coworker told him they were falling behind schedule, and it occurred to him that he had a job to do. "Well then, welcome aboard. You'll be fine if you keep your body straight and hold on tight. Please do not lean too much to either side."

The seats had handles like those seen on a child seat one could attach to a bicycle. Luka sat closer to the tail while Cayna sat closer to the wings. "We're off!" the Insect Tamer cried, and the whooshing of beating wings followed. A momentary burst of speed later, and they had a sweeping view of Felskeilo's south side.

"Whoa, awesome!" Cayna shouted.

"Wowww…," said Luka.

Everything was laid out before them, from the cityscape to the streets packed with people. Cayna and Luka were momentarily captivated by the unbroken view of the vast forest beyond the city's gates and hilly regions that practically continued all the way into Otaloquess.

It wasn't long before they started descending toward the water. The two of them sighed wistfully, eager to see more of the landscape.

"That was so incredible. Thank you," Cayna told the young Insect Tamer when they dismounted their laigayanma.

"It really is, isn't it?" he replied fondly. He seemed to genuinely enjoy seeing such reactions from guests.

Lytt alighted from her dragonfly with the same look of wonder on her face that Cayna and Luka had. When Luka grabbed her arm, she returned to herself and said, "Wasn't the scenery super pretty?" She closed her eyes and clutched her chest as if to hang on to those lingering feelings.

"Sooo awesome," said Lytt.

"...Uh-huh... Awesome," said Luka.

"Sooo pretty."

"Uh-huh... Pretty..."

The girls didn't have much vocabulary to go by and continued their earnest praises of "awesome" and "pretty."

"How about you, Cie?" Cayna asked Roxine.

"Ah, yes... I was surprised—those views were simply stunning." Roxine turned around and watched longingly as the laigayanmas took off again. Cayna found her sincerity touching.

The dragonfly stop was near the entrance to the Academy. Others had ridden dragonflies as well, but most seemed to be heading toward the church. It was safe to safe that absolutely no one was going to Kartatz's workshop.

The guards at the Academy gate remembered Cayna, and after

exchanging a few words through a magical communication device, they opened the gate.

"Might you be the mother of our headmaster?" one of the guards asked Cayna.

"Ah, yes."

"We shall inform her of your arrival, so please come in. The headmaster's office in on the second floor."

"Th-thank you. Pardon me, then," Cayna replied with a light nod. Roxine bowed and said, "If you'll excuse us," as she followed. When Luka and Lytt nodded with similar politeness, the guards smiled and waved.

Everything that had been destroyed during the penguin monster incident was repaired, and the Academy was now back to its former self. In the corner of the Academy grounds where the monster had appeared was a pillar with a sign affixed to it that read DANGER! DO NOT APPROACH! in red letters.

"I'm not sure that explains what's actually in there...," Cayna murmured to herself. Roxine tilted her head quizzically, so Cayna decided to elaborate.

"Hey, see that black pillar over there?" she said.

"What is it?" Roxine asked.

"It was an Occupation Point for the White and Green Kingdoms' forces during the war."

"Ah, I see... Here, of all places?!"

"Yep. So anyway, a little while ago there was this random monster that showed up, and everything turned into a huge mess. The whole city would've been destroyed if I hadn't gotten here in time."

Roxine's eyes went wide in unexpected shock. You were likely to find another country's Occupation Point if you went looking for it, but nothing could be worse than having one right in the middle of town.

The group followed along the wall and did a quarter lap around the grounds to get to the main building. From there they followed the path Lonti had once showed Cayna (with Kee's guidance). Meeting almost no one else as they made their way through the Academy, they finally arrived at a door that had HEADMASTER'S OFFICE written on it. Roxine knocked, and they heard a voice tell them to come in.

Roxine opened the door and urged Cayna inside. Luka and Lytt followed with Roxine in tow before closing the door behind her.

"Welcome, Mother!"

A golden-haired, blue-eyed elf woman sprang up from behind her desk. Her waist-length hair was braided as usual, and she wore a floor-length red robe. She looked like she could be Cayna's older sister, but Cayna was, in fact, her mother.

Mai-Mai quicky sidled up to Cayna and wrapped her in a big hug. "Hee-hee-hee. It's been sooo long!" The Academy headmaster purred like a cat and sprouted dog ears and a wagging tail. Cayna wished she would just pick one animal and stick with it.

Roxine grabbed Mai-Mai by the collar and easily pried her away.

"O-oh?" Mai-Mai stammered in bewilderment.

"Long time no see, Mai-Mai," said Cayna. "Hold off on the excessive touching for a second." She smiled uncomfortably and put her hands to her daughter's waist.

Mai-Mai led them to a parlor in a separate room, and when Cayna and the children were seated, Roxine poured them tea. Once all four guests had been served and Roxine stood at attention behind Cayna, their preparations were complete.

"Ah, a maid summons? I didn't know you had one, Mother."

"Without a base to put her in, a maid summons is kind of a waste. But now I have Luka to take care of, too. And besides, I'm not too great at taking care of myself either."

Cayna was making fun of herself, but Mai-Mai didn't take her

SU
(WHOOSH)
スッ···

comment that way. She clapped her hands together and beamed. "Then you should come live with me, Mother! We have plenty of maids and attendants who could help take care of you!"

"No way. I'm not some trust-fund baby." Cayna quickly turned her down.

Mai-Mai giggled and murmured, "I thought you'd say that. But it's a child's duty to care for their parents. You really are stubborn about the strangest things, Mother."

"Well, sorry for being a stubborn parent." They both burst into laughter.

Luka and Lytt were confused; Cayna held the girls by their shoulders and introduced them to Mai-Mai.

"Mai-Mai, this is Lytt. She's the daughter of the inn proprietress who's been helping me out. And this is Luka, your new little sister. Girls, this lady here is Mai-Mai, my second child. She's your big sister, Luka."

"Hello."

"Hello…"

The two girls were visibly nervous. Mai-Mai smiled at them. "I'm Mai-Mai. It's nice to meet you," she said. "Why don't you two enroll here at the Academy?"

"Where'd that come from all of the sudden?" Cayna demanded.

Luka and Lytt froze in place. They clearly had no idea what Mai-Mai was offering them.

"Oh, but they'll get all sorts of experiences if they start their education now," Mai-Mai retorted.

Canya struggled to respond; she really had no reason to reject this outright. Still, one didn't usually extend such an offer upon meeting someone for the very first time.

After Lytt and Luka had a chance to recover, they swiftly declined her offer. Lytt said she had to help with the family business, and Luka preferred to stay with Cayna.

"Mother! May I hug Luka?"

"I mean, sure, but stop if Luka doesn't like it, okay?"

"Hee-hee-hee, will do."

Mai-Mai embraced the dazed Luka. She then held her up in a practiced manner, smiled, and nuzzled her cheek.

"It's nice to meet you, Luka," she said softly. Luka nodded awkwardly, at which Mai-Mai gleefully exclaimed, "She's just like when my Caerina was little!"

As soon as Mai-Mai said this, Cayna realized, *Oh yeah, she's a mom, too.* The thought tugged at her heartstrings.

As everyone was starting on their third cup of tea, a knock came at the headmaster's door, and Mai-Mai told them to come in. Two familiar faces entered.

"We just heard Lady Cayna stopped by..."

"Ah, Cayna! It's been a while!"

It was Myleene and Lonti—the Felskeilo crown princess and the prime minister's granddaughter, respectively.

What is this, a karaoke booth? Cayna thought when the room suddenly became packed. It really wasn't what anyone would expect the office of the headmaster running the Academy to look like.

When Cayna introduced Roxine, Luka, and Lytt, Myleene and Lonti shouted, "A maid?!" and "Another child?!" in shock.

"I haven't seen you around Felskeilo in a while, Cayna," said Lonti. "I was wondering if something had happened."

"Ah, sorry about that, Lonti. I recently moved to the sticks. That means I won't be able to go around catching Primo for you."

"I wasn't talking about the Prin—er, Primo! I just thought you had gone to another country!"

Lonti must have decided to use the pseudonym since she was in mixed company. The crown prince's prospects weren't looking good if even Lonti was referring to him as Primo.

"Come to think of it, I saw him the day I got here," said Cayna.

"Aghhh...," Lonti groaned as she gripped her head. "I—I suppose he escaped again."

"I couldn't catch him because I had Luka and Lytt with me. Sorry about that."

"No, it's not your fault at all!" Lonti insisted.

Myleene then introduced herself as Mye and asked Luka and Lytt about life in the village.

"By the way, Mai-Mai, I don't see many students around. Everything okay?" Cayna asked. She'd had a strange feeling about this as they were walking through the Academy.

"Yes, attendance has been quite low as of late."

"You think that has to do with the shadow that appeared in the river?"

"Well, I suppose that's one reason, but I believe the primary cause is economics."

"Economics?" Cayna tilted her head, frazzled.

"How did you get here, Cayna?" Lonti asked.

"Um, by dragonfly."

"Dragonfly fare is five times more expensive than a ferry. I imagine commuting from the residential district to the Academy every day must really add up."

"Tuition at the Royal Academy is almost free," Myleene added, "although some students earn a living by becoming adventurers and doing odd jobs around the city. Many are no doubt feeling the pressure of day-to-day food and transportation costs."

"Furthermore," said Mai-Mai, "the nobles are keeping their children at home out of concern over the dangers of whatever is lurking in the river. The students currently in attendance are of a unique category."

Mai-Mai shifted her gaze to Lonti and Myleene. It was rather unusual for the crown princess and the prime minister's granddaughter to be visiting the Academy in the midst of such turmoil.

"I am here as Mye's attendant," Lonti said with a strained smile.

"I'm…well, ah…" Myleene put her hands to her cheeks as her face reddened.

"Ohhh…" Cayna figured out why the two of them were here; her gaze grew distant.

Myleene had most likely visited the church before coming to the Academy. She had a crush on the High Priest Skargo, although Cayna didn't know how the two had even met. Cayna thought getting him to understand romance, let alone win his heart, would be no easy task. There was no question there'd be an unbelievable uproar if he found out; Cayna started spacing out when she imagined this scenario.

"Doesn't Skargo have work at the Helshper border?" Cayna said.

"Did you run into him, Mother?"

"He came to the village, along with some knights and a shiny carriage."

"I knew about that!" the princess piped up enthusiastically.

"Oh…," Cayna replied, bewildered.

If Myleene knew Skargo was out of town, then Cayna didn't see what reason she might've had to visit the church.

"Mai-Mai, do you know anything about the shadow?" Cayna changed the subject after deciding there was no point in trying to comprehend Myleene's logic.

"I haven't seen it myself, so I can't really say that I do. Wouldn't you be more knowledgeable on that sort of thing, Mother?" Mai-Mai asked in turn. She must have been truly at a loss if she didn't know anything despite having two hundred more years of experience than Cayna.

"The closest I can think of is a top-level Green Dragon summoning. But even that only has a wingspan of one hundred meters."

"Aren't Green Dragons flying types? They wouldn't be able to swim underwater," Mai-Mai noted.

"Yeah, you're right…" Cayna sank into thought, and Mai-Mai hugged her from behind. Since Mai-Mai was about one head taller, her slight chest was about level with the back of Cayna's head.

"You certainly are worried about that shadow, Mother. Did something happen?"

"The Adventurers Guild asked me to look into it. Guess I better investigate the river myself."

"W-will you be okay, Cayna?! You might get dragged into the water, or something might jump out and attack you!"

"Don't worry, Lonti," Cayna assured her.

"Please let us know if anything happens. I will inform Father and aid you as much as possible," Myleene said.

Lonti and Myleene were suddenly nose to nose with Cayna and gripped with worry. *Nice offer, but by "Father," she means the king, right?* Cayna thought. She wondered if that would be considered an abuse of authority. Nonetheless, she was happy to see Myleene so earnestly concerned for her.

"Mind if I get your help if I end up stuck in a jam?" Cayna asked.

"Of course!" said Lonti.

"Yes," said Myleene. "Please allow us to be of any assistance."

"Mother! I'll help you, too!"

"Thanks, you three."

Cayna grinned from ear to ear, touched by such kindness.

Roxine also vowed to help out, of course, and then Mai-Mai started talking about having Lytt and Luka stay over at her house.

When Myleene offered, "We can take them in at the castle," Lytt nearly fainted at the gap in their social positions.

Luka, meanwhile, hardly reacted at all—either because she didn't particularly care either way, or because she didn't understand the class system.

CHAPTER 3
A Demon, a Summons, a Tower, and a Project

After they returned to the rental house and finished eating dinner, Cayna stayed with the girls until bedtime. As she gazed at their happy, sleeping faces, she sensed Roxine calling for her. As their summoner, Cayna was able to communicate telepathically with Roxine and Roxilius even from a distance. She soundlessly left the bedroom and went downstairs, where Roxine was waiting in the small area they used as a dining room.

"What's wrong, Cie?"

"I apologize for interrupting," Roxine replied as she poured tea for the two of them. "There were a string of troubling occurrences today that I feel I must report to you."

"'Troubling occurrences'?"

While Cayna sat down, Roxine told her of the hoodlums she had run into that afternoon and how they seemed to have planned to put the girls in harm's way.

"Still, the fact you're safe and telling me about all this means you handled it, right?"

"Well, yes. I did not kill them, but the fate they suffered was likely worse than death."

"Good point…"

Just to be safe, Cayna reached out to Roxilius and asked if anything odd had happened. *"Nothing of note,"* came his reply. Apparently, the village was safe. Since it was possible their foe had already set out for the village and simply not arrived yet, she urged him to be careful and keep her updated.

"Everything's fine on Rox's end."

"That is because these ruffians tried to get rid of me and kidnap the girls. Perhaps they wanted to use them as leverage against you?"

"Against me? For what…?" Cayna hit upon the reason in no time at all. "I bet they're after my wagon golem."

"The men are likely subordinates of the butler who visited the other day. It's not too late. If you give the order, I shall rip them limb from limb."

"We should first find out which noble they work for."

"Tch!"

Roxine clicked her tongue in extreme disappointment. At this point, it was likely she'd lash out at their enemy the moment they figured out who was pulling the strings.

"At any rate, it looks like you crushed their big guns. We should be safe for a while."

"Lady Cayna, you are being soft. Too soft. These are your garden-variety thugs. I humbly suggest we eliminate all suspects tonight."

"Vetoed. That's not what we came here for."

What in the world was putting Roxine on such a warpath? Cayna tilted her head and wondered if she'd always been this relentless. It was likely rooted in her concern for the children. However, no one was asking her to go on a search-and-destroy mission over it. Besides, if Roxine went all out, Cayna would basically have a level-550 monster on her hands. She was stronger than even Shining Saber, meaning no one in Felskeilo would be able to stop her.

"Being a maid is your real calling, so please just stick with that. Keep looking after Lu and Lytt like you did today. Use your combat abilities for protection only."

"...Very well, then."

Roxine looked disappointed, but she still agreed to Cayna's terms. There didn't seem to be any danger of her disobeying an order. Cayna regained some peace of mind, but she didn't think that was the last they'd see of the people targeting them.

"Tomorrow I'm gonna check out the river per the Adventurers Guild's request. I'll have another summoning help guard the girls."

Cayna couldn't look after Lytt and Luka at this rate. She needed to get to the bottom of this strange phenomenon, or else the River Festival was doomed.

"Lady Cayna, won't summoning a high-level creature leave you short-handed?" Roxine asked.

Summoning Magic was powerful, but a summoned creature's level depended on the summoner's maximum available resources. Even a Skill Master couldn't bypass these restrictions.

"As far as I know, zwohms are the largest aquatic monsters out there, and those live in the ocean."

A zwohm was a giant cnidarian with the body of a spotted garden eel and the head of a sea anemone. They stayed on the ocean floor like ancient sea lilies and were rarely seen except on the occasional fishing expedition; their meat was considered a delicacy. Zwohms grew to over one hundred meters long, and it was highly unlikely Cayna would find any in a river since they were ocean dwellers. Plus, zwohms couldn't be summoned in the first place.

"We'll solve this a lot faster if it's indigenous to this world rather than something from the game. Native creatures are usually pretty low-level, so I doubt I'll need a particularly powerful summoning."

"I won't stop you if you're that insistent, but please cancel my summons and focus on yourself if you must," Roxine advised after quietly listening to her master's explanation.

Cayna finished her tea and put down her cup. "Yeah, I will. Thanks, Cie."

"You're welcome."

Roxine nodded politely, and Cayna bade her good night before heading back up to the girls' room. "Good night," Roxine replied as she saw her off, then finished washing the dishes and returned to her own room. "I don't want to be caught off guard later," she murmured to herself as she scrupulously checked her equipment before going to bed.

Meanwhile, at the Parched Scorpions' stronghold...

Their leader couldn't hide his rage at how more than half of the members were now out of commission.

"What the hell happened?!" He grabbed the collar of one of the subordinates among them who was relatively uninjured and mercilessly took out his rage on him. The man cowered under his boss's intense voice and face full of terrifying anger and gave a stilted report of what he saw.

"The maid...was crazy strong...and—!"

The moans of subordinates wrapped in bandages like mummies could be heard everywhere. There were some whose eyes focused on nothing, others who trembled as they hugged their knees, and others still who were so deranged they didn't even notice their open wounds. It was like a field hospital. Beds were brought in from the ruined mansion above, but since there weren't enough, straw was laid on the floor for some to sleep on.

The wounds of key members had been healed with potions, but each one of them kept silent. No one looked at the leader or met his gaze.

The slender, dagger-wielding man was trembling beneath a blanket. He could feel his boss's chilling gaze on him and was too terrified to meet it.

The large man who had wanted to hear the children cry was hunched over and facing the wall, mumbling nonsense to himself. His superhuman strength hadn't done anything for him. In fact, he'd been quickly incapacitated, and being tossed like scrap paper had destroyed his confidence.

The small kobold man had his tail between his legs (literally) and was shaking underneath a bed. He'd seen his life flash before his eyes the moment he met his boss's dark glare. He was now terrified of maids. Even stray cats looked like assassins to him.

The arrogant pickpocket who prided himself on his everyman looks and expressionless face was now frozen in a horrified grimace. No matter how hard he tried to maintain an air of calm, he couldn't dispel the terrifying feeling that he could die at any moment. Fright distorted his features, and ironically enough, that made him stand out even more.

"Beaten by a maid?! You sayin' the Parched Scorpions were done in by a *woman*?!" the leader's voice boomed through the basement of their organization's stronghold.

No one dared object. It seemed that these men who lived by the creed that the weak deserved to be picked on had never expected themselves to be weak. Each one's pride had been smashed with ease, and they had been turned into cowards with a phobia of both maids and werecats.

"Dammit!!" the leader shouted in pure frustration.

This was all because of that one noble's messenger, who gave the organization this job, and the leader resented the two of them for it. He had heard that their targets were an adventurer and a maid, but no one had said they were this strong.

Did the noble and his messenger purposefully not mention that information? Or did they simply not know? The leader couldn't be sure either way.

Just as he was thinking about his revenge against them for this lack of details, he suddenly picked up an unfamiliar smell. He stopped pacing and clicking his tongue; a terrifying silence filled the basement.

The henchmen cowered, thinking their leader was about to explode with rage.

But his murmuring halted their pitiful wails. They heard him say softly, "What's this smell?"

"Smell?"

"Huh?"

"Hm? What's…this…smell?"

Before they knew it, the henchmen were starting to get a faint whiff. The sour, rusty odor made their hearts skip a beat. It was both familiar and foreign at the same time. No one could quite place it.

The henchmen wracked their brains trying to identify the smell but found themselves at a loss. Instead, a third party provided the answer.

"That is the scent of magic."

It sounded like a raspy old man—or maybe like the sonorous echoing heard in caves.

""What the—?!""

The two henchmen who turned toward the source of the voice froze from the shock. Following this odd behavior, the other men who looked over at their comrades did the very same.

Floating in midair at the basement entrance was a pure white skull tilted slightly askew. But it wasn't white like bone—the skull looked as if it had been drenched in white paint.

The floating skull was plenty bizarre on its own, but something about its position was off as well. It was suspended at roughly the height of a grown man's chest.

"Keh-keh-keh-keh. How unfortunate for you all."

The skull's chattering jaw left no doubt that it was the source of the voice. The men near the entrance lost their nerve and scampered further inside the basement.

""Eek?!""

"""Agh...!"""""

""Wha—?!""

""Uwagh!""

The skull moved forward until its full form appeared from the darkness. The tough, fearless henchmen let out petrified shrieks.

It looked like a withered and twisted old tree that had been forced into a humanoid shape. The pure white skull floated in a cavity within its chest. Perhaps because it already had a skull there, no head or neck was to be found.

"A d-d-d-devil..."

That was really the only way to describe it. It looked human, yet it wasn't. Although a composite of different forms, the closest description was indeed humanoid.

Everyone had heard the tales at least once at church as a child—of a being one must never face. Even the organization's leader, who had never been frightened a day in his life, felt true terror and took a few steps back. No one questioned him.

"Uwagh..."

"A-aghh..."

"Why? Why us...?"

Everyone in the room drew ragged breaths, their eyes grew hollow, and they were unable to look away from the grotesque form before them.

"Keh-keh-keh. Even if you knew why, there is nothing you can do."

Creaking and groaning, the ghastly old tree took a step forward. The fear and chaos that instantly gripped the room sapped the men of all their courage. The devil tree turned toward the bed of the delicate man who hid himself under rags and swung its left arm.

"Gyaaaaaagh?!"

A screech rang out.

The slim man dressed in rags began writhing. Flesh and fabric twisted together like water squeezed from a bundle of different-colored towels until he transformed into a long stick. His right eye had moved above his slitted mouth, and his arms were wrapped around his torso. What was once a 180-centimeter-tall man was now a three-meter-long stick.

He still appeared to be alive. He managed to let out a sputtering moan from his mouth with its warped teeth and tongue. The horrific sight alone was enough to drive a person mad. The basement instantly filled with wailing and screaming, crazed laughter, and people begging for their lives.

"Yes, yes. I am happy you are so pleased."

A devil's joy came from the negative emotions of living creatures. Since this place now overflowed with those emotions, it was no doubt a wonderland for the weathered tree devil. The devil then pierced the stick-man into the floorboard and looked for its next victim.

Of all the men, the only one to somehow maintain his sanity in spite of the heartwrenching scene was the leader. The moment he sensed the devil was looking away from him, he made his move. He threw his nearby subordinates who had lost their minds at the creature and ran to a corner of the room. There was an emergency exit here. He never told his followers, but it was a secret path that led to the sewers.

The leader was convinced that if he broke through the thin wall

and made it to the path, he could escape this place. However, before he even had the chance, a thick, bluish-black arm and shoulder burst through the wall and grabbed his chest in a vise grip.

"Gwagh?!"

The boss wailed as the breath in his lungs was restricted and woven together with the air. It wasn't only a right arm that broke through the wall to grab the leader. Three left arms broke new holes through the wall as well. The leader's eyes widened as he realized what this meant.

Finally destroying the walls and ceiling of the underground room, a six-armed dragoid with bluish-black skin appeared. It was two heads taller than the standard dragoid.

"Igzdukyz. Our leader said to not let a single one escape," the strange-looking dragoid rasped as it glared at the withered tree devil. Given their similar static-filled voices, the two creatures must have been in cahoots.

"Keh-keh-keh. Do forgive me for sating myself with their emotions. I have been slumbering for ages; I was so famished, I could not contain my arts."

The dragoid tossed the gang leader with ease, sending him crashing into his trembling subordinates, some of whom suffered broken bones while others were laughing from insanity.

A bunch of city thugs didn't stand a chance against two devils; this was a job for the heroes of legends and fairy tales.

"Finish quickly. We don't have much time," the dragoid spat.

"My arts are not immediate. This leader of ours doesn't understand," the tree argued.

The two otherworldly creatures exchanged brief banter as they left the area. The Parched Scorpions' leader soon lost consciousness.

The last thing he heard was a high-pitched scream.

*   *   *

Word of the incident came early that morning before the sun had even risen. A guard on night duty at the nearby landmark had been on his way home when he noticed a strange sight.

Shining Saber and his knights wasted no time in hailing a dragonfly from the castle to the location in question.

The moment they arrived, the youngest knights threw up their breakfasts. None of the knights could keep themselves from grimacing. Many took one glance and then averted their eyes. Others turned pale and walked away. Some even fainted. Dragoids' expressions were usually difficult to read, but Shining Saber instantly clapped his hands over his mouth.

Now that he'd seen it with his own eyes, Shining Saber understood what the guard who had made the report meant when he said the place was "some sort of bizarre facility." He understood on a logical level, but psychologically speaking, this was unfathomable.

Shining Saber cast several Active Skills to boost his mental fortitude until he was finally able to look at the ghastly sight directly. Most of the knights with him watched with gritted teeth. Shining Saber asked a messenger to fetch a mage who could buff psychological endurance, then entered the scene of the crime.

"You okay?" he asked his co-captain, who looked clearly unwell. The co-captain mumbled, "Well, somehow," through the handkerchief he had over his mouth.

Shining Saber remembered passing through the area numerous times while on his rounds. This specific residence appeared somewhat habitable, but most eye-catching of all were the grotesque objects neatly displayed throughout.

"A 'bizarre facility,' he said… That's what you'd call this place?"

"Captain?"

"Bizarre" was certainly an understatement, considering this facility was not of this world.

An arched sign atop the entrance to the building read WELCOME TO THE PARCHED SCORPION HUMAN ZOO in big bubble letters. Cutesy cartoon animals Shining Saber recognized—giraffes, lions, elephants, hippos—decorated the walls.

"This is some sick joke...," he muttered in spite of himself.

Inside the facility were enclosures typical of any normal zoo. However, the creatures on display were abhorrent and strange, even unnatural. It was enough to make a person sick to their stomach.

In the center was a slightly elevated rest area surrounded by benches—but these were no ordinary benches. These were men, their faces twisted in agonizing pain, their hands and feet seemingly welded into the ground. At their center was an inscription that read THE FOUNTAIN OF MIRACLES—and the man who had been the Parched Scorpions' leader until just hours earlier. He was embedded in a gold-plated wall and pleading a tearful, "Help meee... Help meee..." Each of his tears turned into gold coins the moment they fell; there was already a large pile of them in front of the wall.

A man's face appeared from a fleshy jar within the enclosure labeled SNAKES. One man's body had been stretched thin like rope and coiled into the shape of a pot; another man whose body had been similarly elongated popped in and out of the human pot like a loaded spring.

One man's lower half had been replaced with dozens of human arms; he was gripping his head and wailing, his face covered in sweat, tears, and snot. The sign on his enclosure read OCTOPUS.

The so-called "guide" was a crystal ball two meters in diameter with a man's face set in the center. His mouth spewed explanations of all the displays like some sort of curse.

Dangling from another enclosure was a sign that read HORSE. It contained a creature that had a human face but whose body had been stretched into the shape of a horse. This man—or what was left of him—was nothing but skin and bones.

A two-meter-long red caterpillar was munching away at the bark of a tree that had yet another human embedded within. That caterpillar, too, was a creature-shaped human. The sign on its enclosure had nothing written on it.

The soldiers and knights who had rushed over to the site wanted to turn tail and flee the moment they laid eyes on such horrors. Their repulsion got the better of their sense of duty to keep the city safe. The mage who had been summoned to boost the knights' mental fortitude urged them to step back and avert their eyes.

Shining Saber cleared the area and sent a notice to close the nearby castle landmark, since its highest tower provided an unobstructed view of this human zoo.

Their psyches now buffed, the knights got to work and wiped at the cold sweat on their bodies, mumbling "No way any humans did this," and "A devil, maybe…?"

They set up a simple tent area, and Shining Saber and his subordinates went around talking to the grotesquely disfigured men to see if anyone might be able to provide leads. It was mentally agonizing work, but they finally got the savage perpetrator's name from one of the men who had been turned into a bench.

"This appears to be the work of…Igzdukyz," the co-captain said nervously. He glanced around; everyone began trembling, their faces stiff.

"Dear gods."

"What is the meaning of this…?"

"Please protect us, O Lord."

"What's a big name like that doing all the way over here…?"

One knight after another offered prayers and raised the holy symbol of the church.

Except for Shining Saber, who had his arms crossed and a serious look on his face. Everyone stared at him, impressed by his reassuring candor, though Shining Saber himself hadn't the slightest clue that he was the envy of all these men. He looked over at his subordinates and said, "Hey…"

"What is it, Captain?"

"Who's this…Igzu or whatever person?"

Everyone fell forward.

"D-do you not know?" one knight asked.

"Nope," Shining Saber replied. "He famous or somethin'?"

His fellow knights face-palmed in utter disbelief. Shining Saber felt humiliated.

The co-captain decided to intervene and offer a simple explanation:

The world was said to be split between the Sun God (Lord of Light) and the Dream God (Lord of Night). Igzdukyz was a minor deity who served the Dream God; he appeared in countless legends and fairy tales, most often as a sort of "artist" who used humans to create unusual sculptures.

In one tale he appeared as an elderly traveler who, after spending the night in a village, left the villagers a painting as thanks for their hospitality. Apparently, one look at the painting moved the villagers to tears as if their hearts had been cleansed. However, they became so obsessed with the painting that they lost their minds and wandered the land in search of an equally magnificent work of art. The elderly traveler also turned any bandits or rogues that attacked him into grotesque objects.

"Sounds more like a devil than a god, if you ask me," said Shining Saber.

"That would make the story much simpler. You should visit the church if you want a more in-depth explanation," the co-captain suggested.

Shining Saber frowned. In his eyes, any religious discussion was more trouble than it was worth. Besides, Skargo would be doing all the explaining in this case, and his very presence was a pain in the ass.

However, much more draining than any religious discussion was continuing to witness this atrocity firsthand. Shining Saber believed it was time to settle things; he didn't feel great about it, but the knights couldn't keep this area locked down forever. They decided to transport the victims to a training area outside the city before any nasty rumors could spread. After that, the decision to either quarantine them for research purposes or dispose of them wasn't any concern for a knight captain...at least, not in Shining Saber's mind.

"There should be a reason why that devil or god or whatever went after these guys, right? I doubt it was some old traveler though. Hear anything else?" Shining Saber asked a soldier who had the incident report in hand.

"Well, yes, a few things, but they're rather inexplicable...," the soldier replied as he flipped through the report and tracked down one item. "Apparently, this organization was trying to abduct children..."

"Children? As in, from noble families?"

"Specifically, the children of an adventurer who was accompanied by a maid."

"The heck?"

Several men tilted their heads in confusion, and one knight raised his hand. "Ah, I saw an adventurer with a maid and two children on the sandbar yesterday. They visited the Academy."

The other knights started asking questions. "So they're real people?" "Are they...students?" "Why the Academy?"

But the knight wasn't quite finished yet. "The, um, adventurer in question was...the captain's fiancée, Lady Cayna."

""""Whaaaaaat?!""""

"She had two more kids after Sir Skargo, Lady Mai-Mai, and Sir Kartatz?!"

That one knight's utterance made it sound like Cayna had at least five kids. Suspicions that Shining Saber was having illicit relations with a widow were beginning to rise.

"I told ya, she ain't my fiancée! Anyway, why were they after her kids?"

"That much is still uncertain."

"So does this mean she was around here recently? Guess I gotta ask her myself."

"Yes, yes, but let's finish up here first, Captain."

Just as Shining Saber looked ready to saunter off, his co-captain grabbed him by the collar and dragged him back to the crime scene.

"Uwaaagh, I don't wanna goooo."

Canya had been sulking since that morning and didn't even try to hide her grumbling from Luka and Lytt. Roxine had explained to the girls at breakfast that Cayna would be away for a little while taking care of a mysterious matter, much to the girls' disappointment. However, unless she did something about the shadow in the water, the festival could never get started. It might even get canceled at this rate. Cayna wanted Luka and Lytt to experience the excitement of a proper festival, and she herself wanted to see the boat race. Although she had a bad feeling about the whole thing, the scales tipped in the children's favor, so she decided to prioritize her job as an adventurer.

Still, a bit of complaining never hurt anyone, right?

Cayna summoned a magical creature for Luka and Lytt while they were getting changed. Choosing something small enough for the girls to hold proved to be a challenge.

"*Meow.*"

"Wow...," said Luka.

"Ooh, a kitty!" Lytt squealed. "What's the kitty for, Miss Cayna?"

Cayna ended up going with a snow-white kitten that still had its innocent, angelic looks. Snug in Luka's arms, the kitten narrowed its eyes and meowed. The girls smiled.

"It's not meant to replace me, but I thought it would make a good companion. This kitty is pretty strong; it'll help you out if anything happens."

"It's...strong?" Luka stared curiously at the kitten in her arms. Lytt patted the kitten's head and gaped in fascination when it mewed at her. Roxine had apparently cast Search and held her head in her hands when she realized how formidable the kitten was.

"Lady Cayna, what is the meaning of this? Is this cat...stronger than me?"

"I mean, that depends. But you should be fine taking it around with you. Take it from here, cath palug."

"Meooow."

The cath palug kitten meowed adorably. She and the summoning could communicate telepathically; she heard it reply with a rascally, *"You got it, kiddo!"*

"It's pretty powerful since it's from the Heaven area," Cayna explained. "And as an added bonus, heavily armored knights are its natural enemy."

"That makes it sound like you want it to antagonize the knights...," Roxine said with a sigh.

Cayna appeared to be enjoying this. She was essentially trying to say the kitten's attacks could penetrate any defense, and knights were the first armor-wearing example that came to her mind. It was as simple as that.

"Where are you guys going today?" Cayna asked.

"That is up to the two girls to decide," Roxine replied. "I believe they want to visit the shops in the residential district again."

"You're not gonna take them down the main road?" Cayna inquired.

"As you are aware, Lady Cayna, the main road is full of trash. It is far too dangerous for the girls."

Crowds were no different from trash heaps, as far as Roxine was concerned. Cayna nodded in acquiescence. Might as well let Roxine go where she pleased if it meant she wasn't going to flip out on someone.

"If you have the time, you ought to check out the market and do a bit of shopping. I bet you two would love that," Cayna told the girls. "Definitely try all the different fruits they have, too."

Lytt and Luka were petting the cath palug, which was now in Lytt's arms; the girls' eyes sparkled with overwhelming curiosity about what Cayna told them. The fruit in the remote village was mostly limited to the strawberries and grapes that grew naturally in the forest. Recently, Roxine had been saving the fruit little by little to make jams. She said she'd share the jams with the villagers once she'd collected enough fruit, so it was going to be a long way off before Lytt could get a taste. The process would go much more quickly if she bought more fruit for the jam from the market.

Cayna herself hadn't seen everything the market had to offer, but she was sure the diverse lineup would be a treat for the girls' eyes.

"'Kay, I'm off to the Adventurers Guild!"

"Take...care..."

"See you later, Miss Cayna!"

Cayna patted Luka, Lytt, and the cath palug on the head, set aside her frustrations, and left the rental house. Eager to get all unpleasantness over with as fast as possible, she headed for the Adventurers Guild at hyper speed and charged at Almana, who was sitting at the counter.

"Okay, I'm here, Almana! Tell me more details about what you said yesterday! C'mon, hurry up!"

"Eek?!"

Almana jumped up in shock when Cayna suddenly appeared with double the authoritative force. This was likely due to flickering light of Oscar—Roses Scatter with Beauty and the extra impact it added.

"Umm, well then, please come this way," Almana said before leading Cayna to the same small room they had been in the day before. There, Cayna found a lineup of vague requests such as *"Get rid of the problem so we can have the festival,"* and *"I can't go fishing, so do something about it."*

"Hmm?"

"Have you noticed the requests?" Almana asked.

"Yeah. This shadow thing doesn't exactly *need* to be defeated. Not that I necessarily could do it."

None of *Leadale*'s quests involved a creature that big. Cayna herself didn't know how destructive her biggest attack would be in this world. Testing this out wasn't an option since she couldn't just cast massive spells indiscriminately.

Plus, there was one more thing on her mind.

"The first shadow was much smaller than the more recent shadow, right?" Cayna said. "What's that about?"

"We still don't have any eyewitness accounts, but perhaps the smaller one grew fearful of the larger one and went away somewhere…"

"So basically, you can't confirm anything since it's underwater, right?"

"Yes…," Almana replied, disheartened, but Cayna told her not to worry about it.

"I'll go check out the river," Cayna said. "We'll just have to see what happens then."

"I'm terribly sorry. The guild is looking into things as well, but we've never dealt with an underwater threat before."

"I mean, that's fair enough. People might end up getting eaten by a laigayanma nymph or something."

Unfortunately, the Adventurers Guild didn't have any further information about the shadow. Cayna gave up and figured it was time to bite the bullet.

"Fiiine. Guess I better get over there."

Cayna hopped from roof to roof until she reached a house near the Ejidd River. She looked down at the water; the current was calm, and there wasn't a single boat out of port. The river had a peacefulness disconnected from the tumult in town. The fishermen in their docked boats appeared to be staring at the river reproachfully as they silently repaired their nets. Others cast their lines or simply stared out at the water.

In short: lots of potential witnesses. Brazenly walking onto the water's surface like it was nothing would be a rash move on Cayna's part.

"Agh, I *really* don't wanna do this."

Just as Cayna resigned herself and was about to take action, Li'l Fairy suddenly began kicking up a fuss. Since she couldn't talk, her way of causing a fuss was a little different from most. To get Cayna's attention, she waved her hands wildly and used her whole body to try and gesture to Cayna. The fairy first pantomimed tugging at her pocket and taking something out of it. Then she pretended to put something on her finger, raised her hand, and drew a circle in the air.

"Something in my pocket? My finger? …Ummm, a ring? Ah, that's it? …You want me to take a ring out of my Item Box?!"

Li'l Fairy nodded profusely once Cayna figured out what she wanted. Cayna hurriedly opened her Item Box and saw that one of her possessions was blinking.

"Huh? The heck—? A trial challenger at a time like this?!"

It was an alert from the Ninth Guardian Tower in Felskeilo's Battle Arena. Cayna had no idea how Li'l Fairy knew a ring in her Item Box had been reacting to the alert. That likely had something to do with the game's system.

Eager to find someplace out of the public eye, Cayna took advantage of the pre-festival hustle and bustle and soared high into the sky.

Once she was high enough that the crowds looked like tiny specks, Cayna lifted her ring and called out the password.

"One who protects in times of trouble! I beseech you to rescue this depraved world from chaos!"

Countless shining stars appeared in the shape of a cross beneath her feet before enveloping her. By the time they dissipated, she had vanished from the sky.

Cayna then found herself in a half-circle dome about fifty meters in diameter. Above her was a geocentric miniature model set with a plush sun revolving in the middle. At the center of the marble-tiled floor was a delicately sculpted white flowerpot. The maple tree growing in it was this space's true form.

Smoke burst forth from the maple tree before coagulating into a human-shaped Guardian. The Guardian bowed its head at Cayna. She didn't like how it kneeled before her the few times she'd come by to refill its MP, so she'd asked it to stop. Bowing its head seemed to be the very minimal amount of etiquette this Guardian could offer.

"Greetings, Lady Cayna. A fine welcome to you. I apologize for the sudden message."

"Don't worry about that. There's a trial challenger here, right? I'm kind of busy, so if we could get this done quickly—"

"Forgive me—I did not contact you because of a challenger."

"Huh?"

Apparently, the Guardian had contacted her for some other reason.

Cayna was impressed with how independent the Guardians had become. After all, they couldn't leave their towers. She figured the least she could do as a Skill Master was provide them with a comfortable living environment. Not that a comfortable environment would be of much use in the Third Skill Master Guardian Tower, since its wall Guardian couldn't even move around.

"Lady Cayna?"

"Ah, right, sorry. Please, go on."

"I had you come today because I have a favor to ask regarding a nearby Guardian Tower."

"Right, right, a Guardian Tower. A Guardian—THERE'S ANOTHERRRR?!"

Cayna had been nodding along with the Ninth Guardian's casual statement when she yelled out in surprise. She'd never heard anything from the Guardian about another tower the last time she was in the area. If she was only getting the report now, the tower must have come from somewhere else. In other words...

"This one's mobile?"

"Precisely."

Cayna's Guardian Tower was really the only one that fit the description of a tower. With the proper trappings, the other Guardian Towers were more like actual homes—thus, they were fixed in place.

Mobile towers, on the other hand, were not locked to one location and could freely wander. Just three of the thirteen Guardian Towers were of this type; the only one Cayna had visited was called the Floating Sky Garden, which looked like an old-fashioned Japanese-style house. She didn't know anything about the other two mobile towers.

"You think it might be in the Ejidd River...?"

"Yes. The tower is currently underwater. I attempted to

contact it since it is within my range of communication, but it seems to lack the MP needed to awaken. Could I ask you to remedy this?"

Cayna crouched down, hit by a sudden wave of exhaustion. Just a short while earlier, she'd foolishly thought she had no choice but to use her Silver Ring to take care of the river shadow problem. Fortunately, the Admins were smart enough to make objects of mystique such as Guardian Towers impervious to attacks by high-powered players like Cayna.

Cayna imagined that if she had, in fact, used her Silver Ring on this underwater tower, the only outcome would be a fully intact tower and a half-destroyed Felskeilo. At any rate, she was glad she figured this out sooner rather than later.

Cayna felt a semblance of relief before coming to another unpleasant realization.

She'd have to refill this new tower's MP and take it far from Felskeilo. Plus, there was the added headache of explaining all of this to the Adventurers Guild, as well as putting the public at ease. The entire city would end up in a frenzy if she explained everything, and that would only limit her options.

"The public loves Skargo. He'd be perfect at a time like this... Oh, right. He's out of town..."

The one person whose conversational eloquence and effects would help her come up with the perfect explanation for the citizens was away from the Felskeilo capital, and she had no time to wait for him to return. Feigning ignorance about the tower was one option, but it certainly wasn't a permanent solution. Felskeilo might even experience a food shortage. Dissatisfaction with the ruling king would grow and possibly result in a coup d'état.

Cayna could calm the capital's citizens from the shadows. She decided that was exactly what she had to do.

"…In any case, I'll go and check out this new Guardian Tower and get an idea of what exactly I'm dealing with…"

Worrying wouldn't get her anywhere, so she decided to see what the tower looked like. She might even be able to make it swim away from Felskeilo while everyone watched.

Moreover, Cayna couldn't get inside the tower from here.

"Guess I gotta get near it first before I use my ring, huh?"

"Yes. It can transport you to either this tower or the Third Tower, as these are the only towers in the vicinity."

Other than her own ring, Cayna possessed the rings of the Sixth, Ninth, and Thirteenth Skill Masters. Each ring reacted to their respective Guardian Tower. In order to go to a new tower, its Skill Master had to use their ring and let you in, or you could use your own ring while close to that tower.

It seemed that due to a safeguard feature, the new tower was normally impossible to perceive from above the water. That had to be the source of the large shadow that people were seeing.

The tower was now deep beneath the water and would appear if Cayna drew close. When that happened, according to the Ninth Guardian, the underwater tower would generate a massive wave to conceal Cayna while she used the password to enter. That seemed to be the extent of what this new tower was capable of right now.

The Ninth Guardian sent her outside quickly, to the outer edge of the Battle Arena's audience seats. Fortunately, the soldiers on guard didn't notice her sudden appearance. But now she had to somehow get over to the new Guardian Tower at the bottom of the river in the southern part of Felskeilo. To avoid looking suspicious, she made her way through northern Felskeilo's royal castle and the aristocratic district to the riverbank and looked for a way to cross the river.

However, the dragonfly service here was for nobles only, and a gondola for transporting people hung from two laigayanma. Since she had no intention of visiting Felskeilo incessantly, she came to the firm decision that she'd have no choice but to deal with sticking out a bit.

Cayna used Water Walk to glide across the river as quickly as possible, not even sparing a glance at the startled townspeople as she made her way to the opposite shore. She cut through the sandbank and got the feeling she'd just passed some church officials or familiar royalty, but no one called out to her, so she kept on running.

Once she was back atop the river's surface, she heard a commotion coming from the residential district.

"Ugh! I wish they'd stop getting worked up over every little thing!"

"You were well aware you would become a spectacle, yes?"

"Yeah, but it still makes me wanna complain!"

Cayna never slowed down as she mumbled and grumbled to Kee. She kept a close eye on her Guardian Ring, which would glow as soon as she got near the new tower.

Somewhere over the water between the sandbar and the residential district, the ring emitted a faint light, and she slammed on the brakes. She slid several meters across the river's surface and came to a halt. The moment she looked up and murmured, "Did I pass it?" the water in front of her swelled, and a massive white body broke through the surface. It was so enormous that the wave it produced shook her up and down. She had to be careful not to step on the pieces of stirred-up driftwood that floated by. At around fifty meters in length, this creature was at least twice the size of the penguin monster. Its wide, smooth back sported a blowhole; this was clearly a blue whale, although the inhabitants of this world didn't recognize it as such. Cayna could hear nearby onlookers shouting in awe.

The whale's upper half stood almost completely straight, its round, black eyes looking down at Cayna, and it flopped over onto its back. The resulting tidal wave swallowed everything in its path—including the nearby onlookers.

The innocent bystanders on the sandbar and in the residential district stood frozen in shock, and immediately afterward the whale sank back into the river. The water's surface was soon calm again, but one particular onlooker was now nowhere to be found.

"Ngh… I was a bit too late with the password."

Cayna's hair was dripping wet. Fortunately, she'd chanted the password before the tidal wave engulfed her, but she still ended up getting drenched just as she said the final *"from chaos!"* part.

She'd made it inside the Guardian Tower but was soaked from head to toe. No big deal, though; at least she could dry herself off with magic.

When Cayna took a look around, her surroundings weren't inside the esophagus or stomach of some animal. The rocky walls were more reminiscent of a cave or grotto. She continued further down the path; it was too dark to see much with the naked eye, but not so bad that she'd need to use Night Vision. Nothing in a Guardian Tower was likely to pose a threat to a Skill Master, so Cayna walked along in high spirits.

However, within a little under thirty meters, she arrived at a small room.

There was no door, so she could see everything inside: a small, dilapidated table, a wooden puppet seated in a chair, and a clock so tall it looked ready to burst through the ceiling. The puppet's clothes were shabby, and it was missing its left arm. The cuff of its left sleeve was raggedy, as if that part of the shirt had been torn off. The puppet was also missing its left leg from the knee down. On its head was a dusty tricorn hat, and in place of its eyes were crosses. Most notable of all was its exceptionally long nose.

The large clock at the back of the room had a pendulum in its lower half and a small door above the clockface; not exactly a masterpiece.

"Is the theme of this place fairy tales or something?"

Cayna looked between the puppet and the clock but couldn't tell which was the tower's core and which was the Guardian. If only they were both in the same place, like the wall Guardian in her tower. Seeing no other choice, she poured MP into both the clock and the puppet.

The changes were immediate. The wooden puppet began to shine brightly, and its missing arm and leg had now grown back. However, the table and chair (and the puppet itself) remained just as shabby as before.

"…So the clock is the Guardian?"

The large clock had started ticking, its pendulum swinging back to life.

Cayna was fully prepared for the clock to start talking. Then, the door above the clockface opened.

"Well met!" *Ka-thunk.* **"This is the tower"**—*ka-thunk*—**"of the First"**—*ka-thunk*—**"Skill Master"**—*ka-thunk*—**"Marvelia!"** *Ka-thunk.*

"……The heck…?"

When the door opened, a small yellow bird attached to a bellows appeared.

It would then pop back into the clock after every few words. Cayna was reasonably dumbfounded. "So Marvelia made this place?"

"Indeed"—*ka-thunk*—**"she did."** *Ka-thunk.*

The Guardian's quirk was so annoying that Cayna wished it *wouldn't* answer.

The First Skill Master Marvelia had been a female werecat. She was the type of person who considered anything to be potential data,

139

and she took statistics of everything. Basically, she was satisfied as long as she could test for something.

Marvelia herself admitted she became a Skill Master while searching for patterns in NPC dialogue. She'd even stalked Cayna for a brief period, claiming she was going to "uncover every last high-elf trait in existence."

…Or rather, that was all part of one of Marvelia's tests Cayna helped with.

In any case, it was accurate to say the stand-out players of every race weren't crazy about Marvelia's stalking or "quest for knowledge," as it were.

"A place this bare-bones definitely suits her. And I get why there's a wooden puppet inside the whale, but is the big clock supposed to be the puppet's grandfather or something?"

"That is"—*ka-thunk*—"exactly right!" *Ka-thunk.* "Master Marvelia"—*ka-thunk*—"based this tower on"—*ka-thunk*—"his oldest memories"—*ka-thunk*—"but when she saw us"—*ka-thunk*—"she actually looked quite sad!"

It seemed this Guardian had some self-awareness.

However, the conversation wasn't going to get anywhere this way. Cayna approached the clock and caught the bellows of the little yellow bird as it popped out to talk. "Gwaaaaaawk!" it wailed painfully.

"What are"—*ka-thunk*—"you doing?!" *Ka-thunk.* "This clock"—*ka-thunk*—"is my body!" *Ka-thunk.* "Grabbing me so"—*ka-thunk*—"suddenly is"—*ka-thunk*—"extremely rude!" *Ka-thunk.*

"Sorry. Curiosity got the better of me."

"Harumph!" *Clunk.* This "harumph" was the bird's way of expressing anger.

It then burst back out of the clock and tossed the ring in its mouth at Cayna. Although the color was different, there was no question it was a Guardian Ring. Being manhandled may have upset the Guardian, but it seemed that it had accepted Cayna.

"I'm the Third Skill Master, Cayna. Nice working with you."

"Understood!" *Ka-thunk.* **"You are my"**—*ka-thunk*—**"new master!"** *Ka-thunk.* **"I apologize for"**—*ka-thunk*—**"cutting to the chase"**—*ka-thunk*—**"but please"**—*ka-thunk*—**"give your next order."**

"Next order?"

Cayna didn't know what the yellow Guardian bird was talking about, so she took the time to listen to it tell her about how to beat this Guardian Tower's Skill Transfer Quest and where the tower was normally hidden. She also asked if Marvelia had left any message behind.

The First Skill Master's special mobile Guardian Tower was in the shape of a blue whale. In order to obtain the tower's skill, one had to fish the whale out of the water. However, Marvelia would change the kind of bait needed to catch the whale once a week, so the tower had only ever been caught a total of five times. According to Kee's log, about three hundred players had met the requirements to pass the Skill Transfer Quest in Cayna's tower. Compared to hers, Marvelia's number was incredibly small.

Furthermore, this tower hid in bodies of water such as rivers and oceans. It would reflect an enormous shadow on the surface, and the true body of the tower would be hidden deeper within that. The Guardian itself didn't really understand the principle, but that seemed to be how the tower worked. And if even the Guardian didn't know, then there was no way Cayna could, either. Most likely, the large shadow that had appeared in the Ejidd River was the tower's method of hiding. And since it was just a shadow, you couldn't poke it with a stick and find the actual tower that way.

There didn't seem to be a message from Marvelia herself. The last time she visited, she said, *"It's been fun, you guys. Later,"* and took off. The lid of the table was the tower's storage, which was full of hastily scribbled notes.

"I'd expect nothing less of Marvelia. Always well-prepared, that one."

It turned out that Cayna did have something to do with this tower's appearance in Felskeilo. It had been lying off the coast at the bottom of the ocean when the Blue Dragon Cayna had sent to find the mermaid village happened to pass by. The tower then detected a player's presence from the dragon. Furthermore, since the tower was right off the shore, it also detected a reaction from a Skill Master's Guardian Ring. It then went down the southern coastline, following the ring's signal before heading upstream from the mouth of the Ejidd River. Finally, it tried to pass through Felskeilo only to be contacted by another active Guardian Tower and decided to stop where it was.

"Hey, Nine! Why didn't you tell me sooner?!"

"You appeared to be coming this way. The First still had some energy left in its tank, so I waited until you came closer."

A circular screen had appeared on the cave wall. It showed the Ninth Guardian bowing its head.

This was the intra-Guardian communication network. It was a bit like a video conference between Guardian Towers, although they sometimes used it to exchange idle gossip.

Besides, the First Skill Master's tower arrived in Felskeilo in the middle of Cayna's journey to the royal capital. If the ninth tower had notified her then, she would've had to temporarily leave Luka and the others, something she knew she couldn't do. Thus, Cayna had no issue with the Guardians' judgment.

"Well then, master"—*ka-thunk*—**"where should"**—*ka-thunk*—**"we go?"** *Ka-thunk.*

"Hold on. It's not quite that simple." Cayna stopped the bird Guardian and thought things through. "Did you hear about what's going on in the city?"

"I've already"—*ka-thunk*—**"received word"**—*ka-thunk*—**"from the Ninth."**

"I explained the circumstances in detail."

The Ninth Guardian had informed the other of the geography ahead of time, at least to a certain degree. It had also told the first tower to stay hidden at the bottom of the river.

"Yeah, your body casts a huge shadow and scares the townspeople," said Cayna. "They think there's some giant, unknown monster lurking in the river."

"I see no need"—*ka-thunk*—**"to pay those NPCs"**—*ka-thunk*—**"any mind."** *Ka-thunk.*

Cayna just barely managed to keep herself from screaming, *"You're an NPC too!"* Fortunately, the Ninth Guardian spoke for her.

"You'd best refrain from upsetting our master, First. Your words are insulting, like calling a dwarf a mole."

"R-right..." *Ka-thunk.* **"I'm"**—*ka-thunk*—**"terribly sorry."** *Ka-thunk.* **"Please"**—*ka-thunk*—**"forgive me."**

"I forgive you," Cayna mumbled after taking a deep breath to quell her rising anger. The words came out extremely cold and stiff, but she shook her head and got a hold of herself. "A lot of people will still be anxious if you just up and leave. Even if you make a show of swimming somewhere else, they'll think you might come back..."

"If I am not allowed here"—*ka-thunk*—**"then I shall simply leave"**—*ka-thunk*—**"and never come back."**

"I can't exactly explain you away with 'Hey, blue whales aren't real'!!"

The cave echoed with reverberations of the *"-eal, -eal, -eal"* Cayna had yelled in frustration. She became annoyed with herself for her sudden outburst. There weren't many Guardians like her mural that she could crack jokes with. Just like Marvelia, this Guardian was bad at reading the room. The Ninth Guardian fell silent at Cayna's menacing look.

"Understood, master." *Ka-thunk.* **"In other words"**—*ka-thunk*—**"I should leave"**—*ka-thunk*—**"in a way"**—*ka-thunk*—**"people can understand."** *Ka-thunk.*

The bird Guardian wasn't especially bothered by Cayna's indignation and spoke matter-of-factly.

"Still, this place is just as good as any other…"

If leaving the river was going to be a problem, then Cayna had to come up with a way to keep the tower here.

"You may be right. If someone acknowledges its presence, will the people agree to let it stay?"

"Is there not"—*ka-thunk*—**"a leader"**—*ka-thunk*—**"who can bring"**—*ka-thunk*—**"the people together?"** *Ka-thunk.* **"Someone like"**—*ka-thunk*—**"a guild master?"** *Ka-thunk.*

"A guild master, huh…?"

Of all the people she knew, Cayna's son Skargo certainly had the gift of gab. His annoying special effects aside, he held great authority in this nation as its High Priest. That said, Cayna couldn't help but feel those effects of his would ruin any image he had as someone of a "responsible position."

"The king…? Royalty… Mye… Primo… Hmm. Maybe I should try talking to Mye? Plus, Shining Saber's also a player, so I bet he'd help out, too."

She settled on the Crown Princess, Myleene. Cayna remembered hearing that the monarch's firstborn child inherited the throne, so Primo wasn't next in line, but rather his older sister, Myleene, was.

"This role would also help solidify Princess Myleene's future reign."

"Oh, I see!" Cayna was impressed Kee had thought of it from that perspective.

"So"—*ka-thunk*—**"what shall"**—*ka-thunk*—**"we do"**—*ka-thunk*—**"master?"** *Ka-thunk.*

Cayna paused the bird Guardian for a moment to pay the Ninth Guardian her respects. "Thanks for your hard work. Sorry for calling you here like this."

"Not at all. Please contact me at any time." It then bowed its head.

"Time to go and see if I can get any help with this," Cayna said upon deciding to head out. She had the bird Guardian show her a map of the city on the screen and pointed to a corner of the Academy grounds on the sandbar. It'd be a hassle explaining things to any eyewitnesses if she popped up in the middle of town somewhere.

"So anyway, just sit tight here at the bottom of the river, okay?"

"Understood." *Ka-thunk.* **"The rest is in"**—*ka-thunk*—**"your competent hands, master."** *Ka-thunk.*

"Don't get your hopes up too much."

With parting words that would make anyone nervous, Cayna gave in to the floating sensation that sent her back to the surface.

She reappeared in a corner of the Academy grounds, then looked around to make sure no one had spotted her. When she saw that the coast was clear, she breathed a heavy sigh.

"Okay—I'm doing this so Luka and Lytt can see the festival. You've got this, Cayna!"

She pumped her fist with determination, then made her way over to visit Mai-Mai.

"Mother?!"

When Cayna knocked at the Academy headmaster's door and

stepped in, Mai-Mai noisily rose from her chair and greeted her with a look of surprise.

"What are you making such a fuss for?" Cayna asked.

Mai-Mai rushed over and gave Cayna an unusually tight hug. Cayna was utterly confused.

"Ahh, thank goodness," said Mai-Mai. "When I heard from Mye that you'd been swallowed up in a giant wave created by a strange fish, I was so worried!"

As Cayna suspected, she'd indeed passed by Myleene and Lonti on the sandbar. They must have seen the great rush she was in and thought something terrible had happened, then followed her—only to see the giant blue whale jump out of the river.

"I'm insulted, Mai-Mai. Did you really think some big ol' wave would be enough to do me in?"

"Huh? Ummm," Mai-Mai blustered as her eyes darted about. "Well, I know you're a Skill Master, but, um…" She trailed off.

Cayna smirked and reached out to pat her head. "Okay, okay. Thanks for worrying about me."

"…Mother!" Mai-Mai's eyes teared up, and she once again hugged Cayna tight. Cayna surrendered herself to the comforting warmth and waited for her daughter to let go before asking about Myleene.

"Mye? Right… She was in a huge hurry, and…ah, come to think of it!" As Mai-Mai searched through her memories and hit upon something, she simultaneously struck a fist to her palm and shouted, "She said she was going to mobilize the knights to look for you and then promptly took off!"

"Huh?"

Cayna thought Mye was overreacting. The knights wouldn't necessarily follow her orders, anyway. Besides, Shining Saber was captain of the knights. He knew Cayna would never die from something like this, and therefore he wouldn't have his knights brazenly run off in search of her.

But Cayna soon had other concerns.

Within the knights, the rumor "Cayna is Shining Saber's fiancée" had not yet been dispelled. It wasn't necessarily untrue that the knights wouldn't revolt and come rushing over...

Cayna grew increasingly worried. "I'm off to the castle," she said and tried to leave the room, but a concerned-looking Mai-Mai stopped her.

"The castle...? Mother, don't you hate places like that?"

"I mean, sometimes. It depends. But I'm in a bit of a rush right now. There's something I want to discuss with Mye."

Mai-Mai stared at her mother for a few moments, then after suddenly tidying up her desk, she took Cayna's arm. "I'm going, too," she said.

"Huh?"

"Besides, you can't enter the castle on your own, right? You'll be fine if I'm with you."

Pulling her arm with a "Hurry, come on," Cayna smiled and murmured, "Thank you."

They rode a dragonfly gondola from the north end of the sandbar and headed for the aristocratic district. Since it was Mai-Mai's return trip, Cayna paid nothing.

From there, they went down the main street and toward the castle. For a street wide enough for five carriages across, there were too few people. Other than a carriage occasionally passing by, they only spotted people in standard uniforms swiftly carrying luggage. Mai-Mai explained that these were the nobles' servants and butlers.

"Come to think of it, Mai-Mai, do you use a carriage?"

"Ah, the Harvey estate is within walking distance of a dragon-fly station."

"Really? So can you go from the station to the castle without a carriage?"

"Ah-ha-ha, you care about the strangest things, Mother. Even back when I was with the Mage Corps, I walked unless I was in a hurry."

The nobles in the stories Cayna read always rode in carriages. She realized this was yet another difference between games and real life.

The castle was at the end of the main street and was surrounded by walls of a different design than the ones around the city. The large door at the front entrance was closed. In terms of size, the level-990 White Dragon that her pendant called upon the other day could walk through it with room to spare.

Next to this was a small door with knights stationed on either side. Even though it was considerably smaller, the width and length were such that a carriage could pass through with ease.

"Helloooo!" Mai-Mai called out, arm-in-arm with Cayna. One of the two human guards grimaced.

"Again, Mrs. Harvey?" he said. "How many times have we asked you to please come in a carriage when you visit the castle?"

Apparently, Mai-Mai's ideas of social etiquette weren't typical of this world. She looked like a child who'd been caught playing a prank.

"We have a message for the princess," said Mai-Mai. "May we come in?"

"You may indeed, but do you intend on bringing that commoner with you?"

The knights eyeballed Cayna. Since she looked like an adventurer, he no doubt determined she was unfit to enter.

"Is there some sort of problem?" Mai-Mai asked.

149

"I'm not so sure she should be allowed in the castle. She may be involved with some kind of unseemly organization."

It was better that Mai-Mai's clinginess didn't get them through the gate. Even Cayna understood the guards' wariness all too well. After all, they weren't wrong for treating someone like her, who had more battle prowess than anyone else in this world, as a threat.

"I guarantee that this person—"

"""AHHHH!!"""

Just as Mai-Mai puffed up at their insolence and tried to ask them to allow Cayna through, piercing screams arose from inside the gate. When the guards turned around, they saw three female knights. Joyous, they passed through the side gate further over that was made for personal use and surged through like an avalanche.

"Lady Cayna! It's been so long!"

"Thank you so much for the other day! Everyone owes so much to you!"

"What are you visiting for today? I bet you're here to see the captain!"

"Ah, right. Nice to see you all," said Cayna.

The women's excessive energy shocked not only Cayna, but Mai-Mai as well. These were the female knights who Cayna had accompanied while they were on their campaign. They were a big help and had given her a bed to sleep in while the forces camped outside, and they taught her march etiquette.

The guards at the gate were just as surprised. In an attempt to get a word in, they questioned the knights.

"Do you know this person?"

"Hm? Well, yes... Hey, what are you doing?!" one of the female knights shouted at the guards. The three female knights looked at each other, reviewed the situation, then saw Cayna and Mai-Mai waiting at the gate.

"""P-pardon?!"""

The women apparently outranked the gate guards, who straightened up and began sweating buckets.

"She is High Priest Skargo and Lady Mai-Mai's mother. To think you would treat her as suspicious. Have you no shame?!" shouted another female knight.

""U-understood! W-we apologize!"" The guards nearly fell over from bowing so much.

Cayna once again felt her own children's magnificence. One of them was still unfortunate, however.

"I wonder what Sir Kartatz would say if he heard such a thing... I trust you two are prepared to learn that for yourselves?" said the third female knight.

For some reason, the guards trembled at the mention of Kartatz's name. He had nothing to do with the knights, so what could they possibly fear of him?

When Cayna tilted her head questioningly, Mai-Mai whispered, "Kartatz always baptizes the new knights."

By "baptize," she meant the new recruits were shuttled over to Kartatz's workshop, where their less desirable traits were beaten out of them. Basically, they got screamed at and occasionally smacked until they were whipped into shape.

"Sounds more like boot camp...," Cayna muttered to Mai-Mai. "?"

The female knights ushered Cayna and Mai-Mai through the gate, past the trembling guards. From there, they would take the pair to either Myleene or Shining Saber. It seemed that these lady knights were usually escorts for female royalty.

"What perfect timing," said one female knight.

"Her Highness just went to see the captain," said another.

"She's been persuading him this whole time that we need to rescue Cayna."

"But isn't that Cayna right there?"

"Perhaps Her Highness was going to rescue someone else?"

Cayna was mortified when she heard this exchange. All her frantic running around town had stressed Mye out. She put her face in her hands, and Mai-Mai dragged her by the arm toward their destination.

They were headed to a knight station located about a quarter lap along the western route on the castle's outer wall. A large dragoid and a petite girl were going back and forth about something in front of it, and the conversation could be heard from a distance.

"I told you before, did I not?! Someone was swallowed up by a wave!"

"There's no need to bring out the entire knight corps for one person! Besides, it's Cayna! She doesn't need any saving!"

"Are you not worried about her?! I heard she's your good friend, Captain."

"I'm saying that has nothing to do with my duties! We knights don't go on personal errands. We act only under the king's command!"

Mai-Mai smiled wryly when Cayna suddenly hid behind her. After all, she heard their argument and realized the situation. Mai-Mai herself hadn't been there to see the bizarre fish appear, so it had all been word of mouth. It was only natural that anyone who saw someone they knew swallowed up by a wave would start panicking.

Thus, Mai-Mai took the initiative and called out to Myleene. "Your Highness!"

"Huh?! Y-yes, ma'am!"

Myleene instinctively stood at attention. It was a reaction to the appearance of the Academy professor who valued discipline and conditioned her students through reprimand.

When Myleene turned toward them, Mai-Mai pushed Cayna out from behind her. "My mother is safe."

"Hey, hold on, Mai-Mai!"

"Lady Cayna!!" Myleene flew forward as Cayna was bewilderedly shoved in front of the dragoid and princess. The panicked Cayna hurriedly caught her.

"L-Lady Cayna, you're safe! I'm so glad! Wh-when I saw the scene...I thought—I thought you..."

Overcome with emotion, Myleene began to sob, and Cayna embraced her. Across from them, the dumbfounded Shining Saber grumbled, "See, I told you."

"*Gasp!* Wait, is this considered insulting the crown?!"

"Bit late for that, don't you think?"

Cayna had returned to her senses as she comforted Myleene. Shining Saber's exasperated answer made the nearby knights burst into laughter.

Cayna gently patted Myleene's back until she calmed down.

"Wow, how maternal of you," Shining Saber joked.

"Huh? Don't you see my big daughter right there?"

"Mother... 'Big' is rather harsh." Mai-Mai pretended to break down in tears.

Shining Saber looked shocked at her reaction. Apparently, he hadn't anticipated Mai-Mai joining in their banter.

"Something the matter?" Mai-Mai asked him.

"Oh, uh, I just wasn't expecting you to react like that. I didn't mean nothin' by it. Sorry if I hurt your feelings."

"There's no need to take things so seriously with my mother here."

"That's how this works?"

"Indeed it is."

Shining Saber had apparently only seen Mai-Mai's strict, professorial side. Seeing her be so casual was truly a rare sight.

Myleene had stopped crying, and Cayna said, "Come now, blow that nose," in a very parent-child interaction.

"Man, I wonder if I should be doing this sort of thing when the queen's still around," Cayna mused.

"……Mother……" Mai-Mai was exasperated. Cayna had only realized this now.

"P-Professor! Please don't tell my mother about this!" Myleene begged.

"Huh? Mai-Mai, you know the queen?" Cayna asked.

"Well, sort of."

Cayna wondered why Myleene had pleaded with Mai-Mai. Apparently, the queen invited Mai-Mai for tea on occasion.

"How'd you two get so close?" Cayna asked her daughter.

"The current queen was a former student of mine."

"Oh."

Cayna had thought the queen would be older than her daughter, so Cayna was a bit curious to know how others might be perceiving Her Majesty.

"Oh yeah, didn't you just move to that village? What'd you'd suddenly come to the castle for?" Shining Saber asked, cutting their idle chit-chat short.

"Ah, right, right! Thanks for the reminder." Cayna clapped her hands in remembrance of what she came there for. "Mye, Shining Saber, I'd like to ask you two something in secret."

"Me, you say?"

"And me?"

The crown princess and knight captain looked at one another. "What for?" Shining Saber demanded.

Cayna glanced around. Since it was a guard station, they were surrounded by knights. Most were busy training, but many were listening in curiously on their conversation. Cayna scowled and skirted the question. "Mm, not here."

Myleene realized something was up, and answered, "Right this way, then." She led the three of them to a back door of sorts that went through the kitchens. The castle cooks were shocked to see such an odd group of people. Myleene and the others continued down the hallways, climbed the stairs, then went down another hallway before entering a room.

"Umm, where are we?" Cayna asked.

"I sometimes use it for dance practice, but it is currently unoccupied," Myleene replied with a bright smile. "Will this location do?"

Cayna eyed her surroundings. This place was about as wide as an Academy classroom. Other than rug on the floor, there were only shelves. There were no windows, so it was ideal for secret conversations. Cayna further cast Isolation Barrier. With this, there was no chance of their voices carrying outside.

"So?" Shining Saber prodded.

"You sure are hasty," Cayna retorted.

"I'm a knight captain, y'know. I got work to do. Let's make this quick."

"Okay, okay," Cayna replied as she thought about where she should start. "Um, the giant shadow in the river is the strange white fish Mye saw."

"What? Is that true?!" Myleene cried in shock. Cayna's point-blank revelation took her by surprise. Shining Saber frowned with incomprehension.

"Isn't the size of that fish much different from what we heard about the shadow?" Myleene asked.

"The shadow makes it look bigger than it actually is. The real thing is only one hundred meters long."

"Hold it, hold it, hold it! Quit chatting with her Highness and tell me exactly what's goin' on!" Shining Saber thrust himself in front of Cayna, effectively cutting off her explanation as well as her view of Mye.

"You said to make it short," Cayna told him.

"I was sayin' make it short enough for me to understand. Don't leave me outta your little two-way conversation."

"But then Mye won't be able to keep up," Cayna grumbled, her arms crossed.

Shining Saber heaved the deepest of sighs. "Okay, I get it, I get it," he said. "Take as long as you need, so just start from the beginning. I'll decide whether to help out once I hear the full story."

"Ooh, nice. If I have your help, Shining Saber, this plan will be rock solid."

"I'll help, too, Mother." Mai-Mai, who had remained silent thus far, expressed her willingness to participate. And even though Cayna hadn't even gotten into the details yet, Myleene threw her hat into the ring, too, nodding and exclaiming, "I as well!"

Prefacing with "I'll explain all the details, so just think about what we should do," Cayna began sharing what she knew about the current situation. "Umm, so the big shadow that appeared in the Ejidd River the other day was a Guardian Tower."

"Bwagh?!"

"Oh, was it?"

"A Guardian…what?"

Once she disclosed information regarding the foundations of the world itself, the three others had three separate reactions. Shining Saber did a spit take, Mai-Mai nodded in admiration, and Myleene tilted her head at the vocabulary she'd never heard before.

"Heeeey!" Shining Saber hissed. "You think you can just tell the princess somethin' like thaaaaaat?!" He grabbed Cayna by the shoulders and dragged her to a corner of the room. He darted his eyes about and leaned in close when he admonished her.

"It doesn't really hurt me in any way, and it's not like Mye will tell anyone, right?" said Cayna.

"Even if it doesn't reach the public, she'll tell people—like the king!" retorted Shining Saber.

"I mean, it's kinda late to be worrying about that. Skargo, Mai-Mai, and Kartatz already know I'm a Skill Master. They've probably told the king by now."

"…That's true, but still."

Suddenly feeling drained, Shining Saber let go of Cayna, who returned to Mai-Mai and Mye. The two of them looked concerned.

"May I ask something, Lady Cayna?" Mye said.

"Oh, about the Guardian Towers? So you know that both me and Mai-Mai can use ancient arts, right, Mye?"

"Ah, yes. I do."

"A Guardian Tower is a place where you can undergo a trial. If you pass it, you receive a single ancient art. I'm in charge of one of these places."

"Huh? Wh-whaaaaaaaaaaaaaaaat?!" Myleene shouted with such surprise it was as if she'd squeezed every ounce of air from her lungs. The shock was so great that she forgot to take a breath and soon had a coughing fit. Mai-Mai stroked her back, and Myleene calmed down once her breath feebly returned.

After waiting for the princess to compose herself, this time Shining Saber asked a question of his own. "You said before that you're looking for towers that have stopped operating, right? From what I'm hearing, that's not the case for this one, right?"

"It was on the very edge. It's got plenty of energy to swim around now," Cayna told him. "You have my word."

"Don't promise stuff like that!"

Cayna ignored his comment with a smile and continued on. "Anyway, the topic of this conversation is that Guardian Tower. I'd like to keep it here in Felskeilo and was wondering what I should do."

"And that's what you wanted to ask us about?"

Shining Saber put a hand to his mouth in thought. Myleene remained silent with the same gesture.

"In other words, Mother, are you asking for someone to hide it so it doesn't bother anyone?" said Mai-Mai.

"No, I don't even really mind if you make it a spectacle. I'm hoping it can stay in the river." Since one of the quest's conditions was fishing it out, her thought was that no one would think to fish for something that was already on display. "Depending on the situation, it could be a new tourist attraction."

Cayna thought it could be something that drew people to the tower, like the castle she'd made from scrap materials. Something that, when all was said and done, would be called part of the urban cityscape. Adding one or two more famous sites wasn't going to change that.

"You've got one teeny, tiny problem there," Shining Saber said dubiously.

"Yes, the captain is right," Mai-Mai agreed. "The tower has already made a very poor first impression."

Unsurprisingly, the initial "large shadow" that caused such a ruckus was the biggest obstacle in Cayna's plan. Since the tower had a poor image among anyone in the fishing business, she highly doubted they'd change their tune if she just insisted that everything was fine.

"Isn't trying to force our way past that a good idea?" said Cayna.

"Don't be ridiculous. I'm just a knight captain; what am I supposed to do about a giant thing like that?" Shining Saber retorted.

"I'm not asking you to lift it. Besides, what if I give you two skills as a reward?"

"...Hmph."

Shining Saber fell silent as Cayna held up two fingers and looked at him suggestively. He was no doubt mentally weighing the pros and cons. Thinking she could get him to see things her way, Cayna grinned happily and held up three fingers.

"Three skills. Those might come in pretty handy, wouldn't you say?" she pressed.

"Okay, fine. I'll help. Happy now?"

"Yesss, all right!" Cayna pumped her fist, to which Mai-Mai replied, "Mother, that's improper."

"So then, can we communicate with this strange fish?" Myleene asked.

"You can talk to it if you go inside, but that kind of ruins the whole spectacle."

"The heck?"

It was undeniable that having a conversation with a Guardian that popped in and out of a door with almost every word was more than exhausting; it was a full-on shock to the system.

"If we catch it and get it to tell people it has no intent on attacking them, that should do the trick," said Shining Saber.

"How's the whale supposed to answer if it can't talk?" asked Cayna.

"That's the thing. You're the one taking care of all this. How about you act as its representative or somethin'?"

"Oh, I get it now. In that case, if I put on some shining treasures, I bet it'll give me some majesty."

"You plannin' on being a messenger of the gods or something...?"

"That's it!" Myleene cut into the pair's increasingly ridiculous conversation. She beamed at Shining Saber.

"Which part is 'that'?" he asked.

"What you said just now, Captain. Let's make Lady Cayna a divine messenger!"

"Huh?" Cayna's mouth fell open at the role she was suddenly pushed into.

"I see. If Mother pretends to speak for the gods and says the whale seeks a peaceful life here in this city, Mye can can offer it refuge here, or something to that effect."

"Professor! What a fine suggestion. That's just what we'll do!"

Mai-Mai and Myleene's discussion moved along quickly, leaving Cayna and Shining Saber in the dust.

"Hmm."

"What's up?" Shining Saber asked Cayna.

"I feel like I should give Mye some kind of reward for this, too."

"Yeah, go for it. Two or three skills, maybe."

"Doesn't seem like average citizens can learn skills. After all, they don't have Item Boxes."

"Mm? Ah, I get it. So it's gotta be a real object."

"Something real... I wonder if a poison- or paralysis-resistant necklace would be good."

"That'd practically be a national treasure in this world. Granted, she *is* next in line for the throne, so I guess it works."

"Now just hold on! Mother! Captain! Don't whisper amongst yourselves over there. Please come over here and properly contribute to our discussion!" The pair's talk of reward had angered Mai-Mai.

""'Kaaaaay.""

"The correct response is *Coming*!"

""Comiiiing.""

After that, they discussed several ideas before eventually settling on going fishing for the tower. The plan would begin from there.

"Okay, so me and the knights are gonna fish out the tower," said Shining Saber. "We got a pole or something we can use?"

"I'll ask Kartatz. His workshop is temporarily closed, so I'm certain he'll be happy to assist," Mai-Mai answered. She had become the facilitator of this plan and wanted to attend to every last detail. "Her Highness will wait upon the specially prepared stage, and when the tower is caught, she will ask it to identify itself."

"'What're you doing here?' 'Why'd you go and upset all these townspeople?' ...Does that sound all right? Do I seem impressive?"

"Mye, you're the next queen. You don't *seem* impressive, you *are* impressive," Cayna insisted.

"Next comes your entrance, Mother. Please appear in a ball of light atop the tower."

"A ball of light—got it. So kinda sparkly like this?"

"Gah, you're doin' that *here*?!" Shining Saber exclaimed.

"Lady Cayna, that's a bit too bright. I can't look at you directly."

"She'll be a bit farther away on the actual day, so she'll need to be bright enough to astonish the townspeople."

"And now my knockout blow, Seven-Color Halo."

"That's an obnoxious neon! You ain't a pachinko sign!"

Shining Saber let quite a few dangerous words fly, but since Mai-Mai went on giving orders and confirming the plan, no one commented on this.

"Then, Mother, you will say, 'I apologize for the disturbance. I am in search of a peaceful abode.'"

"Um…like, '**I apologize for the disturbance**'?"

Canya gave Kee a command and tried out one of several eerie, hair-raising samples that sounded as if they belonged in horror movies. This was, of course, the Voice Change skill, but they'd need it to accomplish their objective. The goal was to surprise everyone in the area enough that they turned around.

"What the heck's with that voice? Where'd that come from?" Shining Saber demanded.

"You sound like a villain, Mother."

"I got the chills," Myleene remarked. "Do you think the towns-people will listen to such a voice?"

"Mother, can you sound a bit more like you came from the heavens?"

"How am I supposed to do that?!" Cayna cried.

No matter how grand a Skill Master she was, there was no way she could pull off a perfect, omnipotent voice. Such a request was too big for her to handle. Since people interpreted voices in different ways, they decided she would write in the sky.

"Should I write in the local language rather than *hiragana*?"

"Why not write it mixed with *kanji* first and switch it to the local language later?"

"Hmm, maybe I will."

There seemed to be some lasting influences from the game that caused the writings of Felskeilo to be in *katakana* and *hiragana*. The local language Cayna and the others now spoke used a unique, morphed alphabet. It was a style with alphabet letters that looked like they'd been written with an oversaturated ink pen and then dripped sideways. The reason most players could read this with ease was because of the Word Translator skill they received in character creation.

"Next, Your Highness should then say that you are willing to give the creature refuge," said Mai-Mai.

"'How about you stay here? Think you can watch over this land and its people for generations to come?' How does that sound?" asked Myleene.

"Is that really gonna convince people?" Shining Saber wondered aloud. "I feel like some folks might have doubts…"

"That is why we are crafting a plan," Mai-Mai replied. "If we cut corners, some people may take advantage of the situation. This is a very serious matter, Sir Knight Captain."

"As soon as I answer, 'Very well. I am in your care,' should I get into position upstream of the sandbar?"

"Yes. Please be sure to stay serious, Mother."

"Looks like we've got a lot to do. For now, I'll leave a Wind Spirit with Mye so it can amplify her voice. I'll be wrapping myself in

Additional White Light Level 9 and writing in the sky… In that case, I'll get a Light Spirit to give me a hand."

Cayna confirmed the steps of their plan as she counted on her fingers. Since she wouldn't be able to hear Myleene in the Guardian Tower, Cayna would explain what was going on and have the tower check the screen that showed the events going on outside. That was the only way to get the tower to move. Just to be safe, she was thinking she'd also cooperate with the Ninth and have the two towers stay in contact while coordinating with the outside. Even so, the core of the plan was nothing more than a matter of catching the blue whale tower, keeping it still, and then moving it.

"I heard that flowers make good bait. Do you think that will work?" Myleene asked.

"They'll be easy to throw, plus I'll explain everything to the Guardian Tower. A whole cow or something would be a waste."

"Well then, um… Would it be all right if I told my father about our plan?"

"True, Your Highness doesn't have the authority to mobilize the knight corps," said Shining Saber. "Don't worry—I'll ask to come along."

That was the final remaining concern. No matter how carefully they planned, if the king refused, nothing would move forward.

"We're causing a scene just to fix the issue, after all," said Cayna. "It'll all come to down to whether we get the king's approval."

"It will fine," said Myleene. "Sir Skargo spoke about Lady Cayna so much during our most recent meeting. I'm certain Father will understand!"

"*…Why was he talking about me during a meeting…?*"

It was an extremely reasonable question, but Myleene was in no position to address it. It wasn't like a princess could breezily discuss the internal details of a government meeting. If the king did understand their situation, Shining Saber could contact Cayna through a Friend Message.

Just as Shining Saber was about to accompany Myleene, he said, "Ah, shoot," and returned to Cayna.

"What's up?" she said.

"There's something I wanna ask. Do you know about the Parched Scorpions?"

"What's that, some guild name?"

"You don't know? It's a mafia-type organization. It looks like they were targeting those kids who are with you."

Cayna's eyes glinted dangerously before she slapped her forehead in realization. "Ah, Cie said she knocked some guys into next week. It was probably them."

"'Cie'?"

"The maid I summoned. She takes care of the house and kids."

"Right, one of those cash servants."

"Cash servant" was a derogatory term for summonings like butlers and maids. Since they were possessed by hardcore gamers, they were a target of envy in *Leadale*.

"You've really got nothin' to do with it, then? You sure?" Shining Saber asked.

"You're a stubborn one," Cayna replied. "What happened?"

Shining Saber was pointing at her. He must have thought it was something only players could know.

"Some god or devil or whatever named Igzdukyz appeared and made a big mess of 'em. Thinking about it now still gives me the chills…"

"'Igzdukyz'? Isn't that boss in the Underworld area? Maybe it went rogue."

Igzdukyz was the name of a scheming devil who commanded an army of grotesque underlings. Fairly weak for a boss character, but plenty annoying nonetheless since it made frequent use of traps. Cayna grew weary just thinking about this creature wandering around somewhere like the Terror Skeleton.

"You know what that thing is? Can you summon stuff like that?!"

"Of course I can't! Only demons can summon devils…"

As soon as she said it, Cayna realized something. Back in the game, demon players really were the only ones who could summon devils. If Igzdukyz had been summoned, it was proof there was a high-level demon player still out there.

"Hey, you've got a creepy smile on your face. You okay?" Shining Saber asked Cayna.

"Yeah, you gave me some good intel. So thanks for that."

"S-sure."

He'd just wanted to check that she was all right. With that out of the way, Shining Saber joined Myleene to go prepare for their audience with the king. Mai-Mai quickly wrote down the crux of the plan and handed it to the princess.

"Shouldn't you go with them to explain?" Cayna asked Mai-Mai.

"No one would be here to accompany you back outside the castle, Mother. Still, I think the guards know your face by this point, so I doubt you'd have any issues coming and going."

"Can't say that makes me particularly happy."

The mother-daughter pair made their way out of the castle, receiving odd stares from the various staff members. Upon exiting, they found Shining Saber's co-captain and several other knights waiting for them.

"Oh, what's this now?" Mai-Mai asked.

The knights apparently received word from Shining Saber earlier and would be accompanying them to the dragonfly station.

"There was also the incident this morning, after all. We will be part of Lady Cayna's escort," the co-captain said.

"Doesn't seem necessary for just a regular adventurer," Cayna retorted.

"No, you are the captain's fiancée. It is entirely necessary."

"Mother? What in the world is this talk about a fiancée?"

It sounded like a storm was rolling in; a dark aura enveloped Mai-Mai. The knights all took a step back, pale-faced and twitching at her eerie expression.

Cayna patted Mai-Mai's back to calm her down, said, "It's just a misunderstanding, no need to worry," and started walking off. "Hold on, Mother! I will not simply let this pass!" Mai-Mai shouted as Cayna dragged her away.

"Sorry about the fuss, folks!"

"Listen to me, Mother!"

The co-captain had watched them go off with shock and fear, but when he returned to his senses, he sent his knights off with an order of, "Two or three of you, act as escorts." The three female knights from earlier immediately followed Cayna and Mai-Mai.

""Please waiiiit!""" they called.

"Huh? You guys need something?" Cayna asked.

"We…"

"…will escort you…"

"…to the station."

They caught up to Cayna, who clearly didn't seem to care either way. "Why, thank you!" Mai-Mai brightly replied.

""Yes, ma'am!""" the women said heartily, then split up, with two knights in front of the pair and one behind. Mai-Mai squeezed Cayna's arm tightly.

"You should just accept this, Mother," she admonished. Cayna nodded firmly. The two knights in front of them observed the pair's interaction pleasantly while the third at the rear had a dead look in her eyes.

"Umm, what's wrong with her? Is she okay?" Cayna asked.

"Ah. She's not getting along with her family at the moment," the knight on the right-hand side in front of Cayna replied. The two in front were commoners, while the one in the back was apparently the daughter of a viscount.

"Please, pay me no mind... I am no longer of such high standing."

From what Cayna heard, the knight's parents were pressing her into marriage, and she received demanding letters daily. Even speaking of it had reignited the woman's anger. Her fist raised in front of her face trembled with rage, and from her furious mouth came the sound of gnashing teeth. From the looks of her, no one would ever guess she was the daughter of a noble family.

"Why not...get married?" Mai-Mai proposed with an incredibly cheery smile.

"Huh?"

""""What?"""""

Cayna looked at her blankly, and the knights gaped in shock.

"There's nothing wrong with at least giving it a try," Mai-Mai added.

"Is that the sort of thing you should be suggesting so casually? Marriage is a huge commitment," said Cayna.

"Well, if you and your partner are compatible, you'll stay together for a long time. And if you're not, you just have to get divorced."

As if seeing where she was coming from, the three women nodded. Cayna didn't know how she herself felt about marriage since she'd sort of stopped making big plans following her accident.

That was likely why she seemed so detached as she listened to the conversation.

"Being divorced and never being married aren't all that different, wouldn't you say?" Mai-Mai said.

"Huh?" A question mark appeared over Cayna's head—a type of skill, of course.

"Ah, well, yes. I suppose you're right," the viscount's daughter murmured in understanding. "In high society, divorce can damage your reputation. And yet, remaining single is rather embarrassing. You lose face among your noble peers."

"So why not give marriage a try? Even getting engaged might give you a change of heart."

The other two knights sighed in admiration, and even the noble knight nodded, convinced.

"You have given me much to think about, headmaster," she said. "I will return home and talk this over with my parents."

"That's certainly a fine method. Parents want their children to be happy, after all," Mai-Mai replied, and her gaze turned to Cayna, who realized what her daughter was getting at. She awkwardly looked away and Mai-Mai stifled a laugh.

"Uhhh, sorry, Mai-Mai..."

"Not at all, Mother. I'm not bothered in the slightest."

Cayna felt like she had been a terrible mother for submitting her own children to the Foster System and disappearing.

I can't make excuses for myself. I've got to make up for my mistakes...

Mai-Mai seemed relieved when she felt Cayna's arm relax and saw a gentle smile appear on her face.

The three knights escorted the two of them all the way to the dragonfly station. Cayna was happy to learn various tidbits from them, such as a popular store hidden in the aristocratic district that even commoners could enter.

After Mai-Mai and Cayna returned to the sandbar, they visited Kartatz's workshop, which was quiet save for the sounds of several employees at work. Kartatz was sitting in a chair by the entrance and absorbed in carving a piece of wood.

"Heya, Kartatz! Looks like you've got some time on your hands," Cayna called to her son with a wave.

"Mum! And Mai-Mai, it's rare to see you here. Something happen?" Kartatz got to his feet and walked over to greet them.

"Well, something's about to happen anyway," Cayna said.

"What are you up to…?"

"Oh, you know. All sorts of things. Mother is involved as well, so I'm sure that explains quite a bit."

"Mum, too? Whatever it is you've gotten yourselves into, it can't be good."

He must have gotten a bad feeling about this from the way Cayna was smiling. Mai-Mai stepped forward and placed her order.

"Kartatz, I need you to make a fishing pole as soon as possible. One big enough for about ten people to use."

"Sheesh, might as well be asking me for a million bucks. Sure, we got plenty of materials now that there's all this free time, but what exactly are you gonna do with something like that?"

This was the only part of their plan that required money. As leader of this plan, Cayna was going to pay for the pole. Mobilizing the knights also incurred a fee, but it looked like Myleene was taking care of that.

"At any rate, we'll need it by tomorrow."

"Tomorrow?!" Kartatz's wild yell echoed across the quiet river.

This was probably the most outrageous part of the plan.

CHAPTER 4

Preparations, a Thank-You Banquet, a Festival, and an Idiot

That night, a Friend Message from Shining Saber confirmed they had easily gotten permission from the king. However, he apparently hadn't been willing to blindly accept all their requests. Now just ten knights, Shining Saber included, were going to help with the fishing while the rest of the corps kept public order.

Part of the updated plan was to spread word that the Crown Princess Myleene was leading the fishing effort. Cayna's job was to make absolutely sure no one noticed that she herself was the one behind everything.

"Those three things, huh?" Cayna said absentmindedly.

"Are you talking about what you mentioned earlier?" Roxine asked.

"Yeah. Shining Saber says we'll set the plan in motion the day after tomorrow. I thought we were gonna do it tomorrow, so that's what I told the Guardians, but now I'll have to go see them both again to give them the update," Cayna answered as Roxine waited on her by her side.

Cayna had just returned to the rental house after visiting Kartatz and the two Guardian Towers. She'd barely made it in time for dinner and was currently enjoying some tea after her meal. Lytt and Luka were at a corner of the same table unwrapping their purchases from the day—an assortment of colored ribbons—and trying them on. Each one had cost two bronze coins, and the girls had chosen three each. All six were a different hue, so they switched out one after the other from their hair and asked each other how they looked. If anything, it was mostly Lytt fussing over Luka.

The cath palug curled up in a ball on the table as the girls sorted through their ribbons. They had fastened some ribbons around its neck and tail, but it didn't seem to mind.

"Anyway, Cie, go ahead and try giving the girls different hairstyles. They'll eventually find ones they like."

"Right."

On Cayna's orders, Roxine swiftly took out a comb and began fixing Luka's hair. It was in a ponytail in a matter of moments. After trying out several ribbons, Lytt cried out, "That one!" and the werecat moved on to her next.

"Now it feels like the rest of this plan is gonna overshadow Mai-Mai's contributions."

"I doubt working behind the scenes will earn her much recognition."

"Well, regardless, our goal of convincing the public is a lot like a staged event. Hope we don't have any accidents the day of, though."

Half of Cayna's proposal had been just to get the River Festival up and running. Even though she'd gotten the princess and one of the knight captains involved, Cayna doubted she herself could convince the people. If she tried, there was no mistaking she'd be running around try to pull off a one-woman show.

"Mommy Cayna…do you…still have…work?"

"Yeah. Sorry, girls. If all the preparations tomorrow go off without a hitch, we just might have ourselves a festival the day after that."

"Really?!" Lytt cried. Cayna had only been speculating, but Lytt was nonetheless thrilled to hear it.

"You sure seem happy, Lytt," said Cayna.

"Yeah, 'cause everything's already so amazing, but I heard that once the festival starts it'll be even *more* amazing!"

"W-wow…"

Cayna couldn't keep up with Lytt's energy. "Who'd she hear that from?" she asked Roxine, who leaned over slightly and replied, "The merchant who sold them ribbons." This person had apparently been a stout middle-aged woman like Marelle. "No helping that, I guess," Cayna said and then gave up questioning this further. She couldn't compete with a plucky mother like Marelle, let alone any other plucky middle-aged woman. That was, without question, Cayna's sole weakness.

Although interested in the ribbons initially, the children eventually set them aside and had Roxine teach them how to style their hair. Even with short hair, they fervently learned to tie it back.

Cayna grabbed a lock of her own hair and remembered how it was right after her accident. The nurses and her cousin had tied it back for her since she couldn't do it herself. Seeing her thin, feeble reflection in the mirror day in and day out made her visibly depressed, something that had greatly worried everyone. Now, she had the use of both hands and could change her own hairstyle any way she liked.

And in that case, she figured she should be the one practicing hairstyles with Luka.

"How very motherly of you."

Kee offered an exasperated comment. Cayna felt like motherhood had become just a bit more fun.

The cath palug, now free of any ribbons, took refuge at her feet and meowed. *"For cryin' out loud,"* came its telepathic message, and she stroked its head for its efforts.

*   *   *

Then, the next day…

After breakfast, Cayna entered the First Guardian Tower with her ring. The moment she activated it and recited the password, several rings of light appeared from a magic circle above her head and gathered around her. She soon went flying toward the Guardian, which ended up feeling a bit like a giant ring-toss game.

The Guardian was noisily ka-thunking as always, and she informed it that their plan had been postponed to tomorrow. After checking that the Guardian knew what it was supposed to do and meeting with the Ninth Guardian to confirm all was in good shape, she had the First send her to the Academy.

As planned, the Academy had been shut down over the past couple of days so that Cayna and the others could prepare. Nonetheless, they had only three days total to get set up, put the plan into action, and then dismantle everything afterward.

A long fishing pole had already been rolled on to the school grounds. It was fifty meters long, and the rod had a diameter of one hundred fifty centimeters. Kartatz and his employees had stayed up all night making it. The rod was fitted with a leather belt that required the support of eight people, which would give even the knights a hard time. It was like a slightly oversized cheer flag. The target they were fishing for would automatically react when caught, so the knights likely wouldn't need to pull too hard to reel it in.

Since Kartatz and the others had stayed up all night, they carried out their next task in complete silence. On the riverbank in front of the Academy, they were currently erecting a tall, platform-like pier. It would reach as high as the top of the blue whale's back when it surfaced from the river. They couldn't have the whale looking down on the (fake) divine messenger, let alone royalty.

Cayna then went around the Academy and checked that nothing

would throw a wrench into their plans. Since she couldn't predict what might suddenly happen on the day of, she examined the situation from every angle while she had the chance.

"I won't be able to see anything if I glow at maximum brightness."

After creating a ball of light with her at the center, she realized there were a number of issues with using Additional White Light.

Back in the game, light was applied to weapons when going into battle. Since one's party members were all doing the same thing, they'd always had plenty of light.

However, after casting it on herself, not only did it make her chest glow bright white, it also made her surroundings grow indistinct. Cayna wasn't comfortable having to depend on Myleene's voice just to get around.

She would have liked to use two or three techniques on her own, but in order to ensure she'd be able to see what was going on around her, she decided to summon a single Light Spirit. With the level-600 cath palug still active, Cayna had only five hundred levels left to spare for other summonings. Since the most powerful summoning she could currently manage would be level 110, she was restricted to four spirits at most. One would be assigned to Myleene, so it was probably best to save the others in case something happened. Cayna would have a Light Spirit keep the inner layer of the sphere weak so it would be like looking through a window to the outside. After all, seeing only what was directly in front of her would be enough should a worst-case scenario arise. Mai-Mai, who was helping Cayna test the lighting, said it was so bright that no one would be able to look directly at her even in broad daylight. But Cayna didn't want anyone to notice her inside the light sphere anyway, so she decided the townspeople would just have to deal with the brightness.

Cayna was able to write quickly enough, but Mai-Mai lent a hand by giving directions. It turned out that any messages written in front of Cayna's light sphere were impossible to read, so they decided to display them above her and in letters big enough to be seen from the opposite shore. Before long, Mai-Mai had Cayna enlarge each letter until they reached a whopping five meters in width and height.

The next order of business was the Wind Spirit Cayna gave to Myleene.

Spirits were invisible to the naked eye, save for those summoned with magic—anyone could see those, regardless of their magical capabilities.

However, Wind Spirits never stayed in one spot. This one was certain to float here and there the moment Myleene stepped on the platform. Even as Cayna now summoned the spirit, it joined Li'l Fairy in using every bit of space in the classroom to fly and dance around.

It was a nude, transparent child. It was clothed in a cape like some celestial maiden, but this was pointless since it was see-through anyway. If everyone was able to see this summoned Wind Spirit, no doubt men of certain unsavory inclinations would want one of their own. Looking at its wild and free appearance, Cayna wondered what she should do. Since the sandbar would be open to the public on the day on the plan, they expected there to be a crowd of observers. It wouldn't be good at all for there to be eyewitnesses.

Since the Wind Spirit was going to carry Myleene's voice throughout Felskeilo, it couldn't exactly be shut away.

Cayna weighed her various options until Mai-Mai offered the perfect solution: "What about a Spirit Staff?"

"Oh, right! I do have that."

A Spirit Staff was meant for people (that is, players) who couldn't use elemental magic. In this situation, it was basically a wand that would allow them to use wind magic. There were some conditions involved that required specific jewels for specific spirits. In this case, they would need emerald or malachite for a Wind Spirit, and it would be temporarily contained. However, this was voluntary help rather than force. The active period would last half a day from sunrise to sunset. If you exceeded this time limit, the spirit would destroy the jewel and escape, and you would be temporarily unable to summon it again. Although she had her concerns, Cayna doubted the plan would last from early morning to the evening, so she decided to use it.

Cayna could make a Spirit Staff with Craft Skills if she had jewels, metal, and a rod. The bigger the jewel, the more it could amplify the spirit's power.

Without further ado, Cayna quickly took an emerald from her Item Box, and Mai-Mai's jaw dropped. The gem was the size of a piece of firewood. If converted to money, it would be valued at several thousand gold coins.

"M-Mother...th-that's...," Mai-Mai stammered, pointing a trembling figure at Cayna, who set to work with her Craft Skills.

As soon as her hand lit up, she produced a flower stand that extended into a staff affixed with a giant emerald.

"Yep, this'll do," she said, waving the wand around to test it out. Mai-Mai put her face in her hands and sighed.

A small wand would've been more than sufficient to amplify a person's voice. Adding a precious jewel to such a long staff was downright unnecessary.

The point was that Cayna overdid it. Mai-Mai shuddered to think that if left alone to her own devices, Cayna might offer this staff to Myleene as a reward.

"I know! This staff can be Mye's reward—"

"Mother!!"

Mai-Mai ended up losing her cool. Just as she started scolding Cayna about the staff's value and forced her to promise not to give out ancient artifacts so willy-nilly, Myleene arrived.

"Forgive my tardiness...," she said.

"Oh, don't apologize," Cayna replied. "You had lessons all morning, right?"

"Yes, I did."

"Well then, that's all there is to it," said Mai-Mai. "Princesses have obligations, after all. Unlike my mother, who has endless free time."

Cayna wondered whether Myleene was a bit too humble for a royal. Regardless, she was offended by her daughter's nonchalant diss. She fixed Mai-Mai with an icy glare, but Mai-Mai looked the other way and acted like nothing had happened.

Cayna then foisted the staff she made onto Myleene, who asked, "Umm, Lady Cayna, what is this...?"

"You'll use it tomorrow with the Wind Spirit to amplify your voice. Make sure to keep it with you, okay?"

"Yes, understood... But, erm...don't you perhaps think this jewel is...awfully large...?"

Myleene's movements grew stilted after seeing the massive emerald. When Cayna replied, "I'd say it's pretty normal-sized," the princess's expression grew tight, and she managed to answer, "Ah, y-yes, normal. I see..."

"Honestly, Mother. How many times do I have to tell you? Your idea of normal is anything but."

"Goodness me, I'm sooo very...*sorry*!"

"Hyaaaaah?!"

Cayna pretended to apologize profusely before tackling Mai-Mai from behind with Accelerate and Warp Speed. This surprise combo wouldn't work on most vanguard-type players since they had the Intuition skill, but Mai-Mai didn't have it. Thus, the combo worked like a charm. Cayna wrapped her arms around her daughter's chest in a bear hug, and Mai-Mai let out a rare scream.

The knight on guard duty in the hallway immediately swung the door open and rushed inside. "What happened?!" he shouted.

The knight froze when he saw a shocked Myleene clutching a staff and Cayna grabbing Mai-Mai's breasts. "Pardon me!" he squeaked before fleeing the room and slamming the door behind him.

That prompted Mai-Mai, now red in the face, to break free from her mother's grasp.

"Ugh! Why'd you have to do that, Mother?!" Mai-Mai whined. Cayna looked at her hands, which had just been gripping Mai-Mai's chest, and grew despondent.

"Huh?"

Cayna thought back to when she created Mai-Mai in *Leadale*. Since Cayna herself was flat as a washboard (thanks to post-accident weight loss), she figured her children would be similarly flat chested, and thus she adjusted Mai-Mai's proportions accordingly. She fully expected her daughter's boobs to lack any bounce as a result, but it was still extremely depressing. Cayna didn't think she'd be in for such a shock when she touched them herself.

Thus, the most reasonable thing to do was apologize. But Cayna didn't expect Mai-Mai to misinterpret things and not get angry, but instead cling to Cayna's arm out of concern.

"You two seem so close," Myleene commented.

"*That's* what this looks like?" Cayna said.

"It is." She seemed wistful somehow as she smiled at the mother-daughter pair.

Cayna pondered for a moment before saying "Here you go, then," and offering Myleene her right arm (Mai-Mai was on her left).

"Huh?"

"You look like you want in on this. So c'mon!"

Myleene murmured, "Huh?" once more and looked at Mai-Mai

clinging to Cayna's left arm. With a wave of her hand, Mai-Mai urged her to join them.

"W-well then, if you don't mind…" Myleene curtsied and took Cayna's right arm with such shyness that glimpses of her girlish youth peeked through her royal exterior.

"Well? How's it feel?" Cayna asked the princess.

"It's a bit embarrassing," she answered bashfully. Super adorable.

Her shyness as she voiced her opinion was precious. Cayna nodded enthusiastically and looked at Mai-Mai; she seemed so happy. It was if she hadn't been screaming only moments ago.

"You look like you're having fun, Mai-Mai."

"Doing this together is part of what makes you so charming, Mother."

Cayna responded to this incomprehensible answer with a sour face. Their mother-daughter interaction made Myleene burst out laughing.

The three of them stayed arm in arm as they went over the plan once more and worked out any remaining kinks.

Incidentally, Shining Saber had just come by to get the three ladies. He looked curiously at the extremely red-faced guard in the hallway, then froze when he opened the classroom door.

"Having a little girl-on-girl time?"

"No, we're not!"

Cayna answered Shining Saber's snide comment in the form of a well-aimed fire arrow.

And thus, their many preparations came to an end. Thanks to Kartatz and his subordinates' hard efforts, the platform was completed.

Then, the next day as everything was put into action…

Although it was early morning, the townspeople had been up and about since before dawn, so by around seven o' clock everyone was finishing breakfast at home and beginning to start work.

Next to the platform on the sandbar in front of the Academy, the giant fishing pole that would be supported by eight knights had been set up. Tied to the other end of the rope-like fishing line was a bouquet of flowers as bait.

Cayna was observing the scene from inside the First Guardian Tower in order to gauge the best moment for her to leap into action. Which was fine and all, but…

"…What's with all the spectators?"

"I haven't the slightest idea."

Since Myleene was out on the platform, the people feared the guards and thought it best not to draw closer. However, the riverbanks of the sandbar were filled to the brim with observers. When she moved the screen to view the opposite shores, she observed that those were packed there, too. Some people were leaning too far forward and falling into the river.

"Shining Saber said he didn't send out any kind of special notice about this."

"Perhaps"—*ka-thunk*—**"they saw"**—*ka-thunk*—**"you preparing?"** *Ka-thunk.*

Since she was inside the tower, the Guardian was, of course, right in front of her. Moreover, as he made his sound argument, she somehow felt a sense of frustration welling inside her. Indeed, they had made the platform directly below where dragonflies were flying by, so there had surely been plenty of eyewitnesses. When the knights had gathered in the morning, that also likely drew attention. Cayna also received a report from Roxine that although the preparations for the festival were finished, people were quite pent up since there was no way it could actually begin.

Today, Luka and Lytt were resting in the rental house.

Since they'd only been with Roxine for the past several days, they were told they could have fun exploring with Cayna later. Thus, she had to finish this event within the day.

"You keep a close eye, too, Ninth."

"Understood."

As Cayna spoke to the always connected communication screen, the Ninth Guardian bowed its head reverently. A progress chart was affixed on a wall of its own tower. As the Ninth checked over everything in minute detail, she gave orders to the First.

"Shouldn't you"—*ka-thunk*—**"be going"**—*ka-thunk*—**"master?"** *Ka-thunk.*

"Something like this calls for a little more pomp."

A throng of onlookers stared at the bouquet bobbing on the river's surface with bated breath. Cayna thought they'd be losing the real thrill of fishing if the whale rushed out now, so she held the Guardian back. She had told it to sink once more after taking the bouquet and then resurface after the rope gave a few good tugs. Since there was a chance that the pole, knights and all, would fall into the river if the First tugged too hard, it would sway lightly with the bait in its mouth. The Guardian was so huge that she wasn't sure it would be able to keep the appropriate amount of force, but she advised it to carry out the plan while keeping an eye on what was going on above the surface. As soon as the whale tower surfaced, she would appear on its back as a ball of light. Myleene would ask it to identify itself, and the show would finally begin.

Swearing she'd do this right, Cayna put the unexpectedly large crowd out of her mind and clenched her fist. A Friend Message came from Shining Saber, who was apparently growing impatient: *Hey, you ready yet?*

"All right, let's get this show on the road!"

"Will do!" *Ka-thunk.*

Wrapping and concealing herself in light, Cayna gave the Guardian the signal.

"Well, it's been a long road, but thanks to everyone for all your hard work! Cheers!"

""""Cheers!""""

Everyone raised their glasses and toasted to their success. Seated at the table full of food were Cayna, Mai-Mai, Kartatz and his staff, Myleene, Shining Saber, and several knights. Roxine, Luka, and Lytt were also present.

The plan had safely concluded in about thirty minutes. Six hours had passed, and it was now the afternoon. Mai-Mai had booked an entire restaurant, and the group was currently enjoying a thank-you party.

Earlier, when Myleene had concluded their spectacle with, "Now the festival can begin. Please enjoy yourselves to the fullest," all the people who had been watching the event broke out in an explosion of cheers. Loud cries of, "Long live Felskeilo! Long live Princess Myleene!" had carried on for some time.

Although she'd declared for the festival to officially begin, it seemed that the pre-festival merriment would still continue for the day. Many were of the opinion that the real event should start in the morning, so it would begin from the next day forward.

The whale Guardian was floating upstream of the sandbar and would be officially staying in Felskeilo. Thanks to Cayna inside her ball of light and the letters in the sky, the number of people surrounding it at a distance to offer their prayers was endless. It was apparently authoritative enough that it seemed like the Guardian would soon become a god Guardian of the river.

The fishing pole and platform were left behind afterward.

According to Kartatz: "A rush job like that'll get washed away soon enough. Once the festival's over, we'll either remake 'em or add the proper fortifications."

The plan was for the platform to be disassembled soon after everything was over. The pole would be brought back to the workshop for maintenance. It had bent terribly since the Guardian had misjudged its own strength, and according to the knights would had supported it, they could hear creaking and groaning.

The eight knights had been suddenly pulled and gone flying through the air. Upon reflection, Cayna thought to herself that they should have rehearsed outside of town.

Myleene had performed marvelously as Felskeilo's representative and received praise from the king. He had recounted the event and lauded her in marvelous detail, so he'd no doubt been watching from somewhere.

The boats resumed their sailing, and the river was once again lively with vessels of all sizes sailing to and fro. Yet even so, not a single person approached the whale Guardian Tower. However, since a bouquet of flowers had served as bait, the church placed a flower altar on a bank upstream of the sandbar. It was piled up as high as a person.

"*Phew.* I'm so glad everything worked out," said Cayna.

"Indeed. Once again, it is all thanks to you, Lady Cayna." Myleene raised her glass elegantly and dipped her head with a smile.

Cayna waved both hands and bowed her head. "No, no, not at all. I suggested it, but it's really thanks to you."

"Mother, this is turning into a nodding contest," Mai-Mai teased, grinning. The two of them froze mid-bow. "Also, Mye," continued Mai-Mai, "I noticed you stumbled a bit at the beginning of your speech."

They recalled how Myleene's mouth hung open when she first saw

Cayna's ball of light. A long silence had passed before she finally asked the whale to identify itself.

"W-well, I couldn't help myself. I still cannot believe such a large fish even exists."

Maybe Myleene wouldn't have been so shocked if they'd done a dress rehearsal beforehand, but given the whale Guardian Tower's massive size, it would've been near impossible to pull that off in secret.

"Uh, it's gonna be a bit of a problem if you don't believe in it," Cayna said.

"Well, yes…you're right," Myleene replied. "Now that I've had a proper look at it, I should be fine the next time we meet."

Since Myleene had been the first one to interact with the tower, she might end up as the royal family's go-between whenever they wanted to communicate with the whale. She'd just have to get used to it.

At first, the only people who knew the whale was a Guardian Tower—Myleene, Shining Saber, Mai-Mai, and Kartatz—were those who'd heard about it from Cayna. Now the king was aware as well. The knights, meanwhile, apparently thought the whale was some magical creature that Cayna had subdued in combat.

"At any rate, this sort of thing will never happen again, so let's set that aside for now. All that's left is to reflect on our own individual accomplishments," said Mai-Mai, and with a clap of her hands, the conversation was put to bed. She then said, "This is delicious," and divvied out portions of salad to Cayna and Myleene. The latter poured dressing over hers and took a bite. Her eyes widened in surprise.

"…It's wonderful," she murmured.

Cayna tilted her head curiously. "Don't you always have amazing food at the castle?"

"The castle cuisine isn't nearly this flavorful."

"Hmmm…"

After watching the princess finish off her salad bite by bite, Cayna looked around them. There were about twenty people just barely squeezed into the restaurant—a fancy sort of place with a chandelier that bathed the interior in soft light. There were various decorative plants as well, but nothing too flashy. The leisurely ambiance seemed perfect for unwinding with a drink or two.

"This is that Black Rabbit Tail place you guys always come to, right?" Cayna asked Mai-Mai.

"It's called the White-Tailed Black Rabbit, Mother."

"Sheesh, that's a mouthful."

"You'd do well to remember it. There's nothing cumbersome about the name at all."

Shining Saber, who had been listening in as he gnawed on some boned meat, said with a grin, "You really can't tell who's the kid and who's the mom."

Of course, this was pretty much a sarcastic jab at Cayna's real age. When she scowled at him, he said, "Sorry, sorry," and passed her a plate of fruit.

Roxine took the ripened fruit before Cayna could, peeled the skins, and placed them back in front of her.

"Thanks, Cie."

"My pleasure. Would you two young ladies like some fruit as well?"

Roxine peeled several other fruits with lightning speed, cut them up neatly, and arranged them on a plate. She'd initially tried serving the food herself but reluctantly took a seat at the table after Cayna insisted. The werecat busily inspected all the food as she apportioned the sliced fruit between Luka and Lytt but remained nonetheless faithful to her duties by keeping an eye on the girls as they ate.

Luka and Lytt, the only children at the banquet, were nervous to be dining among royalty and knights. They'd hardly touched any of the meat or fish Roxine had served them, so she instead offered them some fruit.

The two girls exchanged flustered looks, so Cayna brought the fruit to their mouths and said, "Aaah." Finally, they began to eat.

"Well, what do you two think?" she asked the girls. "Tasty, right?"

"...Uh-huh," said Lytt.

"It's...yummy," said Luka.

"We've got all this food today, but don't push yourselves. There's gonna be plenty of goodies when we check out the festival tomorrow."

They appeared to relax a bit when Cayna hugged them close and patted their heads, then hesitantly began tucking into the other food on their plates. Everything they tasted was delicious beyond belief, and soon their mouths stretched into grins. Cayna cheerfully watched them dig in.

The knights also watched this tender scene unfold only to get a good smack to the head from Shining Saber.

""""Yeowch?!""""

"Quit gawkin', you idiots. You'll scare the kids!"

Kartatz did the same to his staff who had also been staring, eliciting similar yelps around the table.

"Oh, by the way, Shining Saber...," Cayna began.

"Yeah?"

"I owe you three skills as a reward. Go ahead and pick which ones you want."

Shining Saber made a face. The question was so sudden, and he still hadn't made up his mind. If this were still the *Leadale* game, his Stats Window would display his skill tree, making it easier to choose among the skills available. This function was gone now, so he had no idea what he could even pick.

"You can always divide them up if you're having trouble deciding."

"Divide what?"

"Y'know, the different skill categories—Magic, Vanguard, Rearguard, Throwaway, that sort of thing. Personally, I'd recommend going for some of the Throwaway Skills from back in the game because they're really helpful now."

Many of the skills Cayna had used around the remote village—such as Spring Water to build the bathhouse—were called Throwaway Skills. Shining Saber looked over his current skillset and began deliberating over what new ones to take.

Myleene noticed that Luka and Lytt were more at ease now and slowly approached them. "Hello there," she said.

"H-hello…"

"…Hi…"

"You two must be Lytt and Luka. My name is Myleene. I may be a princess, but this is a casual gathering. Please don't worry about formalities."

"M-my name's Lytt."

"…I'm…Luka."

The way the girls looked up at her in awe was so adorable that Myleene couldn't help stroke their heads. Then something hit her. "Lady Cayna."

"What's up, Mye?"

"Their hair is so incredibly silky. How did you get it that soft?"

"What?"

Cayna couldn't really answer the question. She'd always thought Luka's hair was simply naturally soft.

Mai-Mai wondered if Myleene was just overreacting, so she stroked the girls' hair as well. It hit her like an electric shock. "What is the meaning of this, Mother?"

"Look, I'm not really sure how to answer that…"

Cayna assumed it had something to do with the bathhouse in the remote village. It was the only one of its kind in this magic-driven world, and just recently a group visiting from Otaloquess had found it deeply fascinating. The use of Spring Water certainly made the bathhouse that much more effective, but Cayna hadn't the slightest clue if those effects did anything to hair quality.

"Did you do something, Cie?"

Cayna wondered if Roxine had used something on Luka during bathtime since she had been charged with Luka's care. She'd anticipated a noncommittal response from the werecat, but ended up with something quite unexpected instead.

Roxine produced a small bottle of golden liquid from her Item Box. "It's this."

"What is it?"

"Just a few drops of this after a bath will make your hair sleek and shiny."

"Huh…"

Cayna then recalled seeing Roxine use it while doing Luka's hair. Mai-Mai and Myleene immediately turned their gazes to the bottle.

"You made that yourself, right, Cie?"

"Yes. It's my own concoction made from honey and several medicinal herbs."

She must have made it with Craft Skills. Since Roxine had several skills that allowed her to make potions, she had deep knowledge of medicines.

The werecat didn't respond to Mai-Mai and Myleene's curious stares. She was willing to show them the potion but had no intention of sharing her process. Cayna tried asking her for the recipe, but Roxine merely replied, "It's a secret." Cayna shrugged and shook her head at Mai-Mai and Myleene, who were quickly disappointed.

"But a potion alone can't fix your hair…," Cayna muttered.

"You're obsessed with potions, Mum," Kartatz interrupted, a bottle of alcohol in hand.

"Good work, Kartatz. Sorry for all the trouble."

"Ah, who cares about the trouble? It helped us kill all that free time. Don't worry about it." Spoken like a truly upstanding gentleman. Even Cayna would have probably fallen for him if he weren't her son.

"Wow, I have the coolest son ever."

"Wha—what're you goin' on about?!"

A flustered, red-faced Kartatz clutched at his head. His employees broke into sly grins; Mai-Mai seemed to be enjoying this as well. Kartatz suddenly felt flushed.

"M-Mum's gotta be drunk. She is, isn't she?"

Mai-Mai and Shining Saber peered into Cayna's glass and took a whiff of its contents.

"I believe it's fruit-infused water."

"Yep, it's juice."

Upon hearing the report that her drink was non-alcoholic, Kartatz's shoulders drooped in disappointment. He could tell Cayna was going to keep pestering him, which would lead to further teasing from his employees. There was no escape.

"C'mon now, Kartatz, all that alcohol isn't good for you," Cayna chided him. "Here, say 'Ah.'"

Kartatz was stuck between a rock and a hard place. The sight of a two-hundred-something-year-old dwarf being hand-fed by his mother would be...a lot to handle.

He attempted to resist before his mind could go completely blank. "C-come to think of it, Mum, I heard you're coverin' tonight's tab in full. You sure you're okay with that?"

"Totally fine. What's a thousand or ten thousand silver coins, anyway?"

"Uh, r-right…"

"Uh-huh. Now say, 'Ah.'"

Trying to forcefully change the subject proved ineffective against his mother. A stunning defeat.

"No way it'll cost that much," said Shining Saber. "This ain't some fancy dinner party."

"That's not true, Captain," said Mai-Mai. "Looking at the food being served, it might easily cost that much. And this is only a light meal."

"This place is that expensive?!" Shining Saber yelled in shock after only just hearing this explanation now. Roxine, meanwhile, just wanted the two children to enjoy themselves, so she took them away from the table and covered their ears.

When the knights saw Cayna feeding Kartatz, they choked on their food. Such an unprecedented sight also caused Kartatz's mind to go blank; he robotically gobbled up the food Cayna brought to his mouth, unable to even taste it.

But Cayna didn't stop there. She hand-fed Kartatz several more bites until he ended up blacking out.

The next thing he knew, it was the middle of the night, and he was in his bed at the workshop.

Then, the next day, the official opening of the festival came.

After Kartatz lost himself the day before, the thank-you party had come to a natural end. Myleene and Shining Saber had to return to the castle before evening, so they quickly offered their thanks as well as appreciation of the food and left.

The workshop employees would apparently go home after putting their boss to bed. When Cayna asked where he lived, they said he had his own room at work.

After thanking everyone involved, Cayna's group saw Mai-Mai

safely home and returned to the rental house. Mai-Mai had said they could stay at her place, but Cayna declined since she had Lytt and Luka with her. After all, if Lytt heard they'd be staying at a noble house, Cayna doubted the girl would be able to relax.

Cayna had decided to sleep with Luka that night, but there was a bit of an uproar once morning arrived. The booming of fireworks woke Luka up in a panic. The terrified girl clung to Cayna, who became enraged, consequently setting off Roxine until the entire house was about ready to go on the warpath. Fortunately, the matter passed without incident after Luka realized the source of the noise and soon calmed down.

For someone who had moved from a fishing village to the remote village they now lived in, fireworks had to be terrifying. If Cayna hadn't cast Soundproof throughout the whole house, Luka would have likely burst into tears.

Lytt, on the other hand, had apparently heard about fireworks from the caravan and helped calm Luka down.

"Luka, that means the festival's starting. It's not scary," she said.

"She's right," Cayna agreed. "It's just loud. You're not in any danger."

Cayna held the unsettled Luka in her arms and rubbed her back to soothe her. Thankfully, she stopped crying soon enough. Her stomach let off a series of grumblings right after, and everyone burst into laughter.

"I'm...hungry," said Luka.

"Me too," said Lytt. "Let's go eat the breakfast Ms. Cie made."

Lytt set off with Luka trudging not far behind. Cayna put a hand to her cheek in slight exasperation. She was really getting a taste of the trials involved in child rearing.

"Okay, we're gonna be together alllll day today, so where should we start?"

After they ate breakfast and prepared to head out, Cayna asked the girls to pick where they'd like to go. The two quickly started deliberating. They had spent the previous day at home organizing their purchases and cooking with Roxine, who told Cayna that they'd heard cheering that day as well. Unlike the fireworks earlier, though, the noise hadn't been loud enough to startle them. When Cayna mentioned the huge whale in the river, Luka and Lytt eagerly declared that they wanted to see it.

"Miss Cayna, what *is* a whale?" Lytt asked.

"It's basically a big, long fish. Sometimes water shoots out of their backs with a *whoosh*."

"It…shoots water??" Luka said incredulously.

Clearly unable to visualize what Cayna explained, the two tilted their heads in unison. It was a funny sight, and Cayna couldn't help but laugh. They started batting at her and told her not to laugh at them, so she grinned and asked their forgiveness.

"What are you doing?" A bit late from cleaning up, Roxine saw Luka and Lytt hanging from both of Cayna's arms.

"Ah-ha-ha, oh, y'know."

It wasn't like their problems weren't all cleared away, but the fact the biggest one was behind them put Cayna in a great mood—so great that she was even willing to let a pickpocket off with just dislocating both of their shoulders. Which she actually ended up doing.

"Never thought a thief would come right at us before we even mingled into the crowd."

The squawking pickpocket was stuck to a nearby wall with magic. He'd come unstuck on his own after enough time, so it was better than handing him over to the guards. If she was being honest, she thought the soldiers had better things to do than deal with small-time thieves. Instead, a paint that was difficult to take off would have the pickpocket's real name and crime written on their face. This information was marked on their status when she used Search, so it was completely obvious. Plus, leaving the pickpocket stuck in a wall was punishment in itself.

After they slowly made their way through the crowd and out on to the main street, they were overwhelmed by congestion Cayna had never seen when she first came to Felskeilo. However, they could still get through with the kids in tow. The crowds weren't so bad you couldn't get past the main drag.

"I knew it," Cayna mumbled. "It's packed since you can't cross the river."

"Ah, there's the ball throwers!" Lytt shouted. She had spotted the performers she'd seen from the carriage. Managing to get close by following the flow of people, they came to a spot where three colorful clowns were entertaining the crowd by juggling and tossing square blocks to each other from atop giant balls. Everyone watched as several small balls were thrown at the clowns' feet, which they juggled while on top of the big ones. The spectators oohed and aahed when the performers started juggling even more balls. Everyone, Cayna included, gazed in thrilled fascination.

Finally, all of the juggling blocks ended up with one clown, who flawlessly alighted from the ball with his arms full. "Wooow!" the applauding crowd cheered as they tossed bronze coins to the performers. The one clown caught the coins without dropping any blocks, eliciting further cheers. Cayna gave Lytt and Luka each a bronze coin for them to try tossing. Lytt's coin flew in a clean arch, but the trajectory of Luka's had it heading straight for the ground. Just when all seemed lost, one clown stuck out his foot, lifted it like he was juggling a soccer ball, and caught it with a block. Luka clapped, and the clown winked at her.

Since they had some time before the next performance, Cayna

and her group left. Lytt and Luka pretended to juggle, but their movements were all over the place.

"Miss Cayna, can you do that?"

"Juggling? Hmm. It looks kind of hard."

Since she didn't know the full extent of her physical specs, she told them she probably couldn't. Juggling wasn't a skill; it depended on dexterity and practice. Not that Cayna had any interest in trying it out.

Lytt said she would practice when they got back to the village. Since Luka nodded and said she would join in, Cayna considered having Roxilius whittle down some trees to create balls.

The next thing to catch Lytt's eye was target-shooting, using throwing knives instead of a gun. One attempt at striking a circular, spinning target was four bronze coins. Five bronze coins got you two throws.

"So is that cheap or not?" Cayna wondered aloud.

"That would depend on the prize," Roxine answered.

Cayna observed the temporarily frozen target. It was split into about thirty-six sections, and only about ten of those won you a prize. Among the prizes on display were pendants and necklaces of blue and green crystal. Roxine had apparently used Search on them, and she sniffed unamusedly.

"What's wrong?" Cayna asked her.

"Those are merely pieces of colored quartz."

"Yikes..."

Cayna got a better look and noticed the couples who attempted the game were failing miserably. She watched them and determined this was part of a never-ending pattern of boyfriends giving up in defeat.

"Hmm."

"What's up, Lytt? Do you want to give it a try?" Cayna asked the concerned Lytt, who flinched as one person after the other lost the game. There would be no challengers unless the whole line was changed out.

Lytt had never used a throwing knife before, so she had no confidence. Just as Cayna was wondering what she should do, Luka tugged on her cloak. She bent down to meet the girl's eye level.

"Do you want to try too, Lu?"

"Here…Mommy Cayna. Me and Lytt…will split it."

Luka handed Cayna two bronze coins. If Luka and Lytt were each paying half, it was clear they wanted Cayna to try.

Naturally, Cayna gladly agreed to the children's wishes.

"Oh-ho, a mother doing it for her children? Step right up! Everyone, please give her a round of applause!" the gamemaster shouted merrily when Cayna handed him the money. Several people clapped.

Cayna was given a single throwing knife and stood at the white line five meters from the target. The person in charge of the target spun it in earnest, and the game began.

Not even pretending to look like she was aiming, Cayna used her Intuition and Throw skills and released the knife.

With a most unusual *zwoosh* sound, it pierced the rotating target with such force that the target immediately stopped spinning. The gamemaster's eyes grew round with surprise when he saw the knife hilt-deep in one of the target's winning sections.

"W-wooow! The mother's knife throw has landed a direct hit! Everyone, please give a round of applause for her fine efforts!"

The ensuing applause was a great deal louder than what she'd received right before the game. Cayna raised a hand in response. For her prize, she chose a necklace laid with a clear, unpainted crystal.

The crowd whistled, and Cayna smiled and waved back. The whistlers blushed, and she could hear their cries from behind her:

"She smiled at me!"

"No, that was for *me*."

"But she's gotta be married, right?"

"""Damn it!"""

As soon as she won, several others decided to give the game a shot and gathered around to try out their luck. The knife-throwing booth soon grew crowded.

After distancing themselves from the throng, Cayna handed Luka the necklace.

"Here you go. Are you two gonna share it?"

Luka shook her head and passed the necklace to Lytt. Cayna thought maybe Lytt had wanted it, but that didn't seem to be the case. Lytt took the necklace and walked over to Roxine with Luka in tow.

"Ladies?"

"Umm, we'd like you to have this as a present for always helping us, Ms. Cie—Roxine. Thank you for everything."

"Thank…you."

Lytt handed over the gift, and Luka bowed deeply.

Roxine stood there blankly at first, but her face instantly turned crimson when she took the necklace. Cayna was a bit surprised by her reaction.

"Thank you very much, ladies. I will treasure it." Roxine held the necklace tightly and smiled, still blushing slightly.

"I get it," said Cayna. "You're fine with those pure of heart."

"…Lady Cayna?"

Cayna thought that even Roxine's glare wasn't so scary when her face was bright red. She'd figured the werecat would take the joke in stride if she got to enjoy a nice surprise. However, Roxine's cold gaze pierced through her, and Cayna pretended she hadn't said anything.

"Anyway, let's skedaddle over to the next spot."

"……"

"Lytt, Lu, was there someplace you wanted to go? Are you hungry?"

"We…just ate."

"Yeah. I am getting kind of thirsty though…"

They looked around for a drink stand but couldn't manage to find one. The main street's setup was primarily for show, so there were hardly any concessions to be found. There'd probably be nothing but trouble if people with food kept bumping into one another.

"One moment, please."

Roxine suddenly produced several long, thin objects similar to test tubes from out of nowhere. These were exactly like the all-too-familiar thin bamboo containers Cayna had used when she made her impromptu potions, and there seemed to be some sort of drink inside. Roxine popped the corks, and the scent of tea wafted by.

The light scent of fruit drifted from Luka and Lytt's drinks.

"You made these? Thanks," said Cayna.

"They sell thin bamboo at the market. I apologize for the poor fare."

They returned the containers to Roxine and continued exploring the festival. After watching blindfolded performers throw knives at a board and tamed wolf monsters jump through hoops and balance on balls, the group made their way to the Ejidd River.

A variety of colorful boats sailed along the water. Among these were sailboats decorated with flowers and vivid sails. Some performers were doing acrobatics atop the masts, while other boats were occupied by bands playing music. There were also venders selling fresh-caught fish to guests on the commuter ships or cooking up fish in their own boats. The tantalizing aroma of grilled fish tickled their noses.

Cayna tried her hand at the archery game by the riverbank. The targets were three small boats out on a river, each with two poles with masks attached to them. The aim of the game was to shoot these, and you could win a live fish depending on the number of targets you hit.

Cayna shot all six targets with the provided bow and won a seventy-centimeter-long ponsu. Ponsu looked like straight-bodied catfish and were appreciated by all citizens either boiled or grilled. Since carrying it around would be a bother, Cayna froze the water, bucket and all, and stowed it away in her Item Box. Doing so shocked many bystanders, and as soon as it disappeared, people mistook this for a performance of some sort and began tossing coins her way. Needless to say, Cayna gave these to the girls.

"Looks like they've been hooked by the festive mood...," Cayna noted.

"I'm sure if you exhibited even a fragment of your magical abilities, you would make quite a killing," said Roxine.

"Don't even start. Anything more than small change for the girls is gonna make us stick out."

The same thing apparently crossed Roxine's mind as she looked out over the crowds. Luka and Lytt pondered over how to use the money that had (literally) come flying at them.

"By the way," Cayna added, "wasn't the Academy going to set up a stall, too?"

She'd heard Mai-Mai mention the day before that the Academy would have their own booth at the festival. After the incident with the Guardian Tower, the Academy started seeing a huge jump in the number of students volunteering for the festival. This was their first day of business.

Mai-Mai would also be at the Academy, helping with the booth. *I think we'll mostly have food stands, so I hope you'll stop by,* she'd told Cayna, who thought her daughter had a lot on her plate, given all that had happened just the previous day.

Cayna, Roxine, and the girls took a commuter boat to the sand-bar and headed for the Academy. The church, in addition to its usual function as a place of worship and sightseeing location, now doubled as a first-aid station. Although the High Priest Skargo wasn't present, there were many other priests who seemed to be managing everything smoothly. Kartatz's workshop would remain closed during the festival period. He had grumbled, *"We stayed open a long time ago but decided to shut down 'cause the noise from the festival kept ruining everyone's concentration and causing injuries."*

A large number of people were on the Academy grounds. The center space was reserved for the students' independent demonstrations, while the outer perimeter was lined with stalls.

The demonstrations included sword dancing and magic tricks. Cayna might understand if this was part of a research project, but she felt like the sword dance made this out to be nothing more than a spectacle. She was never into that sort of thing back in the game either and instead saw it as extra background fluff, so the sight didn't really resonate with her.

The stalls were colorful, and unsurprisingly, filled with standard festival fare likely introduced by past players: *okonomiyaki, yakisoba,* candy apples, chocolate-covered bananas, skewered meat and chicken, *imagawayaki,* and *taiyaki.* The various items in this world had allowed for the development of many distinct specialties, some of which were expensive due to their more valuable ingredients. Commoner children likely never got a taste of those.

Chocolate-covered bananas were one good example: A single banana was four silver coins. Cayna wasn't sure if these were exclusively for nobles, but even an adventurer's salary couldn't easily afford one.

Despite the sign advertising candy apples, there were no obvious "apples" in this world. A variety of easy-to-eat fruits were candied instead. The sugar used for hard candy was expensive, so only a small amount was drizzled over the fruit.

The *taiyaki* being offered was in the shape of a ponsu for some reason, so it was a bit jarring when Cayna was drawn to the booth by the sign only to be met with an unfamiliar shape. Even the contents of the *taiyaki* were different in this world.

"The filling is sweet-boiled potatoes instead of red bean paste," Cayna remarked.

"That is because sugar is expensive," Roxine said.

The cotton candy made from brown sugar instead of white sugar cost one silver coin. Cayna had absolutely no intention of buying that.

She bought several foods that reminded her of home and divided them between Luka and Lytt for them to eat. The plate of *yakisoba* was split among all four of them.

"This is more like *yaki-udon*," Cayna noted.

"The noodles are indeed a bit too thick," Roxine agreed.

"It's really yummy."

"Uh-huh."

The utensils that came with it were not forks or chopsticks but instead long skewers. They were incredibly difficult to use. Cayna used two as chopsticks and fed the girls that way.

"Looks like there's bonito flakes or something in it."

"They sell *yakisoba* sauce at the market, although the flavor varies greatly with each chef."

While they ate, Cayna and Roxine discussed their opinions on different ingredients and food products. The children were unable to keep up with the pair's appetite and soon grew full.

Then, as Roxine was taking the girls to the bathroom:

"Hey, you there!"

Cayna had noticed someone rapidly approaching before she realized they were calling out to her.

It was a young man in his late teens with a butler by his side. He had a condescending look in his eye, which made Cayna's mood visibly worsen. She'd sensed a sickening gaze on her earlier but had meant to ignore it unless push came to shove. Nothing good would come out of this for the children, so she told Roxine to take Luka and Lytt elsewhere.

The loud, yapping man came into view. Cayna regretted meeting his gaze.

He wore a gray jacket with gold trim over a shabby, threadbare shirt along with a red cloak. His eyes angled upward most villainously.

"Hey, you there! You're that adventurer my father told me about, aren't you?!"

She knew this encounter was going to be a pain in the butt because Kee told her the butler behind this teen was *"the one from our first day here."*

As the young man continued to smirk pompously, Cayna heard whispers flying among the people nearby: mentions of "an earl's son," "blackmail and extortion," and "abuses his parents' position."

So he's pretty much your typical young noble…

"A quest classic."

Still, if he was the type of person she pegged him to be, he was going to run away like a scared rabbit. By this point, Cayna wouldn't let him escape instant death even if he tried.

He stuck out in the worst way, and curious onlookers surrounded them at a distance to form a wall of people. The young man arbitrarily interpreted Cayna's silence as fear of a noble's presence and kept running his mouth: "If you give my father what he wants, I'll smooth things over between you. What do you say?" followed by "I know—I should have you for myself. I doubt my father will mind based on your looks alone" and "Hey, you gonna say something? I'm very generously trying to compromise here." His tone grew more and more heated.

To a noble, compromise was no different than blackmail or cutting corners. Cayna was curious what kind of upbringing it took to create such a narcissist. His parents were probably a piece of work, too.

What a pain. What should I do now?

"Why not take him on?"

"I've got a feeling he'll turn to charcoal…"

"This is true."

Already fed up, Cayna completely tuned him out. The young noble then spoke to the people standing at attention behind his butler.

"Hey, you two! Show this lady what you can do!"

"Yessir!"

Cayna was even further confused as to why anyone would resort to violence toward the object of their desire simply because they weren't getting their way. Moreover, he was after someone else's power. Wouldn't it be humiliating for a fox to borrow the might of a tiger? You had to pity any poor person who took down a tiger only to be told they're a huge embarrassment.

The two people following the young noble's commands stepped forward, both dressed in full-length reddish-brown robes. They shared a single wand taller than themselves. It was a bit twisted, and it wouldn't be strange at all if they were to say they had picked it up from the forest floor.

As they raised the wand and chanted a spell, a magic circle appeared on the ground. Cayna used magic circles as well, but hers were much more complex.

She'd never seen one this oversimplified with nothing more than a hexagram at the center. As she stared intently and wondered what sort of magic circle it might be, the ground in the middle of it swelled and sent sediment bursting forth. The wriggling dirt rose higher than a person and seemed to struggle to take form. The onlookers began screaming, apparently already cognizant of what sort of magic had been cast. Cayna strained her ears in an effort to hear if someone might say what spell had been used, but all she picked up was along the lines of, "To think he'd use that," "Is he trying to kill us?" and "How awful!"

So this spell was used often and to terrible effect.

However, the creature's writhing didn't seem like the slighest threat from Cayna's point of view, so her only option was to wait until she knew its true form. She'd considered blasting the spell back with an attack of her own, but she was certain that if she used even the smallest bit of her power, they'd all turn to mincemeat.

After she resolved to remain a bystander, it took a full five minutes for the writhing sediment pouring from the magic circle to finally transform into a humanoid figure over two meters tall—at least, humanoid in the sense that it looked like a ghost made from a blue tarp and a two-meter-high pole. Checking with Search showed this was an earth golem. She was shocked it wasn't even made of stone.

The earth golem was just barely level 6—so weak that going up against it honestly felt like more trouble than it was worth. The thing was slow as a turtle, and it clunked its way toward Cayna. She genuinely wanted to know what about it was so "awful."

However, since these two mages had gone to the trouble of producing a golem for her, she thought it only fair she respond in kind.

Magic Skill: Load: Create Rock Golem Level 1
""""Ohhhhh?!""""

A mix of awestruck and frightened cries erupted from the onlookers. A shocked look swept across the young noble's face, and the mage pair trembled in fear.

Using a stone she threw as a fulcrum, rocks and boulders bubbled up from inside the earth one after the other and joined together to form a humanoid figure. It was one head taller than the earth golem and made of solid stone, unlike its foe's flimsy, poorly protected body.

Cayna had constructed something the earth golem couldn't compete against in a matter of moments. The humanoid figure flexed its arms and gave its first newborn cry:

"BOH!!"

"""It taaaaaaalked?!"""

Everyone present was flabbergasted. Some actually became paralyzed with fear and fell to the ground. The chorus of voices echoed across the entire sandbar, the uproar so great that it wouldn't be strange if the guards came by to see what the fuss was about.

Cayna ordered the rock golem to attack the still-squirming earth golem.

In all honesty, a level 110-rock golem up against a level-6 earth golem wasn't a fight at all. The earth golem was turned to dust with a single punch.

The spectators stared with mouths agape. Even the young noble's expression was cartoonishly contorted; the shock had caused his mind to go blank.

The two mages murmured, "a-ancient arts…," and dropped the wand.

The rock golem wasn't done yet. It lumbered over and seized the dumbfounded mages. "No killing, okaaay?" Cayna warned it. Its eyes glinted in understanding. Grabbing both their shoulders, it lifted the men overhead and used its full might to twirl them around like the blades of a helicopter.

Anyone would feel sick after getting spun around so much. Just as it looked like they might spew ectoplasm, the pale mages' suffering was brought to an end.

The onlookers remained in frozen silence after witnessing the rock golem's moves, which could be considered as nimble as any other

race. Cayna, meanwhile, thought it was quite inefficient as far as rock golems went.

In the end, the mages who had been held overhead by the rock golem were tossed north of the sand bar. The young noble who had been staring in bewilderment soon joined them. He howled about this and that, but the rock golem was loyal to Cayna's orders, so it didn't listen to a single thing its foe had to say. The noble went flying and then landed far off in the water with a splash.

Unsurprisingly, the butler escaped the rock golem's demonic grip hand and chased after his master.

"Well, now what?" Cayna muttered to herself in puzzlement as she observed the silent onlookers. She wanted to meet back up with the girls, although definitely not with this many people staring.

Just as she was thinking about somehow breaking her way though, a voice cried out, "What the heck's going on?!" and the crowd hurriedly came to life. Several knights appeared as they parted the dispersing throng.

Before things could get any further out of hand, Cayna cut off her supply of magic, and the rock golem disappeared. One knight towering above the rest caught sight of her, and his face twisted in exasperation. "Hey, do you get antsy or somethin' if you don't got a problem to stir up? Seriously."

"It wasn't me," Cayna retorted. "Someone picked a fight."

Several familiar knights greeted her with a "hello." She waved at them, and Shining Saber looked even more exasperated when he learned further details about the recent incident.

"Getting into squabbles with nobles?" he asked.

"This noble tried to intimidate and extort me and even attempted to kidnap the kids. Roxine sent 'em packing though."

"You gotta keep that dangerous maid of yours on a leash."

"If someone's rude enough to come at you like that, you've got no choice but to go all out, as far as I'm concerned. I'm not in the wrong here."

"Yeah, you are!"

As she exchanged complaints with Shining Saber, Roxine returned with Luka and Lytt.

"Are you okay, Miss Cayna?" Lytt asked.

"Were you...scared?" Luka added.

The two girls clung tight to her sides, and Cayna patted their heads in comfort. Even though this was the second time the girls had seen Shining Saber, Luka looked up at the big, booming dragoid in fear and shut her eyes.

"Don't bully Lu."

"I ain't bullying her. I'm talkin' to you!" Her words seemed to suffice though, and Shining Saber stepped away from the kids so he wouldn't frighten them. "Anyway, I'll talk to the top brass. Can't have people ticking off the owner of a Guardian Tower who can turn the city to ash in a snap."

"I wouldn't turn it to ash," said Cayna. "What's the point in that?"

"So you're telling me you would if there was a point."

"Anyway, nobles are all idiots, right?"

"There's only a few bad eggs. Look, don't cause too much trouble. It'll just make more work for us."

Shining Saber looked like he had just one more thing to say, but instead he rounded up the knights who had restored public order and left. They seemed to be the star unit in their own way, and the majority of Academy students looked upon the knights with admiration and envy.

"Now what do we do, Miss Cayna?" Lytt asked after Cayna had glanced around and confirmed the danger was gone.

Since the kids were looking tired, Cayna suggested, "Should we go home?"

"Yeah…I'm…sleepy," Luka replied, nodding off.

Cayna picked her up and prompted Roxine, and they headed home. Lytt kept glancing up at Luka in Cayna's arms, so as soon as they crossed the river, Cayna picked up Lytt instead.

"Oh, right. I forgot about the boat race…," Cayna said.

She turned back around to look the sandbar, tilting her head curiously when she saw no signs that any such event was to take place.

"Apparently, many are concerned that the race will cross paths with the Lord of Water, so it's been postponed to another day once the course has been modified," Roxine explained.

"…Lord of Water?"

"Yes, that's what the townspeople now call that whale Guardian Tower."

That was likely enough to happen, given the performance Cayna had pulled off. With the whale now revered as a deity of sorts, that would prevent anyone from getting involved with the tower, which was a huge help to Cayna.

"Was this announced?" she asked Roxine.

"Yes. It's posted all over the walls."

Cayna hadn't noticed in the least and was dumbstruck. In her arms, Lytt gave a questioning look and mumbled, "Race?"

"There's supposed to be a boat race around the sandbar," Cayna told her.

"Is it fun?"

"I wonder? Sounds like it's a popular enough gambling event. It's probably exciting if there's a boat you're sponsoring."

Too bad they wouldn't get to see the spectacle that was Primo and his friends. "Maybe next time," Cayna murmured as she got a better hold on Lytt, who seemed to be slipping. She could've easily held both girls, one in each arm, but she didn't want to stand out. She alternated the girls back and forth until they returned to the rental house.

Retaliation, Fishing, the Road Home, and Secret Talks

A banging echoed in the lightless room.

"Dammit…"

An incredulous mutter followed. Then there was more banging—someone was striking a desk in utter frustration.

"Preposterous…"

The man who owned the room knew that recent unthinkable events had left him in a vulnerable position.

Just as the commoner's noisy festival was reaching its end, the prime minister had bid him to come to the castle immediately. He quickly got his affairs in order and was on his way.

When he arrived, unsure of why he'd been summoned there, he found the king was present as well. The king ended up castigating him for a most unpleasant incident.

The crime in question was his son's attempt to harm a commoner—specifically, someone closely connected to an honored national guest. The man had also collaborated with a seedy underground organization and thereby sullied his noble family's name and dignity. The father, of course, insisted that such accusations were false or part of someone else's scheming.

However, many prominent figures had witnessed the young noble's threats firsthand at the Academy, among them the princess and several knights. The man was unable to evade the accusations against his son.

Among the man's biggest miscalculations had been the fact that the castle had the magical lie detector tool known as Mute Eye, and the underground organization's messenger, who had supposedly been killed to hide any remaining evidence of the crime, had actually survived. Even covered head to toe in bandages, the messenger had been subjected to a thorough interrogation; the Mute Eye confirmed his account and the noble's claims were rejected. As a result, the king and prime minister refused to hear the man's desperate sophisms, and his punishment was meted out then and there. He was demoted from his rank of earl and his lands were confiscated. His family was to vacate their mansion within the month and relocate to a smaller abode.

"What the hell is going on?!"

There was more banging along with the sound of furious kicking. Nothing was spared from his unbridled rage. Was the man's anger born from his family's tarnished name, or was it simple indignation at having his masculine pride sullied?

As the night stretched on, the banging, thumping, and clanging from his office continued, and the servants held their breaths in the hopes of avoiding his ire. Once the next day came, his wrath finally abated. The room that had taken the brunt of his fury for hours on end looked as if a monster had been set loose within.

To ease his hardened heart, the man headed to his private quarters. He would look upon and touch his treasured collection for comfort. The man felt relief before he even opened the door. He was like a child thrilled to receive a present the day before his birthday.

However, his heart froze in an instant once he stepped inside— someone had entered the room before him. The servants were forbidden entry, and he was the only one with a key, so this visitor was clearly an intruder.

The person in question was by the window with the man's treasure in their hand. They passed it back and forth between both hands like a toy. Each time the treasure flew through the air, the man's heart felt on the verge of breaking.

He wanted to scream: "Get your paws off it!" "Stop!" "Give it back!"

However, the man said none of this. Instead, he demanded, "Why—? What are you doing here?!"

He approached the intruder carefully so as not to surprise them and cause them to drop his treasure. Just then, the moonlight revealed the intruder's full form.

It was the messenger who had just endured a harrowing ordeal at the castle—the one he had ordered his subordinates to kill. As proof of their success, they had brought him a unique part of the messenger's body: a red eye. Since half of the messenger's face was still wrapped in bandages, one could only assume he was missing an eye.

"Hello there, earl. It's been a minute, hasn't it? You look downright terrified. Is something the matter?"

The corners of the messenger's mouth rose in a smirk. The earl felt that something wasn't quite right.

Wasn't this messenger the more modest type, he wondered? Indeed, he was more subservient and excellent at reading faces.

When they'd recently reunited at the castle, the earl had confirmed this man to be the messenger. But the person before him now seemed like someone else entirely.

"Keh-keh-keh. Unsettled, are you? I let you mistake me for him in that moment alone. But no longer."

His silhouette suddenly twisted, and an unfamiliar figure overlapped with that of the messenger. A confident voice unlike that of the messenger filled the room, and like tossing away an old shell, someone else appeared from within him.

There was a *thump*. It sounded nearby yet somehow foreign. Several moments passed before the earl realized that he was the source of the sound. He'd gripped the back of a sofa as he fell backward. The reality before him was like a fictitious, hazy sensation that was impossible to grasp, and he lost his ability to stand.

The messenger once before him was now an utterly different and commanding man who stood about two heads higher. His tall collar reached the corners of his mouth, and his entire body was enshrouded in a reddish-brown coat. Only his head and feet were visible. His head was no different than a human's, but he had sharp, pointed ears and peculiar horns. It was difficult to see in the poor lighting, but his tanned skin marked him as a demon. His golden eyes glared in disinterest.

The mere sight froze the earl to his very core. He couldn't stop trembling.

"A-agwah…"

His heart was gripped in an agonizing vise, and his breath came in gasps. He didn't even have the composure to realize he'd been hit with De-Buff, which inflicts a target with a status ailment in a single look.

"Well then, I sincerely doubt the king's punishment will serve as proper atonement for the likes of you."

The demon's gaze swiftly shifted over to a second figure that had unexpectedly appeared. When the earl caught sight of it, he unleashed a massive scream.

It was a humanoid white tree with nothing from the neck up. The cavity on the left side of the chest held a white skull.

"Perhaps you will serve as good material for this one. Or…"

A sword was thrust right before the earl's eyes. The blade alone

was longer than he was tall, and its polished, mirrorlike surface reflected his utterly terrified visage.

"…perhaps you'd like *him* to chop you into tiny pieces?"

Wielding the sword was a six-armed dragoid so tall it had to crouch against the ceiling. Each arm held a weapon, all of which were pointed straight at the earl.

"Eeeeek?!"

His throat grew parched from fear, and panic seized his arms and legs. He wanted to beg for his life but was so stricken with terror that his body wouldn't listen.

Nevertheless, the demon picked up the gold coins scattered on the table and announced his death sentence with utmost indifference.

"I know—let's decide with a coin toss."

His light tone might as well have been discussing the weather. An instant later, the skull's and dragoid's faces were tinged with surprise, but those expressions disappeared quick enough to make one wonder if they'd been there at all.

"Nonononononononononononononononononononononononononononono!"

Only a voiceless scream that threatened to split him open echoed within the earl's heart. The demon flicked a gold coin; it flew unfeelingly through the air, then twirled in slow motion. The earl felt like he could see every detail of the coin's design. He mustered all the strength in his body and released a shriek the moment it landed.

However, when questioned the next day, the servants in the mansion reported not hearing a single sound.

Then, the day after the festival.

When Cayna suddenly woke, she realized she was the only one in bed. Luka and Lytt's warmth from the night before was now long gone. All that remained were neatly folded blankets.

"Meooow."

The cath palug leapt gracefully onto the bed and sent her a tele-pathic message: *"'Bout time you got up."*

Based on the angle of the sun coming in from the window, she had clearly overslept.

"I guess yesterday wore me out more than I thought…"

She stretched with a "Nghhh" and quickly got changed with a few taps of the Equipment field. After twisting her back and rotating her shoulders around, she confirmed there was nothing out of the ordinary. Feeling fine, she picked up the cath palug and left the room.

"Miss Cayna!"

"Mommy Cayna!"

"Good morning, Lady Cayna."

They all greeted her with smiles and sound effects that were along the lines of *"Bubble, bubble"* and *"Shing."*

The bubbling came from Luka and Lytt as she hugged them. The *"shing"* came from Roxine's polite nod after she'd already prepared and arranged their meal perfectly.

"Sorry I'm late. Are you two having breakfast?"

"I…ate."

"Me too. You were super late, Miss Cayna!"

"Sorry about that. It looks like my job yesterday wiped me out more than I thought. Cie, I can look for brunch in one of the stalls. Or did you already prepare something?"

"No, I thought you might do that. What about dinner?"

"I'm not sure yet. Worst comes to worst, we can all go to a tavern or something."

"Understood."

The festival was over, but Cayna planned to go and see how the tower was doing. She'd bring along the girls and the cath palug, of course. Roxine said she had to clean the rental house and would meet up with them later.

"Won't you finish faster if you have some help?"

"Lady Cayna, could you please refrain from doing my job?" Roxine gave her the evil eye, so Cayna decided to gladly leave her to it. "It looks like we'll be leaving by tomorrow, so I must ensure that everything is spick-and-span."

"Right, sorry about that. I appreciate it."

Judging from Roxine's expression as she took out various cleaning supplies from her Item Box, she was ready to get down to business. The werecat maid was prone to bouts of verbal abuse when anyone got in the way of her cleaning, so Cayna and the girls made a swift exit. She led them toward the main drag with the cath palug on Lytt's head.

"Uwagh…"

"Eek."

"……"

When they got there, the three stared in bewilderment at the disastrous scene.

"There's trash everywhere…"

"Yeah…"

"Ah, right. Makes sense, I guess. That's bound to happen when you've got so many people and stalls."

Skewers and paper bags covered the street from one end to the other. The storefronts were tidy for some reason, but everywhere else was a scattered mess of litter.

"I feel like I've seen the dark side of the city…"

The trash at the corners wasn't so bad, but anything in the middle of the street got kicked up every time a carriage passed through. When Cayna spoke with the people carrying around large bags and cleaning up, they turned out to be adventurers who specialized in requests within the city. The guild apparently got a lot of clean-up requests after the festival. Even so, since there weren't nearly enough hands to help with the entire city, it would take several days before the garbage was fully packed away.

Cayna thanked them and went down an inconspicuous back alley to summon three Wind Spirits.

"Make sure no one sees you and use the wind to collect all the trash."

She asked the little Wind Spirit girls to gather up the mess in town. Doing so would save everyone both time and effort.

The spitits flitted about merrily before disappearing and scattering to every corner of the city. Creating a whirlwind to pick the garbage up off the ground was fine, although the powerful gust that sent half-eaten skewers flying was probably not. No one had yet noticed.

Li'l Fairy, who had hardly made an appearance throughout the festival, flew around Cayna; maybe the lack of crowds put her at ease. The cath palug had been startled the first time it saw her, but now it didn't seem to care in the least as she sat on its head. They looked like the Bremen Town Musicians stacked atop one another like that, and Cayna laughed.

"Mommy Cayna?"

"What's wrong, Miss Cayna?"

"*Phew.* Ah, sorry. There was something funny, so I couldn't help myself."

Since the girls couldn't see the fairy, they had no way of knowing what was on the cath palug's head. With a mere shake, Li'l Fairy and the kitten on top of Lytt's head swayed, and it took everything Cayna had to hold back her laughter. This made the girls even more confused, and their unsolved questions grew. Once they started pouting, she decided to fess up. She avoided the topic of the fairy, of course.

"It's just funny to watch the cath palug on your head sway each time you move, Lytt. Sorry, I didn't mean to make you think you were doing anything wrong."

"Hmph!"

Lytt removed the kitten from her head and gave it to Luka, who stared at it for some time before frowning and subsequently passing it to Cayna. However, the cath palug soon twisted out of Cayna's arms. It jumped to the ground, shook itself off, and began trotting toward the riverbank.

"Ah, wait, kitty!"

"It...ran off?" Luka watched Lytt chase the kitten and looked up at Cayna with concern.

"No worries. That kitty is strong, so it'll be totally fine." Cayna gave Luka a comforting hug, and the two of them followed the cath palug, Li'l Fairy, and Lytt.

They found Lytt on one of the riverside piers with the kitten in her arms. Luka trudged over to her and held her tight.

"Don't...run off."

"Sorry, Luka."

When Lytt looked up in apology, she saw Cayna behind Luka with several skewers of salted grilled fish. "Here you go," Cayna said as she handed one to her.

The three of them sat on several wooden crates and barrels on the pier, and for a while, there was only the sound of them munching on the fish. When Cayna looked over toward the sandbar, she noticed the Guardian Tower was surrounded by small boats keeping their distance. She used Eagle Eye and saw that most of the passengers were soldiers. A galley full of sightseers also slowly passed by, all of whom looked terrified. Cayna felt bad that she might've actually created more work for the Guardian.

"Oh!"

Cayna took a look around when she heard Lytt cry out and realized she'd let her mind wander too much. Kee was also more or less keeping an eye on things, so he would report to her if anything happened.

When Cayna turned toward the direction of Lytt's gaze, she found the cath palug gnawing a collection of empty fish skewers to pieces. As soon as she finished eating, Cayna handed over hers as well, and it repeated the process. The kitten then gathered the chopped debris on to a corner of a wooden crate, and a single gust of wind collected the trash and snatched it away. The cath palug appeared to have a good relationship with spirits, and it stuck its nose in the air with a self-satisfied look.

"How'd ya like that?" it boasted.

When she petted its head and told it "Good kitty," the children followed suit: "Good kitty!" "Good...kitty...," they said as they rubbed its head and back. It amused Cayna that this was the one time the cat acted subtle.

While the girls were enjoying some fruit for dessert, Cayna mentally contacted Roxine to let her know their location. The maid wasn't quite done cleaning yet, so the group decided to head over to the sandbar. Now that the ban on sailing was lifted, the commuter boat was back up and running. However, someone on the pier made Cayna a strange offer.

"Will you walk on water if I cancel out the children's fare?"

"Whaaa—?"

She hadn't planned on making herself a spectacle but realized she was already being put on the spot. Weighing the embarrassment of public humiliation against six bronze coins, her mind focused on the former. She could've very well considered the whole ordeal as a personal demonstration rather than a show that forced her to be on display. However, Cayna would need more time to settle into such a mindset.

"Hmm, fine. I'll walk by the boat until we reach the sandbar."

"Ah, I'd be mighty grateful if you did. Heck, I'd even pay you for it. I'll just raise the fare, then."

The nearby passengers who heard the captain laughed out loud.

Having someone walk on water and accompany the boat would make for an excellent marketing opportunity. Plus, since Cayna couldn't join the boat for each ride, her presence would give those trips an added sense of luxury.

"In any case, riding alongside you is enough of a reward for me."

"That's all?"

The old captain said he could offer her more money, but Cayna wasn't willing to be that greedy. She turned down any compensation for the time being.

The passengers' fare would be three bronze coins whenever Cayna walked beside the boat. The cost was round trip, although the passengers didn't know whether or not she would accompany the boat on the return. Only those who didn't mind this boarded.

Once the boat departed, Cayna walked alongside it near where Luka and Lytt were seated. She drew a lot of curious stares. Several minutes in, and she already wanted to retract her previous offer.

The captain and passengers thanked her after they arrived at the sandbar pier, but she quickly said her good-byes and hurried off before others could make similar requests.

"I'm not some pushover who'll do just any favor on a whim."

At any rate, she was only willing to do this service for that specific commuter boat.

Cayna took Luka and Lytt to the sandbar's eastern edge. Large groups of people were coming and going from this direction.

Normally, the top of the blue whale's head was visible at this location, a dome-shaped space surrounded by tall piles of flowers.

"Wow, what is this place?" Lytt asked.

"So many...flowers."

"There sure are, huh?"

Only one spot where you could just barely see the front of the blue whale was open, and people stepped forward to pay their respects. They would then add their bouquet to the nearby wall and leave. The three of them watched as more and more flowers were added to the wall.

Some people were eyeing Cayna and her group suspiciously for not praying, so she and the girls left to avoid bothering anyone further. Just then, the whale spouted water from its blowhole, and those who had gathered to offer it their prayers started cheering. Some of them seemed to consider this a form of blessing. Real whales didn't actually spout water, though.

After stopping by the church to check out the sparkling stained glass windows, they visited Kartatz's workshop. It was then that they finally met up with Roxine.

"How'd it go?" Cayna asked her.

"Everything has been well polished. We will be able to depart tomorrow with no issues."

"Gotcha. Great work. Looks like we're heading back tomorrow, then. Are you two okay with that?"

"Uh-huh."

"Yeah, that's fine!"

The children gave their approval, and Cayna made plans to thank Elineh the next day and leave Felskeilo. Marelle was no doubt worried about Lytt being so far from home.

"Mum!"

"Hey there, Kartatz."

The workshop appeared to be back in business, but things didn't seem especially busy at the moment. Cayna and the others arrived to see the workers resting on the floor or in the shadow of piles of lumber, which was when Kartatz came rushing out from further inside the workshop.

"Thanks for the lumber earlier," said Cayna. "I was able to build a really nice house with it."

"It was your own abilities that made it possible, Mum, not anything I did. Hey there, Luka. How are you?"

"......Hel...lo...Kar...tatz."

"Hello, it's nice to meet you. I'm Lytt."

Luka had approached Kartatz and kept her head down as she spoke, and Lytt nodded next to her. Behind Cayna, Roxine bowed.

"Oh, you must be the innkeeper's daughter. I'm Mum's third child, Kartatz. As you can see, I make boats in this here workshop. Nice to meet you." Kartatz briefly introduced himself while stroking his beard with his arms crossed.

Luka took Lytt's hand and looked up at him.

"Can we...look around?" she timidly asked.

"Sure, I don't mind...but there's a lot of dangerous stuff around here that you could trip on and whatnot. Stay away from the piles of lumber. It might topple in a heartbeat."

"...Okay."

"Got it!"

"Then I shall accompany you ladies."

When Roxine suddenly stood right by them and made this offer, Kartatz chose one of his men to act as a guide. He gave instructions to let them observe as they pleased.

Since both the cath palug and Roxine would protect Luka and Lytt even in the event of an avalanche, Cayna wasn't particularly worried.

"Sorry that Luka kinda forced this on you."

"Aw c'mon, it's nothin'. Besides, that lady with her looks pretty capable herself. If any of the lumber collapsed, I bet she'd handle it no problem."

Lytt asked Kartatz's employee a string of questions, which Luka would whisper to her, like "What's that?" and "What's this?" Behind them, Roxine kept a constant watch. The other workers still on break watched them with smiles on their faces.

"Even though my house is in the village, I made more rooms than I need. You're free to stay anytime. We even have a public bathhouse."

"That right? I'll be lookin' forward to it."

"And we've got *this*!"

Cayna produced a barrel from her Item Box, and it landed with a thud in front of Kartatz. One whiff of the aroma had him lunging at it and crying "Ooh, booze!" with a big grin on his face.

"I decided to open up a brewery in the village, so I thought I'd give you a barrel as thanks for the lumber. You can either drink it yourself or share with everyone. I'll leave that up to you."

"You already paid me for the wood. Isn't this giving me too much?"

"Conscientious as ever, I see… Just accept it as 'profits.'"

"R-right. Much obliged."

"I'll be selling through Sakaiya, so order from them if you want more."

"Got it. Thanks for this, Mum."

Clearly quite pleased with this "profit," Kartatz beamed from ear to ear as he hoisted the barrel up and headed further inside the workshop.

"Listen up, boys!" he called to his staff. "I got some top-notch booze from my mum, so the drinks are gonna be flowin' tonight!"

His men let out a raucous cheer that shook the workshop. Luka and Lytt looked around, startled by the noise. The cath palug meowed and licked Lytt's cheek to assure her there was no danger.

Cayna grinned uncomfortably; she had a feeling Kartatz and his staff were going drink it all within the day. "I guess they drink like fishes," she murmured.

"...Fishes?" Luka repeated, clearly confused.

She, Lytt, and Roxine had returned after taking a tour of the workshop. Seeing Kartatz skipping back to them in high spirits shocked Cayna, although she couldn't relate since she wasn't a fan of alcohol herself.

"It means that you drink all the alcohol in one sitting," she told Luka.

"Hmm," said Lytt. "I don't really like adults who get plastered…"

"You sure don't pull your punches, Lytt." Cayna burst out laughing. Lytt was just as brazen in her opinions as her big sister, Luine.

Lytt unmistakably saw her fair share of sloppy, foolish adults since she lived in a tavern. It was impressive how every employee around them who had been listening in on the conversation clutched their hearts with a groan and looked away.

The shipbuilders had returned to their activities that day, and Cayna decided to stay at the workshop until evening since the children insisted on watching. Roxine said she would keep an eye on the girls, so Cayna decided to spend her free time fishing on the bank of the sandbar. Fishing was a skill as well, and one which Cayna only used when gathering cooking ingredients. Many players had fished with boundless determination in order to snag a rare catch or collect one of each kind.

Fellow Skill Master Kujo had often invited her on fishing trips where he had her spend endless hours helping him look for specific types. Her own friendliness and camaraderie surprised her; one time they visited a beach with a different goal in mind but ended up fishing out a zwohm with Liothek. Kujo hadn't been after the zwohm but rather Liothek, who had been dressed in a sea slug onesie. It was a huge ordeal, with the zwohm subjugated after a great many sacrifices only for them to learn that it couldn't be made into a summoning. Cayna remembered how Liothek had cried with resentment.

These memories came flooding back to Cayna as she got ready to go fishing, and only after Kartatz pointed it out did she realize she'd had a grin on her face.

She put together the fishing bait through skills, and after recalling some of Kujo's past meddling, her fishing gear was ready to go. Given the large variety of fish at the market, Cayna was certain that Kartatz, who had long lived in Felskeilo, would be able to identify which ones were edible.

She caught the Ejidd River's famous catfish (ponsu) on her very first try and realized she'd need something to put the fish in. As time went by, the attention of the workshop employees fell on Cayna. After all, she was sure to catch something with each swing of her rod. Kartatz wisely brought out a washbasin, but Cayna's catches quickly filled up two more. She had put the smaller fish in one basin, which was soon full to bursting.

Luka and Lytt grew more fascinated with fishing than observing the workshop. Together with Roxine, they peered into the basins and listened to Kartatz's explanation of each kind of fish and how to cook them. Four large fish like the ponsu were swimming in one other basin. The little ones were released at Kartatz's suggestion.

"I think I've had enough of the little guys." Cayna switched out her rod meant for medium-size fish and switched it for a rod designed to catch large ones. "Cie, can you pick out several fish from that basin and cut them up for me?"

"You'd like to turn them into bait? Just one moment."

Roxine took out her own knife and cutting board, and then chopped a few fish she had scooped from the basin.

"Miss Cayna, are you going to fish some more?"

"I'm really enjoying myself. It might be seem boring, but wait just a bit longer."

It'd been a long time since she last fished, and it was surprisingly fun once she started. Her expectations went from *"I'll get enough for the whole family,"* to *"Let's get fish enough for everyone."* Now, her plan was, *"I won't stop until the line snaps."*

"Agh, fine! I give! We ain't gettin' any work done like this! Hey, someone grab some burners and leftover wood! People who know how to clean fish, get over here!"

Kartatz, realizing that his workers were captivated by Cayna's huge haul and that any attempt at work was futile, decided to round everyone up for some food prep. Following his orders, they soon collected scrap wood and made a bonfire. Magic stoves were brought from the kitchens, pots and frying pans were set up, and those who knew the proper techniques cut and trimmed the fish. Many of Kartatz's workers were quite skilled; they gutted the fish, skewered and grilled some with salt, and arranged others for fresh sashimi—even readied the fish for frying. A mouthwatering aroma wafted through the air.

Roxine borrowed a stove and started her own preparations. She always seemed to have her own ideas in mind.

Unable to keep up with the rapid-fire pace, Luka and Lytt held the cath palug and stared in amazement as the rough-looking men went about their work.

"So cool."

"Uh-huh. So…cool."

"Meow." Swaying back and forth, the cath palug covetously eyed several fish dishes.

As an added bonus, even some of the fishermen passing nearby were lured by scent and brought their own catches as well. The riverbank by the workshop was instantly filled with people, several bonfires were lit, and an impromptu banquet broke out. When Cayna switched out her gear and immediately caught a nearly three-meter-long pirarucu, the crowd erupted into cheers.

Pirarucu were difficult to catch and very delicious. Such a

high-quality fish went for more than two silver coins at market. Everyone agreed that the one who caught the fish ought to decide what to do with it. Since she didn't really want to bring it all the way home, Cayna urged everyone to eat it.

"Here you go...Mommy Cayna..."

"Oh, thanks, Lu."

Luka brought out the first piece, which had been steamed with herbs inside a hole in the ground. Cayna opened her mouth with an "Ahhh" as Luka tossed it in.

"Gah, hot! *Huff, fwagh.* Ooh, this is tasty," said Cayna.

The herbs had erased any bad odors while the salt had softened the flesh. It tasted of sea bream. After Cayna finished her own plate, she later divided the portion Lytt had brought over between the two girls. They were shocked at how good it tasted.

Later on, Kartatz came over and offered his mother a cup. He'd recently opened the barrel of beer she gave him and was apparently treating everyone to drinks.

"Here ya go, Mum. Haven't you done enough fishin' by now? Why not join the party?"

"Hmm. I'm having so much fun though. I'll keep at it just a bit longer."

"*More* fishing...?"

"Also, Kartatz, I don't drink alcohol."

"Huh?! But didn't you bring this?"

"I brought it and made it, but I don't drink it."

She smiled awkwardly as Kartatz stood frozen in shock. She wished he would stop thinking she could drink as much as a dwarf all because he was her son.

"Mommy Cayna...are you...still hungry?"

"Yeah, I'll have another bite. Could you bring me some of that salted grilled fish?"

"...Okay."

Incidentally, Roxine was producing salt with her skills and using her Cooking Skills to make *oshizushi* and *nigirizushi*. Since it was rare cuisine, people kept coming back for more the moment it was available. However, Roxine's intimidating aura ensured no one made a move. She watched Luka and Lytt take some of the food with a bright smile on her face but stared daggers whenever anyone else tried to do the same, forcing them to dejectedly retreat.

Cayna held the fishing rod in one hand and popped the salted grilled fish Luka had brought into her mouth with the other. Perhaps out of some deeply ingrained habit, Lytt was now serving, carrying food, and pouring drinks. People sang and played ditties on their flutes, and for some reason even a wandering bard joined in to enliven the merry atmosphere.

"It's getting pretty rowdy. Does this sort of thing happen often?" Cayna asked her son.

"Nah, it's pretty unusual. You just...tend to cause a ruckus wherever you go, Mum."

"Well, gee, sorry about that."

"Yeah...this is fun...," said Luka.

Kartatz had joined Cayna at the edge of the river and was sitting on a wooden crate while he ate and drank his fill. Luka sat on a large boulder nearby, staring out at the over eighty members who had joined the party. She was stroking the full-bellied, purring cath palug on her lap. Roxine returned to them with Lytt, who was now dog-tired from serving. Both the maid's arms held several plates of food. She tossed them into the air and took out a table from her Item Box. Catching the falling plates one after the other, she lined them along the table. It was like watching a combination of acrobatics and a parlor trick. Luka and Lytt clapped enthusiastically, and the maid bowed politely.

"You did a fine job, Lady Lytt."

"Uwagh, I ended up serving people before I even knew it!" Lytt moaned.

"Comes with the territory, miss," Kartatz teased.

"Forgive me, Lady Cayna. I failed to assist you here."

"I'll call you if I need anything, so just do whatever you feel like."

As Roxine earnestly apologized for leaving Cayna's side, Luka patted her head consolingly. She probably wouldn't want Roxilius to learn she'd been in such a state.

Next to Cayna, who was visibly confused as to why Roxine was being so hard on herself, Lytt looked at the line in the water and mumbled with boredom, "You're *still* fishing, Miss Cayna?"

"Yeah, I was thinking I'd catch one more before we head back… Hmm?"

Just as Cayna spoke, the fishing rod bent. This type was meant for hauling big fish from the sea and had apparently caught something. The line moved to the left and right along the river's surface beyond the light of the bonfires. Cayna grabbed the rod with both hands and shouted "Light!" at Roxine, who cast Additional White Light over the tip of the pole. The cath palug slipped off Luka's lap and walked across the water with a *tup, tup, tup* to peer at the end of the line. A summoned Light Spirit, which looked like a giant dandelion, further illuminated what lay beneath the surface.

The next moment, a giant swaying shadow rose out of the water. Cayna's group stared wide-eyed.

"Whoa, what is that?" said Cayna.

"It's freakin' huge… Do we have the space to reel in somethin' like that?"

Kartatz quickly looked at the nearby riverbank and told the people there to retreat. "Hey! Somethin' big is comin'. Stand back, you guys!"

"Hold on, I don't even know if I'll be able to catch it yet!" Cayna protested.

"I believe in you, Mum!"

He gave her a thumbs up, and Cayna's gaze grew distant. "I hate when people expect big things of me…"

It wasn't just her son. The merrymakers had also heard the commotion and come running. Cayna became the center of attention as she strained against her big catch. She clutched the rod tight as it swayed back and forth and paused for a moment. Instead of reeling the line in, she kept the fishing rod raised and gradually backed away in order to pull the creature to shore.

Finally, whether out of resignation or desperation, her big catch made its way onto land. As soon as it was illuminated by the Light Spirit, people screamed and scrambled away from the riverbank. Roxine picked up Luka and Lytt and carried them off a good distance. The only ones left were Kartatz with a beer in one hand, Cayna who still held the rod, and the cath palug growling at her feet.

"The heck is that?" said Kartatz.

"Looks like a monster to me," replied Cayna.

It was some sort of alligator creature that looked to be about nine meters long. It had rough, dark-green skin, a shark head, an alligator body, and wide fins like a stingray's. The monster's long, thin, vertical tail was like those you see in cryptobranchoidea.

Its chimera silhouette bore a striking resemblance to a monster Cayna had seen recently; she wondered if this one came from some sort of Pillage Point.

Now with its body fully on land, the chimera alligator-shark snapped its jaws with a clang in an effort to threaten Cayna and her son.

"Ah, now that ya mention it, I got a feelin' there was a warning sent out for the whole riverbank," Kartatz casually recalled as he gulped down his beer. His staff behind him shouted, "Shouldn't you have mentioned this stuff, boss?!" in protest.

He couldn't flip out at his workers and make a fool of himself in front of his mother, so his only reaction was a bulging vein that appeared on his forehead.

"Now, now," Cayna said with a strained smile as she consoled her son. She then glanced at the chimera alligator-shark curiously.

"Hey, isn't this the smaller shadow that appeared before the Guardian Tower did?" she said.

"GRAAAGH!" the monster howled, and went to attack just as Cayna looked away. The onlookers behind her gasped and screamed, "Watch out!"

They shut their eyes, anticipating her tragic end where she would get torn to shreds. Their shrieks echoed through the night as Cayna, the one under attack, calmly leaped toward the creature.

As the chimera soared through the air to make its attack, she slipped beneath its giant body and let a kick fly.

Weapon Skill: Explosive Kick: Guen Van Ti

A sound like "*Bwaahm!*" followed, and a huge hole went straight through the chimera's chest and out its back. An instant kill, it passed straight by Cayna and fell motionless to the sandy soil with a loud thud.

An almost painful silence settled over the area, and the onlookers timidly peeked at the unmoving monster. Finally, a quiet round of applause began to rise from the murmuring crowd. This soon turned into a thunderous cheer that spread across the sandbar.

At that point, a phosphorescence rose from the chimera. The monster lit up in an instant and disappeared before their very eyes. All that remained was a square piece of metal small enough to fit in the palm of one's hand.

"I knew it. So it was a Pillage Point..."

After Cayna picked the metal up and used Search to evaluate it, she tossed it to Kartatz.

"Whoa, what's this for, Mum? Don't just throw stuff at me."

"I'm not gonna use it, so you can have it."

"'Won't use it'? What even is this thing…?"

Kartatz used Search on it and did a spit take.

The metal was actually Damascus steel, one of the hardest of all fantasy metals.

At any rate, the feast drew to a close, and the partygoers and workshop members who had drunk and ate their fill began cleaning up. A soldier who should have been on patrol but had also joined in the revelry collected accounts from the eyewitnesses who saw the vanishing monster.

"He's playing hooky," Cayna stated.

"Yep, no question," Kartatz agreed.

"Wh-what are you talking about?" the soldier retorted. "Th-this is part of my duties, too. Yeah."

"He dodged the issue," she added.

"Indeed he did," Roxine concurred.

The soldier learned from Cayna that this creature might have been the source of the first shadow that sprang up before the ordeal with the white fish and hurriedly went to report this information to his seniors. It would take some time for him to deliver this report, since he had to cross the river; this was one of Felskeilo's pitfalls. The news apparently wasn't too urgent, so the guard couldn't use the dragonfly service either.

"Sounds like a pain to me," Cayna said with a sigh.

"Mum, not everyone has useful skills like you." Kartatz shot his mother an exasperated look. It would take a few days to get conclusive results, so Cayna asked that any reward for her information be sent to Kartatz.

"You can collect it the next time you stop by," Kartatz told her.

"Just go ahead and use it, honestly," Cayna replied indifferently.

"What are you saying, Lady Cayna? Money is a finite resource. Sir Kartatz, please hold onto it for safekeeping," Roxine urged.

"R-right…," said Kartatz. Faced with her stern expression and fervent gaze, he really had no other choice but to agree.

"Well, guess we better catch a boat before they're all gone," said Cayna. "Lu, Lytt, let's go."

"'Kaaaay!"

"Okay…"

Roxine gave a polite bow, and Luka ran to Cayna with the cath palug in her arms. Lytt followed Cayna after accepting some salted grilled fish.

"Sheesh. Never a dull moment when Mum's around."

As soon as he saw Cayna and the others off, Kartatz kicked his workers' butts into gear and had them hurry with the clean-up.

The sun had already set by the time they crossed the river, and it was pitch dark. The city was basking in the lingering post-festival atmosphere, with many people out reveling in groups. Getting through such crowds with children in tow would put any parent or guardian on edge. Many of the revelers were fairly easygoing, but not the ones Cayna's all-female group ran into. Most of them were men who were either starved for female attention or tried to force drinks on her and Roxine.

The group made their way through town, handling those men as they cropped up, although Cayna and Roxine had to resort to force several times when a verbal warning didn't suffice. By the time they got back to the rental house, Cayna was mentally exhausted.

"What is this, the final gauntlet? Gimme a break."

They spotted several shadowy human figures in front of the rental house. Cayna took her magic staff from her earring and gave it a swing. When she brought it back down to a manageable size and glared at the group, a harried voice called out.

"H-hey! Just hold on a sec! Why're you suddenly goin' into battle mode?!"

"Hmm?"

"M-Miss Cayna, it's Mr. Knight from yesterday," Lytt said as she clung to Cayna's arm to stop her. When Cayna strained her eyes, she saw the startled faces of the group of knights as well as Myleene, whom they were protecting.

"Jeez, it's you, Shining Saber? Don't get me all confused like that," Cayna griped.

"You seem pretty beat. What're you doin' out with the kids this late?" the dragoid asked.

"All sorts of stuff. I guess you haven't heard about what went down yet. Anyway, come on in. Sorry, Cie, I know you're tired, but please prepare us some tea."

"Will do."

Although the invitation was extended to everyone, only Myleene and Shining Saber entered. The rest of the knights stood on patrol around the perimeter of the house.

As Roxine was preparing the tea, Cayna brought the two children to the second floor.

"I'll leave the girls with you for a bit, cath palug."

"Meooow."

"You two can go to bed without me," Cayna said to Lytt and Luka.

"Gotcha."

"…Okay."

Once the girls changed into their pajamas, they got under the covers and bade Cayna good night. When she arrived back down at the first floor, she sat down in front of her two visitors at the table.

"Well, what is it?" Cayna said.

"You sure are sulky," Shining Saber replied. "You mess up or somethin'…?"

"I'm tired from dealing with drunks."

Really, it was more exhausting than the uproar at the sandbar.

Myleene giggled as she watched Cayna stretch and stifle a yawn. "Just when I assume it's from the momentous odd job you've taken on, it turns out to be people who have tired you out. You certainly are a peculiar one, Lady Cayna."

It was here that Roxine served them tea before stepping back with a bow. Each took a sip, and just as they all relaxed, Shining Saber brought out a strangely bulky leather pouch.

"What's this?" Cayna asked him.

"The reward from yesterday."

"Oh, okay."

"Huh? That's all you've got to say?"

Without even checking what was inside it, Cayna accepted the purse and stowed it in her Item Box. Myleene's eyes grew large as she witnessed the quick exchange.

"If you're giving it to me, I'll take it. It'd be more of a pain to reject this sort of thing than to just accept it."

"Somethin' happen?" Shining Saber asked.

"Yeah, just a little while ago. I've got a feeling the soldiers won't get back to me soon, since I can't prove my claim."

As soon as Cayna told them what had happened at the sandbar, Myleene got to her feet.

"What's wrong, Mye?"

"I shall speak with the soldiers myself. After all you have done for us, to think they wouldn't take your claim seriously!"

"No, no, it's really okay! There's no reason to get so worked up! Just calm down!" Cayna hurriedly had Myleene sit back down in her chair. "*Phew*, I'm totally wiped…"

Shining Saber clutched his stomach from laughing as Cayna hung her head wearily. "Ha-ha-ha-ha, how's it feel when someone else has all the power?" he taunted.

"By the way, is it really a good idea for the princess to be out this late?" Cayna asked.

"Of course it's not. That's why I'm with her. Quit screwin' around."

"Why're you snapping at me?"

When Cayna looked at Myleene, she had an apologetic expression and nodded. It seemed that Shining Saber or some other knight was only supposed to deliver the reward, but the princess had requested to come along. That's why there was an entire group present. Primo wasn't the only member of the royal family actively trying to run away from home, as Cayna had realized the last time Mye had escaped the castle on her own.

When it was time to return to the castle, Cayna sent her off with one of the Wind Spirits she had called upon that morning since they had already returned. She made it so the summoning would cancel out once Myleene safely returned.

"Well, see you later, Mye." Cayna waved good-bye, and Myleene curtsied. "See ya, Shining Saber."

"Yep. Don't get mixed up in any more trouble." After giving his tall order, Shining Saber waved a hand from behind.

"Good night, Lady Cayna."

"Thanks. Night, Mye."

The knights on guard also bowed their heads or waved back, and the group disappeared into the bustling night.

"Aghh, that sure was a busy way to relax…" Cayna stretched with a "Nghhh" and gave a big yawn. She mumbled, "Time for bed," and headed to her bedroom. There, she was greeted with the sight of the girls and kitten curled up and peacefully asleep.

"My goodness." Cayna climbed in under the covers next to the girls, said good night to the cath palug in the center, and drifted into dreams.

The next morning, they went over to Elineh's company and returned the key to the rental house. Cayna had removed all the traps while Roxine had done some deep cleaning, so it was spick-and-span by the time they had checked out.

"Thank you so much, Elineh," said Cayna.

"Thank you!"

"Thank...you..."

"Ha-ha-ha, I'm so glad to see you've enjoyed yourselves. How was the festival?"

"More than worth it, since we got to enjoy all different kinds of food."

"My, my, it appears food is your true love. How very like you, Lady Cayna."

Next to Elineh was the untransformed Armuna. Just as she interrupted her husband's conversation, she gave her employees an order, and they brought over three wooden boxes.

"Umm, what's this?" Cayna asked.

"Yes, well, I heard you desire food ingredients, Lady Cayna, so I've prepared a choice selection. I do hope you'll accept it," Armuna replied.

"Wow, you didn't have to do all that, but thank you."

"It was nothing. Our company accomplishes this much before breakfast."

When Cayna looked over at the employees who had brought the boxes, her expression stiffened. Some had dark circles under their eyes; everyone looked rather exhausted.

"In that case, please take this," Cayna said, and handed Armuna three gold coins. The kobold blinked and stared at the money in her hand.

"Um, what is this for?" Armuna asked.

"It's payment. I said I would pay next time, didn't I?"

"Goodness me, you certainly don't pull your punches, do you? Understood. I shall accept your payment. Thank you as always for your patronage." Armuna and the relieved employees fell back.

"Oh my, Lady Cayna. It seems my wife is rather fond of you," Elineh commented cheerfully.

"…Please give me a break," a haggard-looking Cayna mumbled.

The wagon was already out of the Item Box and ready for departure. In order to avoid any commotion, this time it would be led by a single horse and look like a normal wagon. To make the appearance more palatable than the stern-looking golem, Cayna used Summoning Magic to call upon an enbarr—a mythological horse that could race across land and sea.

"Well, Elineh. Thanks so much for everything," said Cayna.

At the rear of the wagon, Luka gave a little bow and Lytt waved good-bye. Elineh waved back and told Cayna he looked forward to seeing her again in the village.

Cayna was relieved to find that they were able to exit the eastern gate without shocking anyone.

"Miss Cayna, isn't the wagon going kind of fast?" Lytt asked.

As Cayna relaxed inside their transport, Lytt, who was staring out at the scenery, looked behind her.

It really couldn't be helped. Since the very beginning, the wagon had always had a will of its own and did as it pleased to a certain degree. Cayna had only instructed the enbarr to *pretend* to pull it. She never said to *not* pull it.

Perhaps pleased it had nothing to do in particular, the enbarr raced along. The wagon raced along as well, and the synergy caused it to push forward at a reckless speed.

"It doesn't look like we are about to run over anybody, and we've got countermeasures *(for the inside of the wagon)* that will keep us perfectly safe," Cayna said with a wink.

They were flying much faster than any normal carriage, and the scenery outside passed by in the same way one might see from the window of a moving train. Lytt's expression grew dark. Cayna popped her head out of the wagon and said, "Enbarr, can you slow it down a bit?" Their speed quickly dropped, and the wagon finally moved at a horse's pace. The enbarr seemed a bit dissatisfied, so Cayna considered unhitching it at night and letting it have a good run.

Then, just as they left Felskeilo and were about to spend their first night camping outdoors…

Roxine noticed an elaborate carriage guarded by four knights on horseback coming toward them from the direction they were headed and reported this to Cayna. It stopped alongside them by their campsite, and Skargo, enveloped in a Rainbow Halo, burst out. Cayna offered a strained smile and greeted him.

"Ah, Mother Dear, to think we would reunite in a place such as this… I, Skargo, am ever grateful to the gods."

The knight guards ignored Skargo's little meltdown and started setting up camp.

Cayna hit him over the head and told him not to leave the knights with all the heavy lifting. Her vaguely icy smile prompted Skargo to leap to his feet and run off to help his entourage. As she put a hand to her forehead with a sigh, she called to Luka and Lytt.

"…You…called us?"

"What is it, Miss Cayna?"

"Could you ask the knights if they'd like to have dinner together?"

"Okay…I'll try…"

"Yeah, we'll help!"

Cayna was watching the two amiably walk off hand in hand when Roxine, who had made a bonfire nearby, burst into laughter.

"What's so funny, Cie?"

"Shouldn't you invite Sir Skargo as well?"

"Those who don't work don't eat."

"How very stern of you. Can he even cook…?"

"I'm sure he learned when he was training to be a High Priest. He ought to be fine, right?"

Roxine brewed several cups of tea and passed one to Cayna and the girls once they returned. The knights, who had assumed they'd be managing their own meals somehow, couldn't resist the children's imploring gazes and accepted Cayna's invitation for dinner.

Skargo wound up sobbing tears of agony and asking why Cayna didn't invite him, too.

Luka shot him a steely glare and replied, "'Cause you slacked, off…Big Brother." Skargo subsequently turned to stone from the shock, but never mind that slight detail.

Cayna used her Cooking Skills to prepare dinner. She made a spicy soup from some large shellfish from the Ejidd River along with vegetables and colt bird meat that were in the wooden boxes Armuna had given her. The pot was full to the brim with soup, but the knights emptied it in no time. Her foolish son was promptly silenced when he started grumbling, "Perhaps you could show an iota of self-restraint while enjoying Mother Dear's cooking?" Most remarkable of all was when Roxine served equal amounts of tea to everyone.

Cayna, Luka, and Lytt went down to the stream alongside the main road to wash the utensils, and when they returned, it was time for everyone to sit together and chat. Social status had no bearing here, as Cayna reminded Skargo earlier. However, the bureaucrats and attendants quickly withdrew, insistent that they should abstain.

The knights' commander seemed like the reasonable type. After all, his objections of "Sir Skargo, could you please refrain from sending out stars and rainbows from the carriage whenever we pass by citizens? It's rather embarrassing" put an end to the High Priest's shenanigans from the very outset of their journey.

"Ah, sorry about my idiot son," said Cayna. "You can keep him tied up until you get back to Felskeilo. You have my permission."

"Motherrrr Deaaaaaar…"

"What are you crying over, Skargo? I'm being totally serious."

"You're not going to deny it?!"

Skargo's harried response sent everyone around the fire into roars of laughter as he crouched down and helplessly cried a waterfall.

The knights then asked Cayna what had brought her all the way to Felskeilo. It was no big secret, so she answered that she'd gone to see her daughter and show the children more of the world. Their idle chit-chat continued for some time, but alcohol suddenly loosened one of the knights' tongues. Silence fell after he asked a single question:

"Heeey, I wonder what Sir Skargo's father is like?"

It really wasn't all that odd a topic of conversation, but Cayna wasn't expecting it and clammed up. Meanwhile, even Skargo, who was normally throwing effects around constantly, went silent as well, looking downward with a pained expression on his face. No one said a word. Unsurprisingly, the knight realized his slipup and bowed his head with a "Sorry" at his commander's prodding.

With this, the light conversation ended as well. However, amid the uncomfortable atmosphere, Skargo lifted his head and looked at Cayna. "Mother Dear. My siblings and I have only heard of Father in vague detail—what kind of person was he?"

"Gah!"

It was out of the frying pan and into the fryer.

Cayna froze when her son asked her point-blank about the hazy subject. An emotional response—that is, hitting him with her strongest Flame Magic—wouldn't solve this.

Strictly speaking, the father of Skargo, Kartatz, and Mai-Mai was the VRMMORPG *Leadale*'s game system. Not that they would ever understand that…

Now internally panicking, Cayna used her deep knowledge of men (that is, Opus) and started to explain without thinking of the consequences. According to her, their father was stronger than Cayna and used his wiles to mess around with people. As she spoke, Cayna's mood grew darker with self-loathing. The knights mistakenly thought it was a painful subject and felt bad for her. She was eternally grateful they never asked why the father was gone even though he'd supposedly been stronger than Cayna.

Her mood now thoroughly deflated, everyone decided to call it a day. The knight who had started the whole conversation bowed his head remorsefully, but Cayna had brought this dark mood upon herself and told him not to worry about it. She summoned a Fire Spirit and Lightning Spirit to keep watch over the camp. Skargo had his knights, so what he did with them was up to him.

Cayna held her head and groaned miserably. Luka clung tight to her.

"Wh-what's wrong, Lu?"

"I want to…sleep with you, Mommy Cayna."

"Huh? Oh, right. Well, let's hop into bed, then."

Luka had never seen her mother so flustered.

"No fair, Luka! I wanna sleep with Miss Cayna, too!"

"Wait, don't the three of us always sleep right next to each other anyway?"

She'd apparently become a hot commodity, and an agreement was finally made when she offered each girl one arm as a pillow. With Roxine as mediator, the matter concluded smoothly.

"My arms are definitely gonna be sore tomorrow…"

At their newest campsite two days later, Cayna's group met up with a party of five that included Cohral.

"Yo, Cayna," he called.

"Wait, didn't you have a guard job to do?"

He was supposed to be on bodyguard duty for Sakaiya, escorting an envoy to the border, but he shouldn't have been finished with the job so soon. She had asked him out of concern, but the reason was simple.

"Ah, that was a one-way deal. They'll be at the border a while. We're also heading back to Felskeilo."

"I see. Well, how about some dinner together?"

Cohral noticed the children staring at him over Cayna's shoulder. Following his gaze, she turned around and smiled uncomfortably.

"We're not gonna get in the way?" he asked.

"It looks to me like they're excited to talk to other people. Besides, it'll help get Lu socialized."

Cohral peered over his shoulder and asked his party, "Sound good?" There were no particular objections; they readily agreed.

Cayna once again used her Cooking Skills, this time to create a dish similar to paella. Cohral's party members had never seen so-called ancient arts, and they were completely confounded. To tell the truth, Luka and Lytt had been staring at Cohral and his party in the hopes that they'd all end up eating a meal made with Cooking Skills.

With Skargo's group gone, last night's dinner had been a dried meat and boiled vegetable soup prepared by Roxine. They soon realized they'd be able to eat food meant for guests if someone else was present. The only one who had known this was Roxine, since the girls had asked her what they needed to do in order to eat Cayna's food.

The night stretched on as Cohral's companions relayed their adventures to the children in a most entertaining fashion around a bonfire. Cohral and Cayna excused themselves briefly before heading behind a wagon that overlooked the vast, dark forest. Cohral had agreed to talk to Cayna in private when she'd asked.

"So why all the secrecy?" he asked her.

"You got here ten years ago, right? I want to hear about your experiences…"

"What, again? Look, I've just been keeping my real power under wraps, passing myself off as some beginner, and laying low. I don't know enough to answer questions from a pro like you."

"Um, I was being serious…but okay."

"Ah. My bad."

Cayna passed him a cup filled with some of the beer she'd made earlier. The downside was that she could only produce a whole barrel's worth at a time. She'd still had a lot left over after running into Skargo, so crossing paths with Cohral and his party here made for perfect timing.

"So have you ever faced an enemy only you were strong enough to handle?" Cayna asked. "Besides that one Event Monster from before."

"Hmm? Umm, let's see… Not really, from what I can remember. Have you?"

He threw the question right back at her, and Cayna sighed. She listed all the high-level monsters she'd faced so far. These included the most recent alligator-shark chimera that she fished out the other day, the dark elf who commanded a team of ogres, and the Ghost Ship that led to Cayna adopting Luka. All of those monsters had appeared whenever she happened to be present.

"You don't think you're being a bit too self-conscious?"

"I mean, yeah, that too. The problem is mostly that the Event Monsters appear outside Pillage Points. The Event Monsters appear during a series of conversations with NPCS, so I don't know why they're operating without any NPC involvement," Cayna said matter-of-factly as she looked down at her wine.

Cohral could tell she had all sorts of idle complaints pent up inside. He nodded; unlike Cohral, Cayna had trouble meeting fellow players. They were all adventurers, besides. They had their own home bases and couldn't necessarily meet up. Talking to her maid and butler wouldn't be of much help to her here. Cohral guessed that she probably just wanted someone to vent to. But at the same time, she was looking for some kind of lead, so Cohral mustered up his ten years of experience and knowledge to answer her question.

"Hmm, do you know the Abandoned Capital?"

"Gwagh… Why not just punch me in the gut?!"

"Ah! I forgot that you were the one who turned the Brown Kingdom to ruins."

The social media posts from the Admins, known as the Weather Report, had announced a monster attack would befall a certain city. And sure enough, a monster horde subjugation event soon took place in the Brown Kingdom capital. In order to quell the horde, Cayna, a magic specialist, the game's highest-level high elf, and a Skill Master with unique and advantageous equipment had appeared on the scene.

The problem started right before the event began, following an experimental update that made even ordinary attacks capable of destroying entire buildings. After a few hundred hits of her long-range attack Meteorite Giga Strike, the Brown Kingdom capital was turned to rubble. From then on, the city's remains were known as the Abandoned Capital, and the incident led to Cayna's notoriety as the Silver Ring Witch.

"Well, it's the former Brown Kingdom anyway," Cohral continued. "I heard on my trip to the border that the Abandoned Capital is to the west and lies in between Felskeilo and Otaloquess. Apparently, it's hidden thanks to an agreement between the three nations."

"Huh? The place is so dangerous that three countries need to work together to hide it? Or is it 'cause it's that beneficial for them?" Cayna asked.

"Couldn't tell ya. It's kind of an open secret. There's a pretty even split between people who believe it exists and those who think it's a total fairy tale."

"I understand that much, but what does it have to do with what I'm talking about?"

With an air of importance, Cohral finished off his beer. Holding the empty cup out to Cayna, he smirked as if to say: *You know, don't you?*

"Okay, okay," Cayna said with a nod, then briefly went back to the bonfire. Already guessing what she needed, Roxine filled two cups of beer to the brim and passed them to her.

"Thanks."

"Not at all."

She returned to Cohral and handed him the two beers. He grew more loose-lipped after he gulped down each one in a single swig, and Cayna elbowed him to continue. He obliged. "Makes no difference to me if it's some fairy tale, but they say that when the three nations were established two hundred years ago, the gods sealed the world's remaining disasters inside the Abandoned Capital."

"…Disasters?"

"The word *disaster* didn't mean anything to me either, but you think it might have somethin' to do with the Event Monsters you're talking about?"

"…………Oh! I get it!"

"Right? Makes sense, doesn't it?"

"It really does…"

Cayna had faith in Cohral's long-winded explanation. However, she thought of Cohral, Shining Saber, Quolkeh, Exis, and the bandit leader whose name she never learned and froze, wondering why they were here in Leadale in the first place.

"Huh? What's wrong?" Cohral asked.

"Cohral, what were you doing the day service ended?"

"Ah, the usual mostly. Taking down small-time monsters with some random party, stuff like that."

"…So that's what's going on. What if, on the day service ended two hundred years ago, a ton of people initiated quests and fulfilled the requirements for Event Monsters to appear, which were then sealed inside the Abandoned Capital? The problem though is why they've been escaping recently."

"Whoa, just hold on a sec…" Cohral understood what Cayna was getting at, and he began sweating profusely.

The seven nations in the VRMMORPG *Leadale* had been split among seven servers. The maximum capacity of each nation's server varied, but records showed that an average of several thousand players accessed a single nation during times of war.

On the day service ended, all the cities and villages had been decorated thanks to a special update, and fireworks had been going off in-game throughout the entire week. Cayna had a feeling some, if not most, of the players online then were really into festivals. It was also possible an unprecedented number of people who hadn't logged on in a long time also accessed the servers that day just to fool around in the game.

With all the festivities going on, there had to be lots of casual players online and not just people like Cohral, who simply grinded levels. What if, instead of going after average enemies, a small number of these players saw this final day of operation as their last chance to take on quests they hadn't completed yet? If that was indeed the case and the entire server shut down in the middle of a boss battle, these bosses had likely remained undefeated. And if this had happened throughout all the servers, then those Event Monsters were now scattered across the continent.

It was unknown how closely this world and the game were connected, but considering the rate of random encounters, the so-called fairy tale in question, and the pact among the three nations, Cayna and Cohral felt that had to be the most logical conclusion.

"Shining Saber probably knows this already since he's top brass, right?" said Cayna.

"What about your son, Cayna?" Cohral asked.

"My guess is he's keeping his private life and work separate. He wouldn't be Number Three in the nation otherwise."

Although Skargo was irresponsible and strange, Cayna acknowledged that since he was dealing with national matters without getting his mother directly involved, it was doubtful he'd reveal classified government secrets. Even if she went all the way to Otaloquess, she couldn't just ask Queen Sahalashade questions about this world's origins.

If they were going to get to the bottom of this mystery, then Caerick was the closest national authority. Cayna considered asking him if he might be willing to sell any information to her. She also remembered that she'd have to get Quolkeh and Exis's opinions as well and jotted down a mental reminder (or rather, Kee did). Cohral and Cayna promised to exchange info the next time they met, and they soon called it a night.

Epilogue

Two days after parting from Cohral, Cayna's group finally returned to the remote village. Lux Contracting, located at the entrance, was now both an engineering firm and a sundries store. Luka and Lytt quickly stepped down from the wagon and went to give Latem his souvenirs. Cayna took this opportunity to greet Sunya, who told her their firm was supplying the fortress at the border with everyday goods, and the villagers could shop here as well.

Cayna thanked the cath palug for all its hard work and dismissed it. It meowed back and sent her a telepathic message—*"Lemme know if you ever need help with the kids"*—before disappearing. Enbarr nuzzled Cayna's cheek and neighed before likewise disappearing.

Marelle was happy to see Lytt back home safe. She was even happier when Lytt gave her a souvenir. Cayna apologized for keeping her away from home for so long, but Marelle gave her a hug and a firm pat on the back.

"Don't you worry about it, Cayna," she said. "I might even ask you to take her out again if you get the chance."

When Cayna, Luka, and Roxine arrived at their own home, they found Roxilius prostrated before them at the entrance.

"What the—?!"

Cayna did a double take; he was definitely on his hands and knees. It was some pretty impressive groveling since he didn't seem to mind getting himself so dirty. Roxine looked repulsed as she contemplated whether to step on his head.

"What are you doing, you useless cat?" Roxine spat. "Did you finally have a mental breakdown?"

Startled, Luka clung to Cayna's cloak.

"C'mon, Rox, stand up," said Cayna. "What's going on?"

No matter how many times she called to him, he remained exactly where he was. He continued a stream of barely audible apologies: "I'm so sorry, I'm so sorry, I'm so sorry, I'm so sorry, I'm so sorry."

"No, seriously, what's going on?" Cayna pressed.

Roxine snapped. She grabbed his collar and lifted him up. "Dammit!! If you're gonna upset our master, then I've got no choice—"

She ended her rant mid-sentence; Roxilius had tears streaming down his cheeks. Even Roxine was dumbfounded.

"U-uhhh… Um…," she stammered.

"At any rate, let's head inside," Cayna suggested. "Cie, let go of Rox."

"R-right…"

Cayna patted the dirt off Roxilius and rubbed his back until he calmed down. Roxine felt guilty for roughing him up, so she helped Cayna. She must have been genuinely shocked by his behavior, as she didn't throw a single insult his way. Cayna left Luka in her room for the time being and summoned the cath palug once again. The cat in question sneered as if it knew Cayna would need its help again so soon.

Roxilius sat at the dining table, having finally calmed down, and hung his head. Deeply concerned, Cayna couldn't help wondering what could have possibly happened to him. Roxine stood meekly nearby with a tray in her hands.

After several minutes of silence, Roxilius finally began to speak.

"Y-you see…"

"Uh-huh."

"Th-there was a visitor…"

"Okay… And?" Cayna urged.

Roxine's shoulders slumped as she heaved a sigh and demanded, "C'mon, what the heck did they want?!"

"A-about that… This visitor forced me to make a contract with them, so I can't say…"

"What?!" Cayna cried, jumping up from her chair. "By 'contract,' you mean Contract Magic?!"

Contract Magic was unique to players and could only be used on NPCs. It was meant to keep people to their word, but in the hands of cruel players, it could be used to bind other users' NPCs (such as Foster Children and guild employees) in a contract.

Also known as Servile Magic, it was among the most detested features in the game. The target remained under the contractor's control unless the latter either undid the spell or deleted their account. Contract Magic had been temporarily erased from *Leadale*, but a number of users had managed to hang onto it via illegal programs. Anyone caught using Contract Magic was reported and subsequently banned.

"But you're still here, and the only thing this person forced you to do was not tell anyone who they were?" Cayna said.

"…Yes. I'm deeply sorry for allowing this to happen while you were away."

Now at his wits' end, Roxilius bowed his head despondently. Roxine stormed off, infuriated.

"…So what did the visitor want?" Cayna asked him.

"Ah, right. They left this letter."

Roxilius handed her a manila envelope. Manila envelopes didn't exist in this world. Astonished, Cayna opened the envelope and unfolded the piece of paper that was inside.

———*To my fiancée.*

That was all it said.

A Princess's Firsthand Experience

I am Myleene Luskeilo, the Crown Princess of the Kingdom of Felskeilo and heir to the throne. As such, my education has been far from lacking, and I have had the privilege of a comfortable life—a privilege I believe I owe my subjects in full.

My mother and father are kind but also strict at times. I certainly feel well-loved. My rambunctious little brother looks out for me on occasion as well, for which I am very grateful.

Nonetheless, is it rather indulgent of me to feel as if I'm lacking something? Perhaps that was what led me to say such nonsense to my dear friend Lonti.

It was a mere passing fancy. I very much understand that words cannot be taken back.

And yet, I'm still not sure why those words slipped so easily from my tongue.

"...Pardon me? What did you say just now, Your Highness?"

My childhood friend Lonti is a prominent candidate for inheriting the position of prime minister from her grandfather, Sir Agaido. She currently takes on simple duties, but I hear she receives lots of practice helping the public solve various issues. Sir Agaido claims she gets too enthusiastic on occasion and can be reckless, and indeed, she is the type to rush to conclusions. I think it's wonderful how she can switch between life inside and outside of the castle.

"'Running away sounds nice'...?"

I have no qualms about my station in life, but you know what they say: The grass is always greener on the other side. That's certainly the case with me. I started thinking it would be fun to live a life I could never have in the castle.

I was fully prepared for Lonti's anger the moment I said it. I think I actually wanted her to scold me and say what a ridiculous idea running away was. However, with an exasperated look on her face, she said, "I suppose there's no helping it," and made our preparations for departure. She even tricked one of the knight captains when we left the castle: *"Her Highness would like to make a confession, so we will be going to the church,"* she'd said; surely that was a bit cruel? Did I appear so brooding that I must be in need of repentance?

The knight captain assigned us an escort to the church. *But, Lonti, won't that prevent us from running away?* I wondered.

...Honestly, I can't believe Lonti had already conspired with the female knight chosen to escort us. I'd like her to repay me for all the anxiety I felt en route to the church.

"Now, Your Highness, I shall proceed to become so fascinated with this stained-glass window that I lose sight of you and Lady Lonti."

"But won't you be held responsible?" I asked.

"Indeed, I will surely receive a good tongue lashing from the captain."

"I would feel most terrible if you had to take the fall for—"

"Worry not, Your Highness! Lady Lonti has already provided me monetary compensation!"

"?!"

Lonti, you shouldn't be high-fiving the knight and shouting, "Yay!"
When did you even have the time to devise such a plan? Ah—don't tell
me... My ladies in waiting left earlier than usual this morning; was that
part of your plan, too?

"Let's get going, then," Lonti said. "The guards will be looking
for us."

We kept ourselves hidden within our cloaks and boarded a small
boat to the city's commoner sector.

An adventurer acquaintance of Lonti's apparently bustled about
the city daily, taking care of various requests. Occasionally, the knight
captain would tell me about this person's exploits, such as building a
new tourist attraction.

What sort of individual could build an entire tourist attraction
single-handedly? I certainly didn't doubt Lonti's claims, but perhaps
they were actually several people?

However, my meeting with this acquaintance came surprisingly
quickly. She called out to us on her way to the Adventurers Guild.

The adventurer looked younger than me but was an unrivaled
beauty. She was intimidatingly attractive, and yet she spoke to Lonti
just like any other teenage girl. Regardless, this adventurer had a mysterious air about her. I would only learn later that she was not my
junior at all. In fact, she was far older. Such was the lifespan of elves,
after all...

Her name was Cayna, a high-elf adventurer...

Aren't high elves considered elven royalty?! What's an adventurer like
her doing in a regular city such as this?!

Despite my confusion, Lonti quickly began discussing how
Cayna would serve as an escort on our little outing.

Don't negotiations normally begin with talk a reward?

I couldn't fathom how such a brief chat was enough for Cayna to
agree to be our guard without any compensation. Most inexplicable

of all was how Cayna ended up serving as our guard while she was out on a quest.

Lonti, will we be all right camping for two days without being properly prepared? I thought.

Cayna had a rapier-like sword at her side, but she didn't look especially strong. Furthermore, her quest involved defeating a horned bear... It would take more than two knights to accomplish such a feat.

"Lonti, is that girl okay?"

"Well, even my grandfather has endorsed her strength. She's also High Priest Skargo's mother, so there shouldn't be any issues."

S-Sir Skargo's mother?!

The mere mention of Sir Skargo had me visibly flustered. That was my greatest mistake; thanks to my reaction, Lonti discovered my secret crush.

Aghhhh, why am I so weak when these unexpected situations arise?!

I blushed furiously in a panic. I wasn't dreaming when Cayna gave me her blessing to pursue Sir Skargo's affections, was I?

The high elves I'd heard about only in stories possessed mysterious powers, like opening up paths by speaking to plants, things regular elves couldn't do.

Cayna continued deeper into the forest down an unmarked path. The best word to describe her was "unprecedented." I was shocked to no end when we set up camp and she cooked for us with ancient arts. She even summoned a three-headed creature said to be a gatekeeper of the underworld to keep watch over us at night as if it were nothing. The horse-sized beast had three sets of sharp teeth. Its mere gaze caused anyone to tremble in fear. And yet Cayna petted and spoke so sweetly to this terrifying creature; I couldn't believe it.

Then at night, she created a bath with a thunderous roar that shook the forest.

After a single day together, I got a good sense of Cayna as a person. She was powerful beyond all description. Lonti felt the same way.

Moreover, she was highly considerate and kept us safe. Thanks to her, we were able to spend the night in a forest without the slightest twinge of chill nor hunger.

And she was much stronger than her appearance suggested. No normal person could topple a horned bear with a single kick. Then she offered us a safe place to sleep and summoned a dragon. She could stand to learn some moderation—although I must admit, I had never seen or heard of such bedding before.

And so I learned just how much hard work travelers face. Without Cayna, we wouldn't have been able to enjoy ourselves in the slightest. I learned how to keep myself from feeling powerless or frustrated.

Perhaps I'll be able to do some traveling once I acquire some knowledge and skills of my own. I may never have it as easy as Cayna does, but with experience, I can come close.

The first thing we can do is service the roads.

I spoke with Lonti throughout those two days outside the city, and in that time we found a vast number of issues. She and I planned to resolve them one by one. It would no doubt take an inordinate amount of time, but it would be well worth it.

The two of us were mulling over these issues on our way home when Cayna had a bad feeling about something and urged us to hurry back.

We thus hastily returned to find the city in the midst of a devastating attack. However, Cayna defeated the scourge before we could even despair.

Words fail me. Is there anything Cayna can't do?

When Lonti and I returned to the castle, my father and Sir Agaido were furious. But they somehow were able to sense that she and I had shown some initiative.

"Well then, Lonti. You know what to do, yes?" I said.

"Yes, Your Highness. After we've compiled all the issues in question, we will adopt a strategy to resolve them."

"Then we'll present them to my father and do whatever we can to help."

There was also the matter of Sir Skargo, but this decision took priority.

Should I accomplish even one of these goals, I'd like to ask Lady Cayna's opinion.

Character Data

Roxine

Level 550. Nicknamed Cie.
A female werecat.
Registered age: About 21 years old.

A rearguard-oriented thief who dual-wields daggers; a misandrist with an intense personality and a sharp tongue. Has a volatile relationship with Roxilius. Her present duties include keeping house and taking care of Luka. She sometimes leaves the village to buy groceries. Both her and Roxilius's names come from the number sixty-four in Japanese, as June 4 was Keina's birthday.

Roxilius

Level 550. Nicknamed Rox.
A male werecat.
Registered age: About 16 years old.

A vanguard-oriented all-rounder whose primary weapon is a sword. He has a serious personality, and jokes tend to pass over his head. He boasts an impressive number of butler skills for serving others, although Roxine has laid claim to any household duties. He patrols the village regularly and teaches the children reading, writing, and arithmetic.

Afterword

Good morning, good afternoon, and good evening. I'm the author, Ceez.

Thank you very much for reading the fourth volume of *In the Land of Leadale*. This book covers chapter 35 to chapter 38 of the original Web version. However, I realized the Guardian Tower that appears on the cover doesn't show up for a while after this part of the story. To fix this issue, I added a few new scenes with the tower, which is why Web readers may find the cover odd.

Once again, my poor time-management skills reared their ugly head, and I ended up working over Christmas and New Year's. I came up with a number of good ideas, so I'd be thrilled if you took notice of them.

In the Web version, Roxilius goes on the trip to Felskeilo, but I switched him with Roxine for the published book. I had a lot of fun writing their curt exchanges that always end in fights.

Shining Saber and Princess Myleene have also been very busy:

Mye managed to solidify her right to the throne, and Shining Saber still hasn't been able to clear up the mistaken rumors that he has a fiancée.

Then who should finally show up but *that* one person… This volume is certainly jam-packed with action.

Next up, we've got some craziness with a turtle. This is the turning point of the story in the Web novel, but there will most likely be some differences in the print version.

Tenmaso, thank you as always for the wonderful illustrations. I never expected the cover to be sepia!

I'd also like to apologize to my editor yet again for all the trouble I've caused, and express my gratitude to all those involved with publishing this volume.

And congratulations to the artist Tsukimi Dashio on the release of the *Leadale* manga.

Lastly, an enormous thank-you to everyone who made this book possible. I truly appreciate it.

Ceez

Tenmaso

enmaso here.
considered drawing a scene of
he amazing Human Zoo for this
fterword's illustration.

ogic won out at the last minute,
nd I gave up on the idea. I'm
ind of glad I did. But I still want
o draw it if I get the chance!

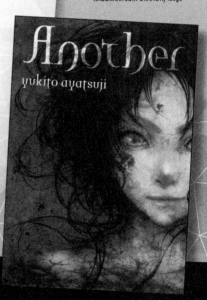